Praise for *Seven Ways to Get Rid of Harry*

"A poignant nostalgia trip to being 13 in the eighties that also has a sharp bite. It tugs at your heart-strings while making you laugh out loud. Never has the attempt to get rid of your mom's evil boyfriend been so charmingly portrayed. A must read!"

—Lee Matthew Goldberg, author of
The Mentor and the Desire Card series

"Jen Conley brought me back to my childhood with this gripping debut. Sometimes harrowing, often funny, this is a great and necessary read for anyone who wants to understand what it's like for boys in that liminal stage, when faced with the challenge of a bad role model."

—Thomas Pluck, author of *Bad Boy Boogie*

"Conley strikes the perfect balance between voice, character, and setting. But technical proficiency isn't what makes the book so special. Her story of a screwed-up kid learning to live without his father is heartbreaking, hopeful, at times hilarious, but above all, flat-out powerful."

—Joe Clifford, author of the Jay Porter thriller series

"Conley's stark, realistic prose transports readers to a time and place when we were all 13 going on 14, and crafts the kind of YA story that feels exceedingly real and unique with a healthy dose of noir."

—Alex Segura, author of *Dangerous Ends* and *Blackout*

SEVEN WAYS TO GET RID OF HARRY

ALSO BY JEN CONLEY

Cannibals: Stories from the Edge of the Pine Barrens

SEVEN WAYS TO GET RID OF HARRY

JEN CONLEY

Down & Out Books
3959 Van Dyke Road, Suite 265
Lutz, FL 33558
DownAndOutBooks.com

The characters and events in this book are fictitious. Any similarity to real persons, living or dead, is coincidental and not intended by the author.

Cover design by Elderlemon Design

ISBN: 1-948235-93-5
ISBN-13: 978-1-948235-93-8

For Jay

FIRST

When I enter the vice principal's office, I do my best to be presentable. My dad once said that a man, when being questioned for trouble he may or may not have caused, needs to stand straight, hands at the side, head up, mouth closed. Make eye contact and shut up. There is no blaming, begging, or weeping. Wait your turn until you are afforded the opportunity to talk. Then when you do speak, speak with your brains, with focus, and with honesty. If honesty is the smart way to go.

"Sit down, Danny," Mr. Cage says.

I sit.

"It has come to my attention that you physically assaulted Richard Plimpton in the locker room."

This is news to me because I didn't do it. And why would I physically assault Richard Plimpton? We were best buddies in second and third grade. We never talk now because that's how things go when you get to eighth grade, but I have no beef with him.

"Richard Plimpton said that you pushed him into the locker room wall, the wall near the emergency exit, then punched him in the stomach three times and gave him a wedgie."

I want to defend myself but it's not my turn to speak. I keep my hands at my side, my mouth closed. There is no window in his office and nothing hangs on the orange walls. On his desk there are four things: a yellow notepad, a ballpoint blue pen, a desk calendar that has today's date, Wednesday, May 4, 1983, and a framed, grainy, colored snapshot of four soldiers standing in front of a tent. They are wearing green fatigues and holding guns. One soldier is a younger Mr. Cage.

I remain silent.

Mr. Cage leans back in his chair. He's a wide-shouldered man with black hair, wears brown-framed glasses and has a handlebar mustache. He never smiles. People say he had eighty-four kills in Vietnam.

"So, son, did you do it?"

I shake my head. "No, I did not."

"You had no participation in this incident?"

"No."

"Were you in the locker room during third period?"

"Yes."

"But you say you didn't do it."

"I didn't do it."

"Did you witness this incident?"

"No. I got dressed and then I left."

"Where did you go?"

"My next class. Social studies."

Mr. Cage glares at me. "Richard sat right here in this office, in the same chair you are sitting in, and claimed that you were the perpetrator."

"I was not."

"Why would Richard lie?"

I can feel my shoulders slump, so I sit up straight.

"Mr. Zelko, answer me. Why would he lie?"

And this is the part where I screw up, completely forgetting my father's advice, which is stupid and I know it's real stupid as soon as the words come spitting from my mouth. "How would I know why Richard would lie? Maybe he's touched in the brain?

It's not like I'm in his head or anything." My shoulders slump again and I lean to one side, feeling my lip curl, completely ticked off. I don't look at Mr. Cage because I know my presentable self is gone and my real self is here. I'm gonna get blamed for this wedgie crap. I just know it.

"Sit up, boy," Mr. Cage says. "Clean up your attitude."

Rage bursts through my veins and I grit my teeth.

"Sit up."

Fine. I'll sit up. But I'm gonna say what I need to say: "I didn't touch Richard Plimpton. I don't know why he's blaming me."

Mr. Cage furrows his thick dark eyebrows and stares me down. "Richard Plimpton is an excellent student and has a clean reputation."

This isn't happening. I'm gonna take the fall for this, aren't I? Nobody cares about my side of the story. I'm always getting blamed for crap, at school, at home. "I didn't do it!" I suddenly shout, frustration screaming out of my lungs. "Why are you blaming me? I didn't give that damn loser turd a wedgie!"

Mr. Cage doesn't move. Doesn't blink. Doesn't react. He's famous for this. But make no mistake, if there's a fight, he's like a superhero—swoops in, wraps you around the neck with one arm, and wrenches you away. I've seen it twice. It's terrifying yet impressive.

I swallow, waiting for Mr. Cage to leap over the desk and put me in a headlock.

Mr. Cage stands. He's a tall, tall man. He moves slowly around his desk, towering over me like Godzilla. My heart knocks against my rib cage. Why did I open my mouth?

"Mr. Zelko," he says, "you appear to be very adamant about this but many a young man has come into my office being adamant. I'll look more into the situation but you will have in-school suspension tomorrow for breaking rule number one."

He points behind me and I swing around, noticing the large, white construction paper taped to the wall. The words on it are written in thick, black magic marker and the only thing it says is:

RULE #1: DISRESPECT WILL NOT BE TOLERATED.

There are no other rules.

Mr. Cage leaves the room to speak to his secretary, Mrs. Panelli. I swing back around and sit there, my heart hammering, trying to get my fear and frustration in check. Then it happens—my eyes start watering. I'm going to cry. On top of everything, I'm going to be a baby. *No weeping,* my dad said, but I can't stop. I try to fight off the tears, trying to figure out why Richard would lie, but my head won't focus. All I can do is hold my tears in my throat. It's painful.

Mr. Cage returns and stands in the doorway. "You can go, Danny."

I stand up and wipe my eyes. So much for following my dad's advice. My dad, who isn't even alive anymore.

The halls are deserted and I head toward the eighth grade wing. My eyes are still wet and I'm not presentable to go to class. I duck into the bathroom, finding some little sixth grader in front of the mirror. Maybe he's a seventh grader, I don't know. He shouldn't be here. He should be on the other side of the school in their wing. They keep the eighth graders away from the younger kids. We're bad news, I guess.

"Do you have a smoke?" he asks me.

"Seriously?" I say to him.

He shrugs. He's got curly blond hair. He wears a Pac-Man T-shirt. His fingernails are dirty.

"Get out of here," I bark. "Go back to nursery school."

The kid shoves his hands in his pockets and leaves. I lean against the bathroom wall and stare at the graffiti written on the stalls. Curse words, phone numbers of girls, but mostly it's this: *OZZY RULES. LED ZEP FOREVER. JUDAS PRIEST. AC/DC.* Like me, the kids in our school like rock and heavy metal, but that's not everybody and that's why you can also see things like *GRAND MASTER FLASH. JUMP ON IT! RAP RULES.* But you have to look hard because that stuff always gets crossed out.

I know I need to get back to class because I'll get in more trouble and then they might throw me out of school for a day. Not that I'd care. Stay home, sleep in, watch TV, ride my bike up to Luigi's for a slice of pizza, take a long ride through the woods, maybe out to Baskro, the man-made lake so deep, a couple of kids died there. Which I never understood because it's not like a sea monster is underneath the water, wrapping its tentacles around your legs and tugging you down to your death. Just swim to shore, for Christ's sake.

I close my eyes and think. Where is Richard Plimpton at the end of the day? I'm gonna get to the bottom of this crap. I'm gonna make the idiot go into Mr. Cage's office and confess.

Then I realize I need to get my brain in check. I can't get into any more trouble because I don't want to stay home tomorrow. It slipped my mind but, yeah, staying home would suck because there's a chance Harry might be there. He works bizarre hours and on his off time, he sometimes hangs out at our house. He's my mom's boyfriend and if there's one person on this planet that I absolutely hate, even more than stupid Richard Plimpton, it's him.

But I don't think about that jerk. First, I need to take care of the present situation.

I leave the bathroom.

After school is over, I locate Richard near his locker. There isn't much to him. I don't mean that he's small or anything; he's actually taller than me. My problem is that I'm small. Not pathetic small, just short and wiry. No match for half the guys in

5

my grade. It sucks. Thirteen and I haven't even grown yet. It's embarrassing. I wish my dad were around so I could ask him when he started to grow, but he's not and I'm not gonna ask my mom because that's just weird. I do have two assets: my attitude and my quickness. For the most part, I don't cower. I got that from my father's family. They were no cowards. They were greasers—walking around the school in leather jackets, chained wallets, and switchblades in their pockets. My second asset, I'm quick. I've had some situations where I've had to defend myself and one thing I can do is duck, dance, and run. My dad used to say I'd make a good boxer. "You've got natural foot work."

Richard is a coward. You can tell by the way he lopes around the school, head down, eyes darting, waiting for someone to jump him. It's not presentable and if I were friends with him still, I'd give him some pointers. But I'm not friends with him. And as of today, you can bet your fat butt, we're enemies to the death.

"Why'd you tell Mr. Cage that I beat you up and stuff?"

Richard turns and looks at me. We're not eyeball to eyeball because he's like five inches taller but he's still shaking like I'm gonna break him in two. If I weren't so pissed off, I'd find it sad.

"Why'd you do it?" I yell.

"Because...because I had to."

"What are you talking about?"

Richard frowns. "I'm sorry, Danny. Jimmy Horak did it. And he made me tell that you did it. He said if I told anyone, then he'd kick my butt."

I'm confused. "Jimmy made you tell Mr. Cage that I messed you up?"

"I didn't mean to. They cornered me in the locker room and all. After it happened, I was just sitting on the floor, you know, sort of upset, trying to get my pants all straight." Richard shrugs and his voice drops a bit. "Jimmy was laughing with Ryan Gumlek and Brian Donnelly, and then Mr. Collins appeared."

Mr. Collins is one of the gym teachers. He has really big ears.

"So what happened after that?" I say, leaning in closer.

"Mr. Collins came over, asked what all the commotion was, and Jimmy said, 'Danny Zelko just punched Richard three times and gave him a wedgie.' Which wasn't true. Jimmy did it. But he told Mr. Collins you did it and then you ran out the exit door."

"I'm still not following," I say. "Why'd you go along with the lie?"

Richard shakes his head. "Then Mr. Collins said he was going to find Mr. Cage and he left the locker room and Jimmy got in my face and threatened me and said that I better stick to the story. That you did it."

"So you just agreed to what they said?"

"What was I going to do?"

I slam Richard against the locker. People look at me, and I know I can get into trouble, but I don't care—even though I should. "You're a coward."

Richard nods and drops his head. "I know."

Oh, Christ. Now I feel bad for him. It must stink to be such a pitiful loser.

My mouth clenches and I suck on my teeth. "I'm not done with you," I growl, pointing my finger in his face.

I march down to Mr. Cage's office, not giving a rat's ass if I miss my bus. But he isn't around so I have to go home. Jimmy Horak lives in my neighborhood so I can go find him anytime I want. Still, he has that older brother, Mark. Mark Horak is psycho. I heard he broke a girl's arm at the bus stop once because she was sticking up for some quiet kid he was picking on.

I take the bus and when I get to my house, I see Harry's motorcycle parked in our driveway. It's black and shiny and slick, like an oversized scorpion. My mom's car is in front of it. She's supposed to be working at the beauty salon but sometimes she has the day off and they hang out together alone when my older sister and I are at school. They're probably drinking.

Suddenly my Richard Plimpton wedgie problem seems like nothing in comparison to my problem at home.

I enter the house and find my mother draped along the couch, a beer on the coffee table.

"Mom?" I say but she's passed out. I hate when she gets like this. It's not like she's an alcoholic. She only drinks when she gets around Harry. When he's not here, she's usually busy moving around the house, picking things up, washing clothes, vacuuming—mom stuff. But she doesn't spend all her time like that. I mean, she's not my maid. She likes to do fun stuff too. We have Atari and my mom loves to play video games with me. Her favorite is *Breakout,* which I think is kind of stupid—it's just a rainbow brick wall of colors and you bounce a ball back and forth trying to break through the top and get rid of all the bricks—but she loves it and I like playing video games with her.

"Mom," I say again, shaking her arm.

She opens her eyes a little and frowns. "I'm sorry, Danny," then rolls over and goes back to sleep.

I want to shake her but she's my mom and I'm not going to shake her. I look around, across the living room to the dining area and kitchen, wondering where Harry is. Dead, I hope.

I head down the hall toward my room but halt immediately when Harry steps out of the bathroom in front of me.

"If it isn't the man of the house," Harry says.

He's holding a beer.

I want to slide by him but the hall is too narrow and Harry is too big. He's not fat, just muscular and thick, like a gorilla. He's hairy like one, too. I should turn around and leave the house, but this is my house and I should be able to go to my room.

"What?" I say.

Even though it's dim in the hallway, I can see his face warp into anger. He rocks a little because he's been drinking. My guess is he's been at it since breakfast.

8

I wait for him to step aside.

He doesn't. He's still rocking and he smiles a bit. "How was school?"

"Fine."

"*Fine*," Harry mimics.

I try to walk by.

He steps in front of me.

"Cut it out," I yell.

Harry smirks. "I'm just playing with you. Don't be so sensitive."

That's what he always says, *Don't be so sensitive*. I don't know what my mom sees in him. He thinks he's all scary and cool with his dumb motorcycle but half the time he drives my mom's car or his puke-green beat up-tank from 1973 that makes gurgling noises when you turn it off. The guy is ugly, too. He's got one of those long faces, a wide mouth, and long narrow eyes with thick rubbery bags under them. His hair is dark, unkempt, thin. He always needs a shave. Yet, the women think he's hot stuff. A few weeks ago, when my mom was trimming my hair at her job, my mom's coworker, Peggy, said, "Oh, that Harry. I love his motorcycle!" And my mom and Peggy giggled.

"Can you let me by?" I ask Harry nicely this time, trying a different tactic. I need to be polite because his biggest gripe with me is that I'm not polite. My mom had a talk with me and said that I had to watch my attitude around Harry, that I needed to use my manners.

"Can you move?" I ask.

Harry doesn't. Just rocks.

"Can you let me by?" I say again, adding, "Please."

This time, he steps aside.

I move by him, as quick as I can, but for some reason, I trip and tumble to the floor. He didn't trip me, at least I didn't feel his foot, but I guess with my rush to get away from him, I went too fast. I land face-first on the carpet and I can feel the rug burn against my jaw.

Harry laughs loudly, bending down toward me, using his hand to steady himself against the wall. "You okay, *Danielle?*"

I hate, hate, hate when he calls me Danielle. It makes my head crack and my blood stiffen, but my jaw hurts too much to tell him off.

I hear Harry slurp his beer.

The door at the end of the hall opens and I see my older sister, Lisa. She looks at us both, ducks back into her room, and shuts the door.

I get up from the floor and glare at Harry. I really want to tell him off but the last time I stuck up for myself when he was drunk and called me Danielle, he threatened to knock me "into next week." He wears heavy black motorcycle boots that could kill a small cat with one strike. I told my mom that he calls me Danielle and that he threatened to hit me but she said that Harry wouldn't hit me and boys and men do that—call each other girl names. I told her Dad never called me girl names and she said I needed to stop comparing Harry to my dad and if it bothered me so much, why didn't I just ask Harry to stop calling me Danielle? I told her, "I tried but he threatened to knock me into next week so why don't you do it? You're the mom." And she said she had a headache and I needed to leave her alone.

Harry grunts, hiccups, and stumbles away from me, down the hall. I go into my room and slam the door, locking it, and switching on my stereo. I've got the station on WCAU out of Philadelphia and Eddy Grant sings "Electric Avenue." I turn it up, loud, so loud that my window starts rattling.

Immediately, there's banging at my door.

"Danny! Danny!" It's Lisa.

I let her in. She goes right to the stereo and snaps it off.

"What?" she hisses. "Did you take your stupid pills today?"

I lock the door again.

"Danny, they're drinking. You know how Harry gets with you when he's drinking."

I plop on my bed and stretch out, looking up at my Pink

Floyd poster on my ceiling. I have a few posters on my walls: Rocky because he's cool; Queen because the song, "Bohemian Rhapsody" is one of the best songs ever made; the horror movie *Halloween* because I like horror; another horror movie poster— *The Night of the Living Dead*; and a Van Halen poster because Van Halen rocks.

But I love Pink Floyd, that's why the poster is on my ceiling, so it's the last thing I see at night. That's my band these days. I connect with the words. *Hey you, out there beyond the wall, Breaking bottles in the hall...*Sure, some of their songs make me sad, make me lonely, but since my dad died nine months ago, I am sad and lonely.

Lisa puts her hands on her hips. She's got feathered blondish hair, a bony body, and a giant head. She'd be okay-looking if it weren't for all that eye makeup she wears—pink eye shadow, blue eyeliner, pink lipstick. She looks like a poison dart frog.

"Danny," she says. "Don't start with him today. Just stay in here, keep your door locked and your music on low. He and Mom will probably go into the bedroom soon and go to sleep."

Why is it always me that starts with him? That's not true. And it's not fair that I have to isolate myself. I'm hungry. I should be able to go into the kitchen for something to eat and not be stopped by some idiot drunken gorilla stomping around the house going, *Oo Oo, Ee Ee...* I tell Lisa this.

"I'll get you a sandwich. Just hang out here."

I let out a loud, irritated breath. "Fine. Can you bring me chips and something to drink?" adding, "Please."

"Okay. But listen. Your school called. Turns out you have in-school suspension tomorrow."

"I didn't do it."

"Do what?"

"Punch Richard Plimpton three times and give him a wedgie."

"Well, apparently you did do it."

I sit up, ticked off. "I did not. I'm being blamed for it. I wasn't even in the locker room when it happened. I was on my way to class."

Lisa rolls her frog eyes. "Okay, okay. I just wanted to tell you that I took the call and pretended I was Mom. That way you don't get into more trouble."

"Please," I sneer. "She's too busy with gorilla guy. It's not like she's gonna punish me." My mom doesn't give a crap about me anymore. If she did, she wouldn't get drunk in the middle of the day with Harry. What kind of lousy parent pulls this garbage?

"Fine," Lisa says. She leaves the room and is back in ten minutes with a peanut butter sandwich, potato chips, and a glass of milk. She sits on the carpet, leaning up against my dresser, while I sit on my bed and munch away even though my jaw hurts from hitting the floor earlier. Soon we hear noise in the hall.

I stop chewing and Lisa looks up. We hear my mom giggling and talking drunken gibberish. Harry is laughing too. They act like idiots when they get together.

Lisa shakes her head.

"Come on, babe," we hear Harry say to my mom. "You need sleep."

Lisa rolls her eyes again.

I put my plate down and listen as they travel the rest of the way down the hall. We hear them move into my mom's bedroom and then door shut.

Lisa stands up.

"Where are you going?" I say.

"Back to my room."

"Just wait a few minutes." I'll admit it, I want her to stay. I don't want to be alone.

Lisa sighs and walks to the window. A light rain falls outside. This makes me smile. Old Harry's motorcycle is gonna get wet and he doesn't like it when it gets wet.

I begin eating my food again. Lisa looks through my cassette collection. Then she drops the bomb.

"Mom says they're getting married."

My mouth, full of peanut butter and bread, falls open.

My sister frowns. "At the end of the summer."

I force myself to swallow. Then I say, "Why?"

"She loves him." Lisa shrugs. "Like an obedient dog."

It's a nasty remark that chills my bones because it's true.

"We have to stop her," I say.

Lisa walks to the door and opens it. "Good luck with that," she says and leaves.

It's quiet the rest of the night and I'm able to step out and watch a little TV in the living room. President Reagan is talking on all the channels but we just got cable so I can watch *Time Bandits* on HBO without it being interrupted. I saw *Time Bandits* in the movies—my dad took me to see it—but I watch it again. It's about a boy who joins a band of dwarves with a time-traveling map. The little people make me laugh but I can't enjoy it because I keep waiting for Harry to come out of my mom's bedroom and start stomping around in his motorcycle boots with a cigarette hanging out of his mouth.

He doesn't.

When the movie is over, I take out the garbage, shut off the lights, and go into my bedroom, locking my door. The window is open and the rain has stopped, but there is a gentle wind. The soft sound of the trees swaying put me to sleep.

"Hey Danny."

This isn't a dream. I'm awake. I'm just staring in the dark because I woke up and I can't get back to sleep. So I pretend my dad is in my room, leaning against my dresser.

"How's it going?" he says in my mind.

"Hi, Dad. How's Heaven?"

"Puffy."

I'm not completely bonkers, I swear, but I like to have fake

13

conversations with my dad and if I concentrate hard enough, for a minute or two, I can believe he's really here. Nobody knows I do this, not even my almost-best friend, Tyrell. Tonight, my dad wears brown-framed glasses, just like Mr. Cage, but he's not tall and he doesn't have black hair. His hair is dirty blond, like mine. He's wearing his greaser jacket from high school. He doesn't always wear it when I conjure him up. He never wore it around me when he was alive but I've seen photos of him in it and I always thought he looked cool.

"I got in trouble for something I didn't do," I tell him.

"I know, but Mr. Cage knows you didn't do it."

"Yeah, good one."

"Mr. Cage believes you. He was just ticked off that you got out of line, yelling at him. I always told you to be presentable, to keep yourself in check. You didn't listen to me."

I don't respond.

My dad grins. "It runs in the family, getting out of check."

I smile back and then frown.

"Hard times, kid?" he asks.

"I hate Harry. He's nothing but a waste, a jerk."

My father nods.

"I wish you were here."

Then I blink and my mind takes him away.

I catch my breath and in the dark, look up and just make out my Pink Floyd poster on the ceiling—the triangle with the rainbow prism. If I try hard enough, I can remember and even think I can smell my dad's scent—Irish Spring soap, a little sweat, coffee.

I lay there, enjoying the memory of pretend-talking to my dad. Then I hear a noise. Harry. He's in the bathroom which is across the hall. He's banging around—I hear the cabinet doors slam, the water running, more cabinet doors slamming.

"Shut up, Judy!" he shouts. "Just shut the hell up!"

My mom must be on the other side of the other bathroom door. The bathroom has two doors: one to the hallway and one to her bedroom.

Within a minute, doors open, the bathroom and my mom's bedroom, and they're out in the hallway, screaming at each other, well, more like he's yelling at her. "No, I'm not gonna listen to you! Shut up!" he shouts. You see, this is the real reason I hate my mom's boyfriend. I know I said I hate when he calls me Danielle. I hate when he gets my mom drunk. I hate his ugly face. But that's half of it. What wrecks my gut and makes my brain split, is when he tells her to shut up. When he shouts at her. When he calls her "stupid" and other names. It's not often—they've only had three major fights I've been witness to—but when these fights twist up and explode, I slip into a whirlpool of worry and panic. When Harry starts shouting, he's cruel and terrifying. He's loud, thunderous, and it sounds like—like he's gonna hit her, or worse, kill her. She tries to argue back, like she's doing right now: "Don't you dare tell me to shut up in my house!" followed by swear words I don't usually hear her say. But he can yell louder, and he does, cursing and calling her cruel names until she can't yell back anymore, until she begins to cry, like she's doing right now in the hallway. I want to help but she doesn't want me to get involved. Last time I jumped in when they were fighting, which was on April seventeenth, my mom begged me to go to my room. "I'll handle it," she said, her face flooded with tears.

I shut my eyes and try to pretend talk to my dad, but I can't focus. Not with Harry banging doors and shouting at my mom. My nerves are twitching and I can't figure out what I should do. Sometimes he's nice, bringing her flowers, hugging her, telling her how beautiful she is. But then these fights happen. Now here I am, sick, the pillow over my head, praying that he doesn't do something awful to her. I don't want to live with someone like this.

Harry shouts again and my mom cries and the bedroom door slams. Soon there is silence except for a few sniffles from my mom in the hallway. A couple minutes later I hear her get up and go into the bedroom. I can't hear anything after that but there's no yelling, so I guess they're all good now. That's how it goes after a fight: things go quiet, they talk secretly, then it's lovey dovey central for another three weeks.

I stare at the triangle on the ceiling. I can't believe my mom is going to marry this beast. I'll have to live with him until 1988, when I turn eighteen. That's five years. I almost start to cry again, like I did this afternoon.

I turn over in bed and gaze through the open window. A breeze blows cool air into my room. We have central air conditioning—something most people don't have—but my mom hasn't turned it on yet. She says it's too early, that she wants to save money. Harry told her to put it on, that the house is too hot, but she hasn't yet.

A hear a car ride by my house and the trees rock in the wind.

At that moment, I have an epiphany: I can get rid of Harry. Scare him away. Threaten him. Something. Like maybe the next time I see him, when my mom is asleep and he's up, drinking his beer, I can get in his face and intimidate him. Like say, "You better get out of this house or when you least expect it, something bad will happen to you." I can play it off, like I'm some crazy wacko kid who will do anything. Then he'll leave and nobody will miss the creep, except my mom. Maybe she'll think he dumped her and she'll start dating other guys, nicer guys who don't look like they just got out of prison. I will have saved her.

It's a bit far-fetched, me getting in Harry's face, but the seed is there: I can get rid of Harry. I can get rid of Harry!

I just have to think up a way to do it.

WAY ONE:
FAKE OTHER BOYFRIEND

The first thing that comes to my mind is really bad, so bad I don't even want to admit it. It's so bad, they can send me to juvie. Or worse, the mental home.

Okay, here it is: An ax to Harry's head. I'm just sitting here in in-school suspension, in my cubby, staring at the wall, when I remember "The Black Cat" by Edgar Allan Poe. We read it last year in literature class. Miss Lewis, our teacher, had to stop like every two minutes to explain some of the more difficult paragraphs, but I got it. It's a pretty simple story to understand. First, this guy says that he's good with animals but he's really not. And one night, when he's drunk, he takes a penknife out of his pocket, grabs his wife's cat, and cuts out its eye. The cat survives but the man can't stand looking at this poor cat that he abused. So he hangs it. Then he gets another cat and we soon realize it's a ghost cat, the apparition of the one-eyed cat he hanged. Long story short, one night the guy is going down to the cellar, his wife behind him, and the ghost cat gets in his way and he almost trips on the steps. He loses it, grabs an ax, and goes to throw it at the cat but the wife stops him. This enrages him so much that he buries the ax in her head, killing the woman on the spot. Afterwards he decides to put her body in an opening

17

in the wall and brick her behind it. The bad part for him is that when the police come to investigate where the woman went, they hear a cat moaning from behind the new wall. They tear down the bricks and there is the cat, sitting right on top of the dead wife with the ax in her head. Ha! He's caught red-handed.

Obviously I can't do what this guy did. I can't throw an ax at Harry and bury him in the basement. My house doesn't have a basement. We just have a crawl space. But if I wait for Harry to come out to the garage and put the ax in his head, I can figure out what to do with his body. Move it out to the woods and bury it. Harry is big so I'd need help. I can ask Tyrell, but he's small like me so I don't know if we could handle it together. I don't think Lisa will help—she doesn't like blood. She can't even sit through the TV version of *The Exorcist*.

Damn. The plan is stupid. I can't murder anyone. That's crazy and sick and I need to get myself in check. I lean back in my chair and tap my pencil, peering through the open doorway at Mrs. Panelli, Mr. Cage's secretary, filing papers in a metal cabinet.

A few minutes later, I hear commotion, yelling, and before I know it, Mrs. Panelli is directing Janine Finn into in-school suspension.

"I hate Mr. Cage!" she shouts at Mrs. Panelli who is about four inches shorter than Janine. "I didn't do nothing! Where is he? How do I know he's making me come in here?"

"Sit down, Miss Finn."

"Sit down, yourself."

The secretary shakes her head. "I don't get paid enough to deal with you." A moment later, she walks away, back to her desk in the adjoining room, leaving me alone with Janine.

You have to understand something about Janine. She's hot, real pretty. She's got long dark hair that goes all the way down her back and her lips are really red. I don't even think she wears lipstick like my sister does. But Janine is bad and she's mean as spit. What makes her even more deadly is that she is one wild and crazy loony chick. Wacky. Batty. Off the deep end. Not playing with a full deck. My sister heard she was dropped on her head when she was a baby, like for real. Janine was about nine months old and it was night and her mother heard this strange noise downstairs, like something prowling around the outside of the house. She was holding Janine in her arms so she went down to the kitchen, takes a knife out of the drawer for protection, and starts creeping around the house in the dark, peering through all the windows. She gets to the front window, peeks through, and immediately a head pops up! It's old man Lafferty from down the street. He's wandered outside again, thinking he's up in Brooklyn making milk deliveries—no kidding, he was a milkman in his younger years. Anyhow, this scares the hell out of Mrs. Finn, who screams, drops baby Janine, who knocks hear head on the window sill and falls to the hardwood floor. Janine hit her head twice. So she's twice as crazy as the normal crazy person. They didn't do anything with old man Lafferty, though. He only just died last year.

"What's up, Zelko?" Janine says to me, scrunching up her face like a rabbit. She smells like cigarettes and bad perfume. Probably caught smoking in the bathroom. She wears blue eye shadow and black eyeliner on the inside rim of her eyeballs. It's liquid (my sister wears it sometimes) and in her left eyeball, the liquid has smeared into the white of her eye. Now it's all brownish and horror-movie looking, making her appear like a once-hot pretty chick now bitten by zombies.

"Nothing's up," I say, turning away from her.

I hear Janine take a seat in a cubby behind from me.

"You got a girlfriend yet?"

I don't answer.

"Probably not. You're too short. No one wants to date a midget." She cackles at her own joke.

"Shut up," I say.

"Shut up yourself," she snaps.

"That's all you got?" I ask, swinging around again. "Shut up yourself?"

19

"I'm in no mood for morons."

"Same to you." I face my private wall.

"Did you just call me a moron?"

I look back at her. "No. You called me a moron."

Janine squints her weird eyes at me, like she's trying to figure out what the heck just went on. She's mean and crazy, but I still think she's pretty, even with her zombie eye. We turn away from each other.

"Hey!" Mrs. Panelli hollers from her desk in the next room. "No talking!"

Janine grows quiet and she stays that way for a long time. I keep peeking over my shoulder waiting for her to do something insane, like start pulling out her eyelashes or stab me with a pencil. Then I realize she's asleep. She has her head on the cubby desk and she's snoring.

I take out a piece of paper and return to my plan. I organize it like an official outline:

Way to Get Rid of Harry

AX

> a. Basic idea: I will hide out in the garage, behind my sister's old toy kitchen set, with ax.
>
> b. When: must be done when Mom and Harry are drinking. Wait till Mom passes out.
>
> c. How to get him in the garage: Use bait. Move all the beer in the house fridge into the old garage fridge. I'll leave a note in house fridge that will say: Beer in garage fridge. He might be mad, but who cares? He'll be gone soon.
>
> d. When he walks into garage, I will hold the ax and then tell him to leave the premises and never return.

I lean back in my chair again and look at my list. It's not bad. But what if he refuses to leave? I let my mind go back to the dark side and as a joke, I go forward with my murder idea.

e. I go through with it.

f. Afterwards: Drag body onto plastic toboggan and pull it out to the woods behind my house. Call Tyrell. He'll meet me at designated spot and I will bring shovel.

g. Blood in garage: Cleaned easily with bleach. If not, tell Mom you killed a really big rat. She hates rats.

That's funny because Harry is a RAT!

I remind myself I can't kill the guy so I put an X through items e-g. Still, it was fun dreaming it up, even if it is psychotic. At least I have a rough draft. I know all about rough drafts because Miss Lewis used to make us write rough drafts before writing the final essays. My eighth grade literature teacher makes us write essays but she's not crazy about rough drafts like my seventh grade teacher was.

"Who's Harry?"

I swing around and see Janine standing over me, her left eye even more brownish horror-like. I grab my paper, fold it in half, then in fourths, then once more. I stick it in the front pocket of my jeans.

"You planning a murder?" she asks.

I stare hard at her. "Yes."

She grins. "Excellent."

"If you tell anyone, I'm gonna murder you."

Janine steps away and takes her cubby seat. "Please. You're too small to murder anyone. You couldn't murder a slug."

Like I said, she is crazy. She may even be dumb. Smallness has nothing to do with being able to commit murder. Plenty of murderers were small, I bet.

I don't say that, though. I just say, "I've murdered plenty of slugs." But that's not true because I used to have a soft spot for slugs. Poor things, just innocently crawling along. When we were little, Jimmy Horak used to come to my house to play and his favorite thing was to kill bugs and slugs, even butterflies. Sicko.

21

Suddenly, I feel a presence in the room. I turn around and see Mr. Cage standing in the doorway, taking up most of the space. Oh no. What if Janine tells Mr. Cage that I plan to kill Harry with an ax? Why did I tell her that I planned to murder someone? I'm not really gonna murder Harry. It was just a joke. *Wait,* I tell myself, *Calm down.* Mr. Cage won't believe Janine. Nobody believes anything Janine says.

"Danny," Mr. Cage orders, "come with me to my office."

I stand and leave, shooting Janine the evil eye when I pass her.

"Shut up, Zelko," she yaps.

"Enough, you two," Mr. Cage says.

I leave the room feeling bummed. I wish she were nicer to me.

In his office, Mr. Cage explains that although he didn't approve of my outburst, he doesn't believe I gave Richard Plimpton the wedgie.

"I told you!" I yell.

"Stop while you're ahead, Mr. Zelko."

I remember to keep myself under control and even apologize.

"I'm letting you out of in-school suspension but I'm going to remind you to watch that attitude."

I'm out in time for lunch. I head to the cafeteria, get my food—day-old cheeseburger and greasy fries—and find Tyrell Colton sitting near the window by himself. I won't lie, I hesitate, because although Tyrell is turning into my best friend, it's sort of upsetting to see him sitting there with no one, reading one of his thick science fiction books. It's not because Tyrell is black and nobody will sit with black kids—it's majority white in my school but there are black and Hispanic kids too. Tyrell and I used to sit with Raymond Tipple but Raymond moved over to the table with the cool black kids so now it's just me and Tyrell. If I really wanted, I could probably sit with some okay white kids, like Shawn Stinson and Lou Barth, but I'm having trouble hanging with those guys this year. They both have dads and it's painful to hear them brag about how their dads are gonna take them to a baseball game or how their dads promised to go fishing with them. Last summer I slept over Shawn's house a couple of times, but after my dad died, just seeing Shawn's father in the kitchen, drinking coffee in the morning like my father used to do, makes me too sad.

"What's up, dude?" I say to Tyrell when I sit across from him.

"You out of jail?"

"I was found innocent."

Tyrell grins. He's got a bunch of large white teeth, naturally straight. I need braces because my teeth are crooked but we don't have the money for braces.

Tyrell leans forward and whispers, "Can you move a little to the left?"

I go to ask why but then my mind moves back thirty seconds, when I was standing holding my tray, contemplating whether to sit with Tyrell or Shawn and Lou. I see it now. Iris Cruz is sitting behind me with her girls and Tyrell has a thing for Iris Cruz.

I scoot to the left and give him the vantage point he needs.

"Dude," I say, "she's never gonna like you if you have your head in your alien books. She'll think you're a dork."

Tyrell frowns. I've insulted him. But honestly, he has no game. I mean, he dresses way nicer than me—today he's wearing a kelly green polo shirt with the collar turned up, clean jeans, and white high-top sneakers—but he's got no confidence. Fourteen and he still has trouble having conversations with people, except me. Like I said, he's small, so that might be the problem. Or his father's story. Tyrell doesn't have a dad either. Suicide. Way worse than my dad dying of cancer.

"So, do you wanna hang out after school?" I ask.

Tyrell shrugs. "Sure."

I bite into my cheeseburger. It tastes like I'm chewing on a leather shoe but I'm hungry. When I swallow, I study my friend, wondering if he's trustworthy enough to let into my plan— scaring Harry with an ax. I won't kill Harry, like the guy in "The Black Cat" did. I'll just scare him off. Like in olden times when people would ride up on your property. You'd brandish a

23

sword or shotgun and just make them go away. I glance at Tyrell's science fiction book and decide that he must secretly want to hear something interesting instead of reading about aliens.

"Hey. I gotta tell you something."

Tyrell chews and swallows his food, because he always chews and swallows before he speaks, then says, "What?"

I take a long breath, then spill, sort of. My voice is very grim. "I'm planning to scare the hell out of someone."

Tyrell grins slowly. "Jimmy Horak?" He knows about Jimmy and Richard Plimpton and the wedgie crap. I told him this morning on the way to in-school suspension.

I'm silent, contemplating again whether I should divulge my plan.

"Well? I'm listening," Tyrell says.

"No, I'm planning something else. Something worse," I finally answer, seeing myself in the near future, holding the ax up in the garage and scaring Harry. "Way worse."

Tyrell pushes his tray forward and folds his hands on the table. "You've definitely got my attention now."

I'm not going to tell Tyrell the details in school so I promise I'll reveal everything when we get to his house. "It's top secret."

Tyrell sighs like it might be stupid. "It better be good."

At the end of the day, when I'm at my locker, Richard Plimpton lopes up to me and hands me a Milky Way bar.

"Sorry you had to take the fall for what happened."

I snatch the candy bar from his hand. "Get out of my face."

He does. He drops his head and disappears into the crowd. I'm not gonna feel bad about this. I appreciate the candy bar gesture but he was out of line.

I meet Tyrell in the library because after school he hides in there. Tyrell is a walker, meaning he doesn't get to take the bus because no buses go to Pine Park, his neighborhood. It doesn't make sense to me because Pine Park is like a twenty-minute walk down the road and through the woods. I shouldn't really say through the woods because the township cut down a bunch of trees and made a dirt road for the Pine Park kids to walk along, which, again, I don't get. Why can't they just send a bus to the Pine Park neighborhood? Walking on a nice day is fine but what about rainy or snowy days? On top of that, if you're a walker, you get harassed. Kids on the buses are mean and they yell curses and crap out the window when the walkers go by. That's why Tyrell hangs out in the library until the buses are gone.

Once it's all clear, we make our way down the long school driveway, down the paved road, then onto the long dirt road, which is a little muddy from last night's rain. There are a few kids ahead of us, a couple behind us, but they don't give us trouble. Our school is surrounded by nothing but ugly scrub pine trees, trees so rubbery and squat, you can't climb them. You can't even break a branch off to build a fort. I mean, you probably could, but you'd be covered in pine sap. It's because we live on the edge of the Pine Barrens, miles of nothingness, just ugly trees that cover south Jersey.

"Didn't Iris look good today?" Tyrell says. "She looks good in pink."

Iris Cruz is pretty, but a different type of pretty than Janine Finn. Iris has a bi-level haircut, short on the sides and a little long in the back. She wears pink sweaters and tight jeans a lot. As far as personality, she's nothing like Janine. Iris is nice and she's very good in school. Her parents don't speak a lick of English, I heard.

"Yeah, she looked hot," I say.

"She always looks hot."

We don't talk about my plan because Tyrell respects what I said: I will reveal all information at his house, in private. Besides, Tyrell is in Iris-land. It's best to let him hang out in Iris-land until he gets it out of his system. Same thing for science fiction-land. Tyrell is a thinker and when he is thinking, he's no good for conversation.

So we walk and walk until we reach his neighborhood. His house is a couple blocks away from the dirt road. Most of the houses in Pine Park are boxy and small. Pretty much only black people and Hispanic people live in this development. We live in the North so I don't understand why we have segregated neighborhoods, but we do.

Tyrell's house is like the rest of them: small. Inside, there is a small living room, tiny kitchen and dining area, two bedrooms, and a bathroom. There's a detached garage in the back that his dad built. It's also the place where his father killed himself two years ago. The guy did a two-year tour of Vietnam and survived but he couldn't survive real life. Just walked out into the garage one night and shot himself. I knew this before I became friends with Tyrell. Many people talk behind his back, snicker he's a weirdo, that he's cursed because his father committed suicide, like Tyrell is gonna go berserk one day and stab everyone at school, which is absurd. Because if all those people would get to know Tyrell, they'd realize that Tyrell is a nice guy and he's real peaceful. He doesn't talk much about his father's suicide but he does talk about his father. He says good things, like how his dad turned him on to science fiction books and how he was really good at math. He could add complicated math problems in his head, with no calculator. When I started hanging around Tyrell and told my mom his story, she wasn't thrilled I had a friend whose dad shot himself in the garage. "You give up your right to kill yourself when you have kids," she said. Yeah, but it's okay if you start dating a dickweed who shouts at you, makes you drink too much, and calls your son Danielle.

Anyhow, like I said, Tyrell talks about his dad but he doesn't speak about the suicide. I wonder how he feels about it. It must hurt big time but I don't pry. That's not right.

We go into the kitchen and Tyrell makes macaroni and cheese from the box. He pours us each a large cup of milk and we sit at the table eating. He talks about the book he's reading—it's about a teenage boy named Bill who moves to Ganymede, one of Jupiter's moons, to live on a farming colony. Only when they get there, the situation isn't good.

"What do you mean it isn't good?" I ask.

Tyrell shoves macaroni in his mouth and then holds up his finger until he swallows. The reason why he does this is because his mother doesn't allow him to talk with food in his mouth. His mom isn't here and I don't care if he talks with his mouth full, but some habits are hard to break.

Tyrell says, "There's too many people there, in the colony, on Ganymede. And the soil isn't good."

Interesting. "So they're gonna turn into cannibals?" I say.

"I don't know. Haven't finished the book." He knits his brow and thinks. "Maybe."

"That would be cool," I say. "They can bite each other and then turn into zombies. So when the next people come to the moon colony, they land and find out they have to fight them off." I stand up and pretend to swing a bat, smashing zombies. "Grrrr! Die zombie man, die!"

Tyrell laughs.

"And maybe," I say, sitting back down, "their ship doesn't work and they can't get back to Earth. Now that would be scary. Can they survive until the next ship arrives? Can they kill every last zombie?"

Tyrell shakes his head. "This is science fiction. Not horror."

I shrug. Like I said before, I like horror. *Halloween* is my favorite, although I do love *The Shining*. It's about a man who goes around this hotel trying to kill his wife and son with an ax. I must like ax stories. I never realized that before.

"So what are you planning?" Tyrell asks after he finishes swallowing again. "Your top-secret plan?"

I put my fork down and look Tyrell in the eye, doing my best to be serious. "You know how I hate Harry, right?"

"Yep."

"So, I'm planning to get rid of him."

Tyrell's face goes stone stiff.

"For real," I add.

Tyrell nods slightly. "Um…"

"Let me tell you the plan." I go into it. I explain about moving the beer into the garage as bait, hiding behind Lisa's old kitchen set, holding the ax, standing in the garage, and threatening him.

"Um…"

"What?"

Tyrell makes a sizzling sucking sound in his mouth, like he's really cringing, like it just pains him to listen to me.

"What?" I say again.

"Don't you think that's a bit…"

"What?"

"Insane?"

"No. Why?"

"You just can't be holding an ax to a grown man's head. And besides, they put kids in juvie for that stuff. You better bet your butt he'll call the police on you."

"I'll say I didn't do it. I'll lie."

"And Harry will say you did do it and the police are going to believe an adult over a kid. That's how it works."

"How do you know?"

"Come on," Tyrell says, fixing his shirt collar which has flopped down. "I like you, Danny, you're my friend, but you know how you are."

"What do you mean by that?"

"You get in trouble sometimes. Even if you didn't do it, like yesterday. You have anger problems."

I sigh and rub my forehead, then lose it. "So what? Maybe I got my reasons to be angry!"

"I know, Danny…"

"Well, you don't know that Harry and my mom are gonna get married! Then he's gonna live with us." My gut tightens and I get sick just thinking about it and I start yelling, feeling my eyes water. "He's such a dickhead!" I tell Tyrell that Harry was screaming at my mom last night. That it scared the shit out of me. That he called me Danielle. That he drinks beer around our house like it's his own personal saloon. "He's got no respect."

Tyrell shakes his head in disbelief. "I'm glad my mom doesn't have a boyfriend."

"You should be glad! Because Harry's gonna end up moving into my house and trying to be my dad!"

"All right, calm down." Tyrell shifts nervously in his seat. I see him eye his science fiction book and I know he'd rather be reading than talking to me.

"Forget it," I say.

"Listen," Tyrell says, lowering his voice. "I know he's bad but you can't just threaten to kill a man. Not unless you have a reason. Like he hit you or your mom."

I shake my head in disgust and frustration. "No. He hasn't hit us." I pause. "Yet."

"So you have no good reason. If you threaten him with a weapon, you'll go to the mental home or like I said, juvenile hall."

"I don't care."

"You will when you're in there. I heard some bad stories about juvie. It's a jail for kids who commit crimes, like murder. Or threaten to kill people."

I slide down in the chair, to the side. "So what?"

Tyrell scratches his chin. "I can't let you do this."

"What kind of friend are you?"

Suddenly, Tyrell grins. "You are one crazy person."

I sit up and push my plate away. "Thanks a lot."

But I see it. My plan is dumb, stupid, idiotic. What makes me think I can threaten Harry with an ax? I am a moron, just like Janine Finn said.

Tyrell takes our plates away. He returns with a Devil Dog in the wrapper and hands it to me. "Let's watch some TV. It'll make you think of something else."

We go into the living room and watch television and I eat my

Devil Dog, licking the cream off my fingers. *Star Trek* is on, which you can guess is one of Tyrell's favorite shows. Science fiction at its finest. I like *Star Trek*—it's pretty good—so for a half hour, my mind goes off on the Starship Enterprise. Of course at the end, Captain Kirk has to say goodbye to the hot female alien woman. He always hooks up with the hot female aliens.

After the show, Tyrell says to me: "Instead of threatening to kill him, why don't you make up a fake boyfriend for your mom?"

"A fake boyfriend?" He's got me interested.

Tyrell thinks for a minute and then says, "Yeah. Write a letter to your mom and sign it some guy's name. Leave it on the kitchen table so Harry can find it. Better yet, buy a card and write, 'I love you so much! I had a great time the other night at dinner. Love, Donald.'"

I smile.

"You can even say, 'You have my number. Call me, love Donald.'"

"Yeah!" I say. "Harry will think my mom met someone else."

"Then he'll break up with your mom. And even if she denies everything, the suspicion is in the air." Tyrell holds his hands up and slowly moves his fingers like a wizard casting a spell. "Just suspicion hanging over them, like fog."

It sounds great but then it makes me feel bad. I know this will hurt my mom. She'll cry and beg Harry to believe her. It will be a scene. I will feel awful.

"I'll think about it," I tell Tyrell.

He shrugs. "I think it's better than the ax threat."

I know he's right.

"Keep you out of juvie. Or the mental home. 'Cause I'm not gonna visit you."

I shoot him a mean stare.

"Sorry, man. I have to draw the line somewhere."

Tyrell's mom will be home soon and although Tyrell says she likes me, she prefers to arrive at a quiet house. Mrs. Colton is a nurse but not for a hospital. She works at a nursing home, a place for sick older people. She works the day shift and when it's over, she likes to walk in the door, take off her white shoes, put her feet up on the coffee table, and watch the six o'clock news. That's her routine, Tyrell says, and she doesn't want it messed with.

"Don't forget your bike," Tyrell reminds me as I get up. I rode it over here last Saturday and left it. It started to rain so Tyrell's mom drove me home. She's sort of quiet like Tyrell.

I step outside into the chilly spring evening and close the door behind me. It's still light out and I make my way around the side of the house to the small detached garage. I'm going to scrap the ax and go with the new plan. I know it will hurt my mom but it will be better in the long run.

The door to the garage is dirty and the bottom corner kicked in. Don't ask me how that happened. I stop before it and freeze. I don't like going into Tyrell's garage.

I stare at the closest pine tree, its branches sticking out in all sorts of ways. A couple of crows are sitting in it and one caws. Creepy.

I need my bike so I take a deep breath, bend down, and pull the garage door open. There's not much in it: just some cardboard boxes, a couple of buckets, a snow shovel. At the back, there's a tool area with no tools. I think Tyrell's mom gave them away to family members. I look at the concrete floor and try to make out any evidence of the suicide, like dried blood. It's too dim to see but I've been in here before so I know it's all cleaned up. I don't know why I think I'm going to see blood now when I've never seen blood in here before.

I hear those crows again and a breeze blows, rattling an old wind chime in a neighbor's yard. A shiver goes down my spine and I quickly grab my BMX bike, push up the kickstand with my foot, and move my bike out, pulling the door down behind me. I pedal as fast as I can from the garage, jetting onto the street. I like Tyrell but I have to admit, I hate his garage. A man shot himself in there. It's got to be haunted.

I ride up the block, passing the three little kids who always call me names. Three boys, probably second graders. They start screaming at me: "Booger head! Green booger head!"

"Shut up!" I snap, zipping by them.

"Booger head! Sloppy green booger head!"

I ignore them and continue toward the highway.

Crossing Route 37 is tough. It's a pretty busy road and you have to be careful. A guy named Martin Jenkins got hit last year. He's okay but he was in the hospital for six weeks with two broken arms and a broken leg. He was a baseball player but it looks like he won't be playing until next year.

I cross successfully and ride along the highway until I find the trail that will lead to my neighborhood. I love riding my bike through the woods. It's quiet except for the sound of my pedals and my breath. I go fast, zooming along the trail. We have a lot of sugar sand here so you have to watch where you're going, moving to the side when you see it coming. Sugar sand is gray but it's like beach sand, thick and hard to get through. It will trap your bike wheels so you can't move.

I burst out of the woods and onto the road. At the corner of Elizabeth Avenue, I have to stop because Elizabeth is the main road that goes through my neighborhood. You've got to be careful when you cross Elizabeth. It's almost as busy at Route 37. I know a kid who got hit here. Well, I *did* know him. We were in third grade together. He's dead now because he got hit by a truck.

Why can't Harry get hit by a truck?

I race across Elizabeth and make my way down Fourth Street, slowing down, realizing I don't want to go home.

Before I know it, I'm passing Janine Finn's house. It's a two-story thing but it's a mess. There's no grass, just a dirt front yard surrounded by a chain-link fenced. This is because they have a mean-ass German shepherd named Orson that comes racing out front, jumping up to the edge of the fence. It barks and howls at me. I pick up my speed and get by. One day Orson is gonna get over the fence and rip someone to pieces.

When I arrive home, the sun is hanging just over the tree tops. Harry's motorcycle is not in the driveway, nor is his puke green tank, which is a relief. I remember it's Thursday and I smile because Harry works double shifts on Thursdays. He works at some factory up in north Jersey. I keep hoping his arm will get caught in one of the machines at his plant and pull him in and tear him up.

The garage door is open and I put my bike inside. I turn on the light and stand, scanning the place until my eyes settle on the ax hanging on the wall. My dad hung it there. I don't know what he used the ax for. We don't have a fireplace so it's not like he was chopping down trees for fuel.

I go inside and the house smells good. My mom made tacos.

"Just in time!" she says happily.

I want to smile because I love tacos but I'm still angry at her for getting drunk yesterday. I walk by her and say, "I'm not hungry."

"You're always hungry, Danny," she says. She's got her dyed blonde hair in a ponytail and she's wearing a T-shirt and sweat pants. She smells like chemicals from the beauty salon, but not bad chemicals. She always smells like this: shampoo, hair spray, hair dye. I can hear the TV in the living room.

"I'm not always hungry," I say, stopping by the refrigerator and looking for a can of soda—no soda. Instead, there's a six-pack of beer in the back of the fridge. They usually keep their beer in the extra refrigerator we have in the garage. Why is their beer in the kitchen fridge? This makes me angry and I turn and face her. "Is Harry coming over tonight?"

My mom blinks at me and says no.

"Good."

She lets out a deep breath. We're standing just a few inches apart from each other. "I'm sorry about yesterday. I have no excuse to act like that."

33

"You're right. You shouldn't act like that."

My mom nods. "I know."

"Then don't do it again."

She nods once more. "I won't." Then she hugs me. I remain still, not hugging her back, but I smell the nice scent of the salon on her shirt. It makes me feel like a little kid again and without thinking, I put my arms around her and hug her back.

"I love you, Danny," she whispers. "I'm so sorry."

I don't say anything. I just let her hug me for a long moment until she releases me.

Lisa comes into the kitchen and we sit down at the table, just the three of us, eating tacos and drinking iced tea like old times. Lisa starts telling us about her new history teacher and how cute he is and my mom laughs. "Oh, I had a crush on my history teacher in school. How funny!"

Life is good for a while. Until the phone rings and Lisa answers it. "It's Harry," she says, holding out the receiver. My mom jumps up like a rabbit, grabs the receiver, taking it with her to the laundry room which is adjacent to the kitchen so she can talk privately. The long red coiled cord trails after her like a snake.

Lisa and I sit at the table, playing with our food until my mom gets off the phone, her face flushed and glowing. How does a woman forgive a man for yelling at her and telling her to shut up? I'm sure they made up earlier and this wasn't the apology phone call. This was the *You're so beautiful, Judy, I love you so much, I want to apologize again for telling you to shut up* phone call. I've heard him apologize to her before. She always buys it.

Before I go to bed, I pull the folded paper from my jeans pocket: Way to Get Rid of Harry. I read it over again, crossing out the entire ax plan and rewriting it:

Way to Get Rid of Harry

Fake Boyfriend

    a. Buy a card at Marsha's Card store and write Thank you for dinner and Love Donald in it.

b. Put it on the kitchen table when Harry is around.

c. Make sure I'm out of the house because there will be a fight.

d. Pack a bag because I may have to hide at Tyrell's.

e. Harry will break up with Mom.

f. She will be sad but I will make her a cake. She likes chocolate cake.

g. I will talk to her and remind her how mean Harry was to her.

h. She will realize that she can meet another guy.

When I'm satisfied with my plan, I fold the paper and stick it in my special shoebox under my bed. It's full of important things, mostly pictures of my dad. I look at one photo. My dad is standing at the kitchen table, his hands in his pockets. I'm next to him. It's my fifth birthday and I've got a red cone hat on my head and a big chocolate cake in front of me. I'm not looking at my dad who is wearing his brown glasses, a wide-collared mustard-colored shirt tucked into brown corduroy pants with a thick brown belt. It's the seventies so that's why he looks so goofy. Brown and mustard yellow were in style then. I shake my head and laugh a little—why did they think those clothes looked good? What was with the seventies? Sometimes I watch old sitcoms, like *The Jeffersons* or *The Brady Bunch* and I think, what made them think that striped bell-bottom pants and bright green shirts with wide collars looked cool? Nothing matched in those days.

I put the paper in the shoebox, place the top on, and slide it under my bed. Then I take my jeans off and lay back, my hands behind my head, looking up at my Pink Floyd poster.

What the hell is wrong with my mom? Like why is such a nice woman dating such a creep like Harry?

Here's the complicated story in a nutshell: my mom and my

dad divorced when I was ten. She started dating guys right away but they didn't call her back or they dumped her. This made her really sad. Then when I was twelve, my dad was diagnosed with cancer and died last spring. It was very quick. Believe it or not, my mom was really crushed when my dad died. She cried for weeks. Then, around January this year, she met Harry. And believe it or not even more, Harry made her happy.

Okay, why did my parents divorce?

I don't want to admit it, but my dad was cheating on her with some woman called Debbie. They were having an affair for over five months so my mom kicked my dad out and divorced him immediately. "I will not stand for this!" I remember my mom screaming. Debbie was twenty-three, and that upset my mom because she's thirty-nine (thirty-six at the time) and she says men don't like women who are over thirty, which I don't believe is true. I don't think my mom should've divorced my dad for cheating. I mean, yeah, cheating is pretty bad and I don't blame her for getting mad and kicking him out, but maybe they just needed a few months apart to hang out and think, maybe date other people, see how much they missed each other. I'm sure being married to the same person must get old. You gotta get bored. On TV all married people get along. In real life, that's not the case. People might love each other but they hate living with each other because they'd rather be out or doing something exciting, like traveling to a foreign country, than staying home, paying bills, cleaning up the house. I think my mom and dad really loved each other but didn't like living with each other. Right before my dad moved out, he said he would always love my mom. Lisa told me that my mom confessed one night that she shouldn't have rushed into the divorce.

I guess my mom settled for Harry because after my dad's cheating and the divorce and the other men dumping her and my dad dying, she just felt lousy. I don't know. My mom is pretty and she dresses nice, and I know if she would just get rid of Harry, a nice dude will come around and be cool to her.

Trouble is, she's got no confidence. She doesn't believe in herself. She doesn't believe that she's good enough to hold out for a nice man. I told her this once and she just smiled and fed me the standard adult BS line, "You're too young to understand."

Tyrell's mom doesn't go out on any dates, like he said earlier, but he also says that his mom is lonely. "I wish she'd go out on dates. Sometimes I hear her crying." I told him that her crying over being lonely was better than crying over some man.

"That's true," Tyrell said.

There's also the problem of money. Lisa explained that to me too. When my dad was alive, he used to give my mom money but now that he's dead, that stopped. My mom doesn't make a lot as a beautician and after paying the house bills, there isn't much left. This past Christmas, she couldn't afford to get me anything but a pair of jeans, a pack of socks, and a Pink Floyd cassette. Harry gives her money now, Lisa says.

So am I mad at my dad for cheating on my mom? Well, I can't be mad at him now because he's dead. I was mad at him for leaving us but I was only ten so I didn't stay mad for long, especially since I got to spend some weekends with him. I do know that even if he didn't cheat on my mom, he still would have gotten cancer and my mom probably would have still met Harry and we would still be in the same crummy predicament we are in now.

The next day at school I see Mr. Cage. I remember I want to tell him what Richard Plimpton told me but after all this thinking about getting rid of Harry and my life, Richard Plimpton's lie seems unimportant. I wave to Mr. Cage and he nods.

"Behaving yourself, Mr. Zelko?" Mr. Cage says.

It irks me that he says this because it means he doesn't quite think I'm innocent, not about the Richard thing but innocent in general. I'm not going to get mad. I keep myself presentable. I nod and say, "Yes."

Mr. Cage says, "Good," and keeps walking.

Tyrell and I eat lunch together again.

"So have you thought about what I said?" he asks.

I look around to see if anyone can hear. "Yeah, I thought about it."

Tyrell bites into his pizza. Friday is pizza day at my school but it's the worst pizza on the planet. It's barely cooked, the cheese is not even melted. It's like they took it out of the freezer and stuck it in the oven for two minutes. I eat it though. It's all they serve on Fridays. I have to remember to make myself peanut butter and jelly on Fridays.

"I'm going to buy a card today and leave it on the kitchen table tonight," I explain to Tyrell. "But I was wondering, if things get kinda crazy, like maybe if there's a big fight, I might need a place to stay. Can I come to your house?"

"I guess." Tyrell seems unsure.

"Your mom won't mind?"

"Yeah, she'll mind."

"So, should I not come to your house?"

Tyrell shrugs. "I don't know." He thinks for a minute. "Only if you really need to. If it's your last resort."

He's frustrating me. Tyrell is a bit of a Mama's boy. Not like he can't do anything without his mom. He cooks and washes clothes and takes care of himself all the time. What I mean is that he never wants to upset her. Doesn't like to make waves.

"I'm sorry, Danny," Tyrell says.

"Whatever," I say, looking across the cafeteria at my old friends Shawn Stinson and Lou Barth. They're laughing and I realize I miss hanging out with them. They like to play baseball, football, soccer, basketball...Tyrell doesn't really play sports. Not that he can't play sports, he's just not great at it. He can throw a baseball and we play catch sometimes in his backyard, and he likes basketball, and sometimes we'll play ball at the old net in front of his neighbor's house. He won't go down to the baseball field or the court in his neighborhood because it's full of guys who give Tyrell a hard time because he's not that good. And on account of his father. Kids make fun of him for it. I've heard them. One time this kid, Keon Dawson, an older brother of one those little kids that call me green booger head, said to Tyrell, "Anyone shoot themselves in your garage lately?" It was cruel as cruel gets. I can't blame Tyrell for hanging out in his house and escaping into his science fiction world. Another thing he'll do is ride his bike or hike through the woods out to Baskro Lake with me, but that's it. I like Tyrell because he and I have things in common, and Tyrell has interesting things to talk about and he's smart, and I like when he tells me about the alien books he is reading, but sometimes a person just wants to throw a ball around and not think about what would happen if you set up a colony on one of Jupiter's moons. Sometimes a person feels better after swinging a baseball bat and smacking a ball across the sky. Sometimes a person wants to hang out with people who don't have too much inside stuff to carry, like Tyrell does, like being an outcast and having a dad who committed suicide and making sure his mom doesn't get upset. Sometimes a person just wants to hang out with people who have no idea what and where Ganymede is.

During the bus ride home, I sit by Shawn and Lou. We're just talking about stupid stuff when Shawn brings up his dad and starts telling us that he's taking him to a Mets game up at Shea Stadium in New York. Lou is going with them and Shawn invites me, but like I said before, I can't hang around Shawn and his dad. It's too depressing. So I decline and slide over to the window, watching the world go by as the bus bumps along the roads.

At home, I let myself in with my house key. No one is there. My mom is working and Harry isn't in the house and my sister is probably working at McDonald's. She just turned sixteen and the first thing she did was get a job to help out with expenses.

Well, her own expenses so she doesn't have to ask my mom for money to buy clothes and makeup and other things she might want. She says she's saving for college, too. Lisa said she isn't sure what she wants to be, only that she doesn't want to end up like my mom, barely getting by. Lisa said my mom was supposed to open her own beauty salon but then she started hanging out with our dad and he talked her out of it. When I asked why, Lisa said that he was afraid she'd make more money than him, owning a business and all. When it comes to my dad, Lisa doesn't think he was a wonderful guy. "He cheated on Mom and broke her heart. He didn't even try to get her back." I choose not to believe that last part.

I drop my backpack in my room. Even though it's Friday, I still have math homework. My math teacher, Mrs. Mullins, is a jerk for giving homework on the weekends. She's a good math teacher but she's mean as mean gets—always yelling at kids for trivial things, like forgetting a pencil or sticking your legs out in the aisle. She seems to like me, though, because I always have my math homework. Math comes easy to me. It's probably because I like money.

I find some cash in my piggy bank—it's actually not a pig but a ceramic baseball with red stitching. There's only five dollars and a little change left over from shoveling snow this winter because in January I gave my mom most of the money to help pay the electric bill. I'll have more money soon. Lawn-mowing season is starting and by next weekend, I should be working. I have my own mower and a list of people who use my services. I even get rid of the bags of grass and sweep up. It's a small business but I plan to expand it this year by adding more customers.

It's about four o'clock so I get on my bike and ride up to Marsha's. The card store is in a small strip mall with a bakery, a small bank, a beauty salon (not the place my mom works at) and a convenience store. We have many senior citizens who live in our township because for some reason we have seven special neighborhoods for older people. Sometimes in the summer, if you look at the arms on the old guys, you can see worn, green tattoos representing World War II. Like an anchor or a ship's wheel if they were a sailor in the Pacific Arena, or an eagle or gun, or the fuzzy outlines of a sexy 1940's girl. Once, and this is really frightening, I was in the supermarket with my mom and the older lady checking out in front of us had numbers tattooed on the inside of her wrist. She was wearing a long-sleeve shirt but you could see it when she reached into her cart and grabbed the food to ring up. I looked at my mom and she looked at me. The lady noticed that I was staring at her wrist and she appeared to get annoyed. I felt bad about being nosey but I didn't know how to apologize to her so I looked away. I'd never seen a Holocaust tattoo. I still wonder what concentration camp she was a prisoner in.

I go into the card store and find the love cards. I pick a small one because I don't want to spend all my money on this. It's pink with a goofy poem on the front and another on the inside. The girl working at the register smiles at me. She's got brown hair and she's wearing a gold heart necklace.

"For your girlfriend?" she asks.

"Yeah," I say, figuring it's easier than making up some story that I'm buying it for a friend.

"How long have you been going out?"

I shrug. "Four months."

"That's sweet." I give her the money and she hands me my change and she slides the card into a thin paper brown bag. "See ya, loverboy," she says and I'm completely embarrassed.

I pedal along the highway and onto the trail through the woods. I have the bag with the card in my hand and I realize it might have been better if I wore a backpack to the store. That way I could've put the card in it.

At home I drop my bike on the front lawn. I left the house unlocked and I'm hoping my sister isn't around to yell at me. She isn't. I'm alone. I go into my room, lock the door, and sit at my desk, pulling the card from the bag. There's a sweat stain from my hand at the corner of the bag and it has leaked into the pink envelope. It'll dry, I tell myself. I find a blue pen in my desk drawer and I'm about to write what I plan to write, but I realize I have to use grown up handwriting. So I take out a sheet of paper and try to write like an adult. I don't need to use cursive hand-writing because I'm Donald and Donald doesn't write in cursive. I think. I should've gotten Tyrell to come over because he has neat handwriting. My handwriting is terrible—print or cursive.

I practice writing what I'm supposed to write. *Judy, I enjoyed dinner last night. Love, Donald.* I write it five times on the scrap paper, printing because I print better but I also use mostly capital letters because I saw Harry write once and that's what he does. When I feel confident, I slide the card over and begin writing. I can't make any mistakes because then I'll have to go back and get another card. It takes me a long time to finish. I slip the card into the envelope, seal it, and write *My dear Judy* on the front. (I think the *My dear* is a nice touch.) It's six-thirty and still, no one is home. I put the card in my desk and go out front to put my bike in the garage. I come back in and watch TV until seven o'clock and then I eat the leftover tacos—cold because I'm okay with cold tacos. I clean up after myself and watch more TV. It's dark at this point and I step outside to calm myself because my mom is usually home by seven-thirty on Friday nights. Now it's eight. I look at the stars and try to find the Seven Sisters. I go back inside and pick up the phone and call the beauty salon—sometimes it's open late. Nobody answers. I wish I knew when Lisa was going to be home. McDonald's closes at eleven so maybe she's working until then? I find the number to the McDonald's and call. The manager answers and says, "I'll get her." It takes three minutes before Lisa gets on the phone.

"Where's Mom?" I ask.

"How would I know?"

"Because she didn't leave a note. She didn't even call."

I hear Lisa sigh loudly. "I'm sure she's out with Harry."

My head goes to a dark spot. "Maybe she's been kidnapped by a killer?"

"I doubt it. She's probably out with Harry."

My mind is still in the dark spot. "Maybe she's tied up in a van?"

"Danny, I'm at work."

"Are you coming home soon?"

"No. I'm staying at Robin's tonight. Mom knows this."

Now I'm really ticked off—was anyone going to tell me I was hanging out by myself tonight?

"I wish someone would tell me stuff!"

"Goodbye, Danny. Don't call again." She hangs up.

I hate my sister sometimes. She's such a jerk.

I want to punch something but I have to pull my head together. I sit at the kitchen table. A minute later, the phone jangles. It's my mom.

"Danny?" she says.

"Where are you?"

"Harry and I are out to dinner."

That's a lie because I can hear a bunch of commotion in the background, even music, so that means that's she's not at a restaurant but a bar.

"When are you coming home?" I say.

"I'll be home in another hour."

I peer at the clock over the kitchen stove. She'll be home around nine-thirty.

"Okay."

"Love you, sweetie," and she hangs up.

I place the phone in the cradle and return to the living room to watch TV. There's not much on except this really dumb movie about fashion models being frozen. It's creepy for about five minutes until it gets ridiculous. I watch the time on the cable box: 9:24, 9:38, 9:57, 10:09, 10:27, 10:46, 11:01. My stomach is tight and my heart is rattling—I'm nervous about going through with my plan. I get up and look through the windows. I even go outside and check out the stars and the moon, which is high in the sky. I pace the front lawn, not caring if my neighbor

George across the street tells my mom I was out on the front lawn at eleven at night. (He told my mom that Lisa was sneaking out of the house at night. That was a couple of years ago when Lisa was fourteen. She doesn't do that anymore.)

I go inside and sit on the couch. 11:07, 11:17, 11:28, 11:36.

I haven't put the card on the kitchen table yet. I'm worried about hurting my mom.

Screw it. She told me she would be home by ten.

11:43, 11:56, 11:59. Midnight.

I go in my bedroom and take the card from my desk drawer. I march into the kitchen and leave it on the table. I return to my room and get into bed. I don't care how much she cries.

"Danny! Get up now!"

My mom is standing over me, holding the card—it's not in the envelope. The light is on in my room. "Where did this come from?" she demands.

Crap. I forgot that detail. I make up a lie: "I found it on the front porch."

"Just lying on the front porch?"

"Yeah."

"Get up and come into the kitchen. Now."

In the kitchen, Harry is sitting at the table, lounged back in a chair. My mom is leaning against the counter still holding the card.

"So," she says, sounding pretty straight for being at a bar until one in the morning. The kitchen clock says 1:07.

"So," she says again. "Where'd this come from?"

I shrug. "I told you. The porch. Why are you home so late? You said ten."

"You better watch your tone," she hisses. "I'm the mom here."

I can't help it. I roll my eyes. I see Harry shift in his chair. He doesn't look angry. He looks amused. My stomach sinks. I

44

think my plan didn't work at all.

"I don't know a Donald," my mom says.

"I don't know who you know," I say.

"Knock it off," she snaps.

I eyeball Harry and I see him shake his head.

"Did you buy this card and make this up?" my mom asks.

"Why would I do that?"

"Oh, I don't know!" she screams, her face completely red. "Maybe because you don't want me to have a life!"

I see Harry shift again in his seat. He's wearing a black shirt and jeans and his big motorcycle boots. His jean jacket is draped over one of the kitchen chairs.

I notice my mom is wearing tight, dark Sergio Valente jeans, a striped V-neck shirt that shows off her boobs and makes it hard for me to look at her, and summer sandal heels that look like they're made of cork. I bet she borrowed that tight shirt from someone she works with at the beauty salon. She never used to wear shirts that showed off her boobs. I hate that my mom gets dressed up for Harry and I hate that she lied to me about what time she'd be home. I bet that was his idea.

I'm about to keep going with this—start saying, *Come on, Mom, you know Donald has been here and you've been hanging out with him. That you've been cheating on Harry with him...* But she's tearing up and wiping her eyes and shoving the card and envelope in the garbage can.

So I say nothing.

She points a finger in my face and yells, "Admit it! Admit you did this!"

I swallow and see the tears rolling down her cheeks and I can't be crueler to her than I've already been. "I'm sorry," I say. "I did do it."

"Why?"

Because I hate Harry and I don't want you to marry him.

I don't say that. I just shrug and try another tactic, to make things easier on her. "I was playing a joke," I lie. "I thought it would be funny."

My mom sniffs. "Oh, for Christ's sake."

"I didn't think you'd get all upset."

Harry now speaks: "Oh, is that so, boy?" His words are oozing sarcasm.

"Don't start with him," my mom says. For a second, I see hope. She's sticking up for me.

Harry shifts, glowers at her.

She drops her head, like a scolded child. "I'm going to bed," she mumbles as she walks away.

I don't know what to do, so I stand there, letting the silence roar in my ears. I'm nervous Harry is going to start shouting at me. I wish my sister were around.

Harry chuckles. "Oh, you're gonna have to be smarter than that."

I look at him.

He stands up and stretches. His T-shirt rides up revealing his hairy stomach.

"Your mom and I are in this for the long run," he says, moving close to me.

"It was just a joke," I say, trying not to look at him.

Harry pats me on the arm. "No, it wasn't. You were trying to get rid of me."

"No," I croak, staring up into his thin eyes, really noticing the bags hanging heavily underneath them.

"It's okay. I understand," Harry says. "You and I have to get along and we haven't been. Truthfully, your mom told me that you were a little out of control and that you needed a firm hand. I was doing what she said. Trying to help you into manhood. I know it's tough coming up in a house without a dad. My father took off on my mother when I was nine. She remarried but not until I was out of the house. I can't imagine what it's like to be in your shoes."

I can feel my shoulders slump and a lump grows in my throat. He's being nice to me and I don't know what to do. I've hated him since February. That's a long time to hate someone.

He pats me on the arm again. "I'm going to step outside for a cigarette. Your mom asked me to not smoke in the house anymore because she doesn't like the smell. So I'm going to abide by her wishes."

I nod.

"We okay?" he asks.

I shrug, nod again.

"Cool." He grabs his jean jacket and pulls a pack of cigarettes from the inside pocket. "Get some sleep, son. We'll forget the whole thing." He winks.

I watch him step outside into the front yard. Through the front window, I see him stare up at the moon and the stars while he smokes.

I'm confused.

WAY TWO:
KILL WITH KINDNESS

In the morning, I hide out in my room. I really have to go to the bathroom and I'm very hungry, but I don't want to face my mom or Harry. I feel dumb about the whole card thing.

It doesn't make me feel any better when Lisa bursts into my room.

"More stupid pills?" she says, her hands on her hips.

I roll over and face the wall.

"So you're hiding out in here? It's after eleven."

"Go away."

She doesn't. "You should've picked a better name than Donald and you should have gotten someone else to write it. Anyone could tell it was your lousy handwriting."

I turn back and look at my sister.

She raises her eyebrows. "At least it was a start. A bad one, but a start."

"I know," I mumble. "I'll think of something else. Another way."

"Sure." She leaves.

I flop over in bed, thinking about how understanding Harry was last night. He didn't get mad, didn't call me Danielle. Maybe he's okay. Maybe I just have to get to know him.

My bladder is about to explode so after my sister leaves, I put on my jeans and go into the bathroom. It's a relief to pee and it's a relief to know I have work to do today—I'll be out of the house for a few hours. I have to visit my lawn customers from last year and make sure they want me to continue mowing.

In the kitchen, I take a seat at the table. I'm nervous because Harry is there and I don't know what to say. He bought us doughnuts for breakfast—he must have because my mom would never buy us doughnuts. I snag a chocolate frosted one but I'm so nervous, the chocolate just sticks in my mouth and I can't swallow.

"What are you up to today?" Harry asks me.

I drink some milk to wash the doughnut in my mouth down. I tell him about my list of lawn customers and how I need to check and see if they still want to hire me this year.

Harry leans back in his chair. He seems impressed. "So you have a little business going?"

"Yep."

We don't say anything more and I'm out the door on my bike, making my way through the neighborhood. I have four customers on my list. Everyone who is home says yes to another season and the one who isn't home will probably say yes because she's an older lady. I shoveled snow for her and she reminded me to come back in the late spring for the mowing. I even get a fifth customer, the neighbor of the older lady who tells me she and her husband hate mowing and they're willing to pay me. I do everyone's lawn once a week or once every two weeks, depending on the request, so that means I'll get at least twenty dollars a week. Last fall I gave my mom the lawn money I had saved up but this summer, with Harry around, I can keep it all to myself.

During the ride home, I bike by Richard Plimpton's house. He lives in the same type of ranch home as I do—you know, three bedrooms, one bathroom, a living room, kitchen, garage— but his parents keep it nice. The grass is always perfect with no brown spots and the bushes are trimmed so neatly they look like upside-down parallelograms. As I coast by, I see his dad and mom planting flowers underneath the parallelogram bushes. His dad looks like he's a doctor and I bet he plays golf.

That night, Harry and my mom take Lisa and me out to dinner. We have to dress up and I have a bad feeling I know what this is about. We go to the Old Time Tavern in Toms River and sure enough, right after the waitress brings us bread, my mom spills: they're getting married at the end of August.

I glance at Lisa and she forces a smile—I know her forced smiles. But I'm okay. It's not that bad. Harry has been nothing but nice to all of us and he's not even drinking beer. He's drinking soda and he kisses my mom's hand after she tells us about getting married. I decide I'm going to be cool. Maybe things have finally turned. Maybe my joke card sort of scared Harry, made him think like: *Hey, this kid isn't so bad. He loves his mom enough to do a dumb stunt like make up a pretend boyfriend.* Or maybe not. Probably not. I just like that things are going well for once. Keeping with the upbeat mood, I grab a piece of bread and some butter and say to my mom and Harry, "Congratulations!"

I feel Lisa's eyes on me but I ignore her and keep eating. I'm going to be a better kid. I'm going to try to like Harry. Especially since he's paying for dinner. I love the Old Time Tavern. They have the best bread in the world. We haven't been here since my parents split, way before my dad died.

After dinner, Harry takes us for ice cream. Since he's paying, I order a super sundae with soft chocolate ice cream, marshmallow and hot fudge topping, chocolate chips, whipped cream, sprinkles, and a cherry. Harry doesn't complain. It's a little chilly for ice cream but I sit on the bench and enjoy every spoonful even though my stomach doesn't. I'm a little sick going home and when I get into the house, I go right into the bathroom and throw up.

After upchucking, I feel like a new man and everyone sits in the living room and watches a movie on HBO, *Jaws*. I love *Jaws* and so does Harry. My favorite part is when they're on the boat and the old man is telling the story about how he was left in the water after their ship was torpedoed by the Japanese. The old guy tells the tale like a ghost story: his voice is really low and serious and in the background, you can hear the boat rocking and creaking. It makes me shiver every time I see this scene.

Harry says that the sinking actually happened and I'm like, "That true?" and he says, "Yes. It sure did." I like how we're getting along and when I get ready for bed, I don't even turn on my music. I just lie there with my hands behind my head thinking about the movie, and how cool it was when the old man just slipped into the shark's mouth. I'm about to drift off when Lisa bangs into my room, flicking on the light and shutting the door.

"So you're using kindness. I like it."

"What do you mean?" I say to her. I'm a bit drowsy and it takes a minute to wake up again.

"Kindness," she says. "You're trying to be super nice to him so he gets sick of you and maybe he'll break up with Mom. I think that's really smart."

I prop myself up by my elbow. "I wasn't trying to do anything. I thought we were getting along."

Lisa rolls her eyes. "Come on now."

I sit up completely. "No. I think he likes me."

"He doesn't like you."

"Yes he does."

"What?" She scans my room, her big head twisting from side to side. "Do you have an entire year's supply of stupid pills in here?"

"Shut up and get out of here!" I hate this stupid pill garbage. And why wouldn't Harry like me now? I'm being polite, I'm trying to be better, we both like the same movie.

Lisa chuckles. "And for a brief, shining moment, I thought I had a clever brother."

51

* * *

On Sunday, Harry and my mom drive down to Philadelphia to see his brother and his wife. Lisa takes off for Robin's and I call Tyrell but there's no answer. I immediately remember he goes to this church up in Newark. It begins to rain so I hang out in my house, playing video games, listening to music. I even take out my old box of Legos under my bed and try to build a fishing boat. I have to lock my bedroom door when I build things with my Legos because I'm in eighth grade, about to be fourteen in a few months and I can't be playing with Legos. It's embarrassing that I do this but it makes me feel better. Reminds me of being a little kid, when things were easier. When you didn't understand much and you believed everything everyone told you.

It gets dark and I heat up two frozen French bread pizzas for dinner in the toaster oven. I take a shower and get into bed. I hate being alone. It's still raining so I just listen to music and pretend-talk to my dad.

"Harry seems okay now," I tell him.

My dad is wearing the yellow mustard wide-collared shirt and corduroy pants he was wearing on my fifth birthday.

"That's good," he says.

"Lisa says he doesn't like me."

My dad doesn't say anything. I turn on my side and stare out the window into the darkness where it is still raining.

"Do you like *Jaws*?" I ask him. "Because Harry likes *Jaws*. We have that in common."

"Danny, that's not much of a stretch," my dad answers. "Everyone likes *Jaws*."

I stop pretend-talking to my dad. It's not him anyhow. It's me.

I'm going to try to be better and like my mom said, I can't compare my dad and Harry. It isn't right.

* * *

The school week is long. Summer break is still weeks away—it's taking forever. My head doesn't focus on my classes. I'm bothered by what Lisa said even though when I see Harry, he's nice to me, saying, "How's it going?" Lisa is sometimes around when he says this and she makes faces at me behind my back, saying, *Still taking the stupid pills, are you?*

All of my teachers are boring. My literature teacher is the worst. I like that we don't have to write so much but she's such a drag compared to Miss Lewis last year. She used to talk to us about things, not just literature things. Like, I remember President Reagan used to have these commercials on TV about raising money to buy more nuclear weapons. It went like this: the screen would be black and the announcer would talk about how many nuclear warheads the USSR had. "The Soviet Union has this many weapons." And bap, bap, bap, bap, bap, bap, bap, bap... About a dozen red pictures of nuclear bombs would come on the screen. Then it would say: "The US has this many." Bap, bap, bap. Like five would come up in blue. "We need to arm ourselves..." Anyhow, I remember I asked Miss Lewis why we were bothering to spend money on something that seemed pointless. Even if we made the same amount of nuclear weapons as the Soviet Union, we'd still wipe out both sides, so what was the point? She said it was like making snowballs. Like when you're younger and you make as many snowballs as possible so that your enemy, the kids you're fighting against, see that you're well-armed and they're less likely to start a snowball fight. "It's like King of the Mountain," she said. I said it was stupid and she said, "I completely agree with you, Danny." And that made me feel good, especially since she didn't get angry that I used the word stupid.

I hate thinking about nuclear war. About just hanging out with your friend and all of a sudden the sky will light up in the distance and you know, That's It. We're all gonna die from the nuclear fallout. Those Soviets are scary. Nobody knows anything about them or the countries they took over, like Poland

and Romania and East Germany. I heard you can't get in or out of Communist countries. So wait, how do we know how many weapons they have if nobody can go in to see them? Maybe they don't have any weapons. Maybe they're just as scared as us. Maybe some kid in the USSR is sitting down right now, just like me, and maybe he's watching a commercial that says the same thing I watched but it's reversed, like his leader is telling his people that we have more nuclear bombs and they have to make more and that kid is scared of us. I bet that kid lives sort of like me, likes to ride his bike and listen to Pink Floyd or whatever they do in the USSR, and he's thinking the same thing as I do: this nuclear bomb thing is stupid. I want to grow up, not die at thirteen. I think it's completely idiotic that the USSR and America spend all this money on nuclear warheads.

At lunch, I tell Tyrell about how his fake boyfriend plan backfired but in a good way.

"Scoot over," he tells me.

Iris Cruz again.

"But it worked out good. Harry's being nice to me."

Tyrell puts a fish stick into his mouth.

I put a fish stick in my mouth.

Then, after he swallows, he says, "It's a good thing you didn't use the ax."

"Why?"

"Because he wouldn't be so nice to you."

I laugh loudly.

On Wednesday Tyrell says he's going roller skating on Friday. "Do you wanna go? We can meet there."

I don't have enough money to pay for the admission or to rent skates so, that night, I ask my mom if she can loan me some money and I'll pay her back after I start mowing lawns.

She says she doesn't have it. "I'm sorry, honey."

Harry comes in the door a few minutes later and he sees me sulking on the couch. I don't mean to sulk, I never mean to sulk, but sometimes it just happens. It's hard to hide disappointment. I love roller skating. I haven't been in two months, not since I had snow shoveling money.

Harry and my mom talk in the kitchen and the next thing I know, Harry is handing me a ten-dollar bill. "Go have fun."

I'm so surprised. "Really? Thanks!"

Lisa isn't around to give me one of her faces.

Friday arrives and a bunch of us are all set to go roller skating. I'm going with Shawn Stinson and Lou Barth because Lou's mom is driving us and taking us home. Tyrell is going with a couple of kids from Pine Park, Marcus Flynn and Raymond Tipple. Marcus is okay. Tyrell says that Marcus, because his dad is a master mechanic, knows a lot about cars and that's pretty much the only conversation you can have with him. Raymond will probably dump Tyrell and Marcus to go hang out with cooler kids.

The roller rink is on Route 70, about a fifteen-minute drive from my house. It's huge inside, like an airplane hangar, and they have video games and pinball machines and you can even get food: pizza, French fries, cheeseburgers...the usual. I never eat there because I usually only have money to get in and rent my skates. But I'll have enough left over from the ten to buy a soda at the end of the night if I want.

Shawn and Lou have their own skates and when we go inside, we have to split up so I can go to the rental booth. The music is pumping and kids are already in the wooden rink, going around, and some are doing tricks in the middle. I love it here. The ceiling is very high and a big disco ball hangs from the ceiling. They spin the disco ball for two reasons: if a cool song is playing and when it's couples' skate.

I look good. My hair is just at the right length and it feathers a bit. I'm wearing jeans, a black Pink Floyd T-shirt with three-quarter white sleeves, and I have a comb in my back pocket in case my hair gets too messy from skating. I'm wearing a gold chain around my neck with a cross on it. I'm supposed to be Catholic but I refuse to go to church anymore. I dropped out of Catechism classes in third grade after I made my Communion. I just wouldn't go. They tried to tell us dinosaurs were around the same time as humans. I mean, seriously? What kind of religion tries to make us believe something the scientists have already confirmed? And besides, the Catechism teachers were mean. They told us it was a mortal sin if we skipped church on Sundays. Like you can go to Hell for eternity if you skip church. It's got the same penance as murder. My dad said he always thought that type of teaching was crazy and I agreed with him and he took my side against my mom about quitting Catechism. I believe in Heaven and Hell. I just don't believe the Catholics have it right. Still, I like my necklace with the cross. It makes me look cool.

I get my skates and see Tyrell standing along the bars, on the outside of the rink. Marcus is with him and they're both dressed in polo shirts with the collars turned up—Tyrell's is bright blue and Marcus's is hot pink. Pink?

"Hey," I say to them.

Tyrell and I high five and low five. We don't do that often but with the music blasting and everyone rolling around, you get a good vibe in your body and you gotta do things like this.

No Raymond Tipple. "Where'd he go?"

Tyrell doesn't answer.

"Tyrell's looking for Iris," Marcus says.

"She out there?" I say.

"Was," Marcus says. "Don't know where she went. Raymond's too cool for us."

I scan the rink and see Raymond out on the floor, spinning around, talking to some girls I don't know. They're probably from another school district.

"Yo!" Shawn says, skating up to me. He puts his foot down to stop himself. Lou is behind him. We all have the same kind of shaggy hair, feathered on the sides. Shawn is wearing a polo shirt and a gold chain. He looks at Tyrell and lifts his collar.

Lou is wearing an Iron Maiden T-shirt. He's a heavy metal fan. He's even wearing a black wristband with silver cackles on it.

"Twilight Zone" by Golden Earring comes on. Way cool. Shawn, Lou, and I go out on to the rink, leaving Tyrell and Marcus on the sidelines because they're being losers. Round and round we go, zipping in and out of girls, spinning around and skating backwards, sideways. The disco ball starts spinning, and the lights start going blue and red. "Twilight Zone" is a great tune. In the middle, there's thunder and lightning, then it goes into synthesized sounds, a guitar solo, never losing its kick-butt beat.

"Zelko!"

I spin around and see Janine Finn skating up to me. She's mouthing the words to the song, *Help, I'm stepping into the Twilight Zone, this place is a madhouse, feels like being cloned...*

I grin at her, noticing she looks really good in her tight jeans and black V-neck shirt. Her dark long hair is flowing behind her back and when she spins around, she looks like a hot witch.

"Who-hoo!" she cheers.

We skate near each other, going faster and faster, zipping in and out of other skaters. It's more like I'm chasing her, while she keeps looking back at me, mouthing the words to the song, yelling out to me. We're going so fast, sweat is dripping down my face but I don't stop. She's laughing and waving. Round and round the rink we go. When I pass Tyrell and Marcus, they shout out to me: "Go, Zelko!" Round and round, the music pumping, the disco ball twirling. I'm weaving in and out of people, really moving, speeding. I see Iris Cruz and her girls down by the pinball machines with Raymond and some other dude and they're cheering as I go by. Some girls I don't know, scream, "Go, go, Zelko!" Then, right near the end of the song, that little sixth grader I saw in the bathroom after I got in trouble about the wedgie crap comes flying from one of the skating entrances and I crash right into him. We both topple down, over and under each other. It's a hard fall on my side. I land on my arm and for a moment, it's like my shoulder is dislocated. The pain is bad and my eyes start watering. But I can feel everyone looking at me and I know I have to save face and get up. I start moving but out of nowhere, Lou and Shawn come swooping in and they lift me up. "You okay, man?" Shawn says. I feel like the entire rink is laughing at me and I know my face is red but the song has moved into something else, a song I don't like, and the disco ball stops. Lou and Shawn still skate but I just go around once. Janine zooms up from behind, whipping around me, crisscrosses her legs like scissors.

"Nice fall, Zelko. You suck at this!"

"Shut up, Janine."

She cackles and flies away. She is a witch. A loony crazy witch. And I hate her. Why is she such a jerk to me?

I make my way over to Tyrell, who sits by himself on a bench near the rink. He has his feet kicked up against the bars. I skate over and plop down, kicking my feet up on the bars too.

"You all right, man?" Tyrell asks.

I attempt to roll my shoulder. "It hurts." Just a little, actually. The pain quickly faded. I try to act cool, like it was nothing. I drape my arms along the bench, keep my feet on the bars.

"You need a doctor?" Tyrell says. "That was a bad fall."

"No." That comes out mean and Tyrell holds up his hands and makes a face.

"Excuse me for living."

I lean my head back and sigh. Everyone saw me take that dive on the rink.

"Where's Marcus?" I say.

Tyrell shrugs and looks around. "Don't know."

I shift my feet, still keeping them on the bar.

A referee skates by with his whistle and halts in front of us. "Take your feet down!"

Tyrell does immediately but I'm in a bad mood from falling and Janine Finn making fun of me. So I don't take my feet down.

"Take the feet down!" the ref says again.

I think about this and come to the conclusion that I don't have to. A: I'm not in school. B: I'm not hurting anyone. And C: the ref is a dork.

I leave my feet propped up.

"Take your feet down!" the ref shouts.

"Why?" I say.

"Because I told you to!"

"So? Who are you? President Reagan? You're not my boss!" I know I'm being bad but I can't help myself. I just feel like being bad—it's like a snake crawls up inside of me and chokes the good sense out of my brain. From the corner of my eye, I see Tyrell fidgeting, ducking his head underneath his hand.

The ref lowers his chin, slits his eyes at me, and rolls closer He places his hands on his sides. His mouth is twitching. "If you don't remove your feet from the bar, I'm going to have you removed from the rink."

"Danny," Tyrell says. "Just take your feet down."

I eyeball the ref and slowly remove my feet, placing them on the carpeted floor. The ref nods and says, "Thank you." He skates away.

I cross my arms over my chest.

"Man, oh, man," Tyrell mutters. "You're just asking to get punched."

"Be quiet."

I sit with Tyrell until they play "Candy Girl" by New Edition. Now things get interesting because Iris Cruz and her girls come skating by. Tyrell stands up and rolls to the bar. I follow him.

"Let's go skate," I say.

"Nah. I just like to watch."

So we watch Iris, wearing red jeans and a pink top, gliding around the rink, clapping her hands to the song and singing the words. It's a new song but it sounds like something the Jackson 5 would do, including Michael's high voice. The girls go round and round and there's my goofball friend next to me, just rocking to the beat, pressing his lips together, watching pretty Iris

Cruz skate. I wonder if she even realizes half the guys in the rink are watching her. I can see a bunch of guys standing by the edge—Lou and Shawn are by the food area, and they're being all sly about it but I think they're watching the girls and Iris. On the other side of the rink, Jimmy Horak and his dudes are perched on the top of the benches, smoking cigarettes and acting like it ain't nothing, but I bet they're eying her. Even Bobby Kovacki, hanging out across the rink with Paul Mazziotti and Tommy Wicky, they're slumped on some benches and they seem to be sneaking looks. I don't know. Iris is cute but Tyrell likes her so much, I would be a rotten friend to like her too. Besides, there are so many girls in the school. I don't need to like the one Tyrell loves.

"You wanna do a couples' skate?" It's Janine again, popping out of nowhere.

"With you?" I crack. "No."

She grins and goes away.

"That girl is downright crazy," Tyrell says.

"Yep."

"But I can tell you like her."

I look at Tyrell. "I do not!"

Tyrell laughs, doubling over, pointing at me. "Yes you do!"

"Be quiet," I tell him.

The DJ announces a couples' skate and I don't do it. I just sit on the bench next to Tyrell. But I dare him to go out in the rink. He says no, then flips the dare. "I dare you."

I take the dare because I actually want to try to the couples' skate. I've never done it before. This is how it works: they lower the lights and spin the disco ball; kids go out on the rink and stand against the bar; and about ten kids—five girls, five boys— begin the skate. They pick a person to skate with and when the ref blows the whistle, they drop hands and pick new people. This goes on for three songs, so you've got about ten minutes to be chosen. I've never gone out on couples' skate because I'm always afraid I'm not going to be picked.

I'm real nervous when I inch my way out there but to my left, I see Lou. He nods and I nod. They've got some really bad love song playing. I don't even know what it is but it's terrible. Lou and me lean against the bar through the entire terrible song, watching as girls and guys pluck people from the sidelines and then go skating off. One girl, who looks like she's nine, comes up to Lou and asks to skate. He shakes his head. She looks at me and I shake my head. I feel bad for her. Some guy must have picked her off the side as a joke, or a dare.

The song moves into another sappy tune and Darlene Rowan asks Lou to skate. He does this shoulder head nod, which means *Sure, whatever* and off they go, under the disco ball. I lean back and glance at Tyrell, who is still on the bench. Marcus is sitting near him now and they're both laughing at me.

Whatever.

I'm about to sneak off the rink when Janine zips up. "Come on, Zelko."

My heart skips. I'm frozen.

"Did you turn deaf in the last five minutes?"

"Okay."

For the first time in my life, I'm skating couples' skate. It's cool. Her hand is sweaty and she's about five inches taller than me, but I don't mind. We skate slowly and Janine doesn't talk. For a moment, I wonder if she'll ask me about my plan to kill Harry—because she saw my original list—but she doesn't. She grips my hand a little harder but then the ref blows the whistle. We let go and she says, "Bye, Zelko."

Now it's my turn to pick a girl. I scan the sides of the rink and I don't know who to pick. There are several girls left but what if I go up and ask them and they say, *No way, get outta of here* and I look like a moron? I won't put myself in that risky situation. I see Janine doesn't pick anyone. She actually skates off the rink. I decide to do the same but I don't follow her. I'm happy. I zip over to Tyrell and Marcus.

It's time to go. They play one more song but I return my

skates and put my sneakers back on. It feels strange walking now. My feet are lighter but I'm moving slower.

Outside, I look for Lou and Shawn. Tyrell is with me and he's searching for Marcus and Raymond, who we lost coming out. All the kids crowd in groups under the fluorescent light of the streetlamp. Cars are parked in front of us—parents coming to pick kids up—and a few horns blow. Tyrell finds his friends and they wave goodbye to me, heading to their car.

I see that little kid who made me trip earlier and I want to tell him off but I'm tired and I really shouldn't care about a little twerp who can't skate properly. So I stand, my hands in my pockets. I search the faces for Janine Finn but I don't see her. I feel relaxed, actually. Skating with her calmed me down. I keep thinking about holding her hand. How she squeezed it at one point.

"Zelko!" Jimmy Horak's voice.

I turn around. "What?"

"Nothing. Just, why are you such a faggot?"

He's flanked by his two idiot friends, Kevin Donnelly and Ryan Gumlek. There's another guy but I think he's a seventh grader. A big seventh grader.

"Because I like being a faggot," I say to him. Why does he have to start with me? I was in a good mood.

"You like guys?"

"Yep." I find it's better to agree with idiots like Jimmy Horak. I wonder if his older brother Mark is around. Probably not. High schoolers don't go skating.

Ryan Gumlek starts singing "Ebony and Ivory" by Michael Jackson and Paul McCartney.

The guys laugh. I peer behind them for Lou and Shawn. It's so crowded and the light is dim, but I can see a few kids have circled around us. They smell a fight brewing but I'm not about to get into a fight—four against one—that's not happening. I'm not stupid. I try to remember what my dad said about this type of situation. Something about distract and flee.

"So, Ivory, you and Ebony, Tyrell, are you faggots together?"

I'm getting pissed off but Jimmy and the tight group is closing in, stepping closer, waiting for the fight. I can see Jimmy's fists balled up and I'm getting scared. I don't let on, though. I lift up my head and straighten out my shoulders, press my lips together. You can't cower.

"Danny!"

Believe it or not, it's Janine Finn. She didn't even call me Zelko.

She's yelling over some kid. "Lou is looking for you!"

"Ooooh, Lou is looking for you," Jimmy sings.

"Shut up idiot," Janine says.

I follow Janine and see Lou waving to me by his mom's car. Before I know it, Janine is long gone.

Lou's mom drops me off at my house and immediately drives away. Parents should wait until kids are in the house—that's what my mom always says—but Lou's mom doesn't. She's nice but she seemed tired so I suppose she didn't remember to wait.

The porch light glows but the door is locked. The curtains are pulled across the front window but the bluish light from the TV flickers through. Someone must be on the couch. I jog around back to the other door but that's locked too. I look through that window. The kitchen light is on and I can see the table is littered with beer cans. My stomach sinks. They got so drunk, they forgot to leave the door open for me.

I run back up front and check the garage door but that's locked so I have no choice but return to the front door and ring the bell. Nobody answers. I lean on the bell a few times but no one comes. I try banging but nothing.

I slide through the narrow opening between the bushes and the house, and start bang on the front window. I peek through a gap between the curtains and to my surprise, I see Harry sitting on the couch, eyes open, just watching TV and holding a beer. I bang harder and yell, "Harry! Let me in!"

He doesn't even look my way. Could you be passed out with your eyes open?

I squeeze behind the bushes back to the porch and then hop over to my window. I usually leave it open but it's locked shut. I go to Lisa's window and bang but she's not even home. I race around back again and bang on my mom's window but she's in bed, sound asleep.

I'm really angry now but also sick to my stomach. It's gotten really chilly and I'm only in a three-quarter sleeve Pink Floyd T-shirt. I could freeze out here.

I start pounding on the front door again. "Let me in! Open the door!" I'm shouting and screaming and there are tears in my eyes but they're not real tears because I'm not really crying.

I'm just so frustrated and desperate and I bang and shout and before I know it, I hear, "Danny? What are you doing?"

It's George from across the street. He's in his pajamas and slippers and he tells me to calm down after I tell him I'm locked out.

"Harry—he's right there, right on the couch!"

"All right, calm down."

George approaches the door but just then a car pulls up and my sister gets out—her friend Robin is dropping her off. Lisa's got her McDonald's uniform on and she marches up to us.

"What's going on?"

"I'm locked out and Harry's right there!"

"What do you mean?"

The front door opens and Harry stands in front of us, beer in hand.

"Hey, George," he says to our neighbor.

"Oh, hi, Harry," George says awkwardly.

I go right into it: "I've been banging and you wouldn't open the door!"

Harry rubs his face. "Oh, I'm sorry." He lifts up his can of beer and grins at George. "I had too many tonight. Sorry for the commotion."

"No trouble," George says, eyeing the beer. "Been there my-self." He smiles but it's one of those, *I'm trying to fit in and be cool* smiles. George is a doofus. He was never cool, I bet.

Harry clucks his tongue and says, "You know it, brother."

George remains in our front yard, standing dumbly in his pajamas and slippers for an awkward ten seconds. Then he shuffles away. Lisa and I remain in front of the door. Robin drives away.

"Well, get in," Harry says, waving his hand with the beer in it.

I burst into the house and start yelling. "You were awake! You saw me!"

Lisa turns on the living room lamp.

"You saw me!" I shout.

"Shh, you'll wake your mom," Harry says.

My heart is rapping, my breath is thin and my fists are clenched. I can go at him right now and I know he senses it because he places his beer on the coffee table.

I glance at Lisa and she appears scared.

Harry shrugs. "I was just joking, Danny. Kinda like you were joking about Donald."

Gusts of air punch at my lungs. I can barely breathe right.

"You gotta go to sleep," Lisa says, taking my arm and pull-ing me away.

Harry sits on the couch. "Lisa. Get me another beer before you go."

She pushes me down the hall and goes off to the kitchen. I stomp into my room and slam the door. A minute later, Lisa sneaks in and quietly closes the door behind her.

"You gonna throw away that bottle of stupid pills now?"

I feel like an idiot. I throw myself on the bed and punch at the pillow.

"That's what I thought." She shuts the door when she leaves.

WAY THREE:
MEAN DOG

I don't even bother to tell my mom that Harry locked me out of the house. She won't believe me anyway. Or maybe she will and turn it around, insisting that I deserved it.

I just spend the weekend mowing my lawns, avoiding Harry, and keeping to myself.

But I do tell Tyrell on Monday.

This time Tyrell doesn't ask me to scoot over so he can see Iris. He just stares at me with an open mouth of chicken sandwich.

When he swallows, he says, "Wow. What a—" He stops himself from saying anything because his mom has taught him not to curse, not even the gateway curses.

"Dickhead," I finish for him.

"Yeah. That."

I rub my eyes.

"You gotta do something, man," Tyrell says. "That ain't cool, locking a kid out of the house. I mean, you can kind of see his side. With the fake boyfriend card."

I shift in my seat, growing ticked off. "It was your bright idea."

"Right. Yeah." Tyrell goes off to thinking land for a second and then says, "It just seems so..." He stops. Continues. "He locked every window and door in the house and let you scream your head off. You don't lock your window, right?"

"Right."

"That meant that he went into your room and purposely locked your window. You see what I'm saying? His revenge was premeditated. So was your fake boyfriend thing but..."

"What?"

Tyrell touches the collar on his red polo shirt. "He's a grown up. He said he forgave you about the card, he was nice to you and then he still inflicted his revenge." Tyrell pauses. "That's just cruel and twisted."

I stare across the cafeteria and see Lou Barth and Shawn Stinson. I wonder what would happen if I told their dads. Would they come over and kick Harry's butt?

Probably not. It's not like Harry really hurt me.

"I just don't know what to do."

"Well, you can't use that ax. Just remember that."

The rest of the afternoon goes from bad to worse.

First, I see Richard Plimpton in the hallway. "Hi, Danny."

"Shut up," I tell him.

Richard frowns and shrugs and I feel like a creep for being so mean. Like I need to feel any crappier. I could fix it by apologizing, but I don't. I just keep walking.

Second, I see Jimmy Horak.

During seventh period, they make all eighth graders attend an assembly in the gym about our class trip. We sit in the bleachers and wait for the principal to arrive so she can inform us where we'll be going. The choices are:

A Broadway show in New York City
The Ben Franklin Museum in Philadelphia
Great Adventure, the amusement park in Jackson.

Pretty much everyone wants Great Adventure because a Broadway show and a museum sound boring compared to a day at an amusement park. Besides, if you watch the news, New

York City isn't safe. Something is always on fire and people are always getting mugged and killed. I heard that over a thousand people were murdered in New York City last year.

I sit next to Bobby Kovacki.

"Where do you think we're going?" I ask him.

He shrugs. Bobby is one of those sporty kids that doesn't talk much. He lives a couple blocks away from me and we've been in the same classes since kindergarten, but I barely know anything about the guy.

I turn around and scan the crowd behind me but my eyes home in on Jimmy Horak. Immediately, fury claws at my bones because I'm remembering how that dickweed called me faggot Friday night. How he and his buddies were going to beat the hell out of me. I jerk my head around and stare straight ahead, forcing myself to stay in check. I could honestly swing around and leap over all those people and beat the crap out of him. That's how angry I am. I tighten up my fists, squeeze and release—it's a trick I read somewhere. That calms me down and stops me from kicking Jimmy Horak's butt. Besides, Mr. Cage is standing at the bottom of the bleachers, his arms crossed over his chest, looking like a bodyguard. When our principal, Mrs. Rosen, arrives, the room goes quiet. Mr. Cage steps back.

Mr. Collins, the gym teacher with the big ears, hands her a microphone and Mrs. Rosen smiles, says the introductions about what wonderful young men and women we've been this year. Then she adds, "Well, for the most part." Finally she says, "I'm very proud to say that you have earned a trip to Great Adventure!"

Everyone cheers and high fives each other, even Bobby says, "Cool!" but I'm still angry about the faggot remark. It's like the word has slithered into my head and taken over my mind. I see Jimmy jumping up and down on the bleachers, being all happy and suddenly I can't deal and my brain goes haywire. I push my way through some girls, climb up a few benches, and face Jimmy. A flash of worry flits across his face and I could laugh but I keep to the plan: "This is for calling me a faggot," I announce and throw a hard, quick punch straight at his face.

The hit hurts my fist but I've stunned my enemy. Jimmy trips backwards, slipping between the planks, onto the floor rest board. He tries to pull himself up but I push him down with both hands, and the surrounding crowd starts to hoot. "Fight! Fight!" I give them what they want: I lean my knee on the plank, move closer, where Jimmy's good and trapped between the boards, and when he lifts his head up, I throw a jab to his chin, another at his gut. He cries out and covers his face with his arms and I'm thinking *good, you coward*...I'm possessed with how much I hate everyone—Jimmy, Harry, my mom...I go for another hit and then I can't breathe.

There's an arm around my neck—I'm in a choke hold and there's another arm around my chest. I'm being dragged down the bleachers, my feet automatically trying to find footing but can't. The neck hold releases but the chest hold is tight. All I see is the steel ceiling of the gym with its gigantic metal lights, then my feet are down on the gym floor. Kids are yelling and booing and the choke hold on my chest is released and I'm staggering, the world rocking before me. I can't get my bearings but that doesn't matter because I'm being dragged out of the gym, into the hallway.

"I told you to behave, Mr. Zelko," Mr. Cage rasps.

I want to plead my case but I know I'm in the wrong. I stand up straight and look presentable, or the best that I can, and close my mouth. Mr. Cage shakes his head in disgust and gestures with the nod of his head that we're going to his office.

My punishment is in-school suspension for eighth period. And the next day. Mr. Cage tells me that if I incur any more infractions, I'll be barred from the class trip to Great Adventure.

"Do you want that, Danny?" he says.

I sit up in the office chair in front of his desk and stare at the photo of the soldiers. "No, sir." I don't know where *sir* comes from. It just feels like it's the time to say it.

"Do you like Great Adventure?"

"Yes."

"I thought so. I bet you even have a favorite ride that you're looking forward to experiencing. However, if you get yourself in any more situations, you won't be having the favorite ride experience. Am I being clear?"

"Yes."

"You're not confused about anything?"

"No."

"So, enlighten me. What is your favorite ride you might not experience?"

I shrug. "I don't know."

Mr. Cage wrinkles up his handlebar mustache. "Think hard, Danny. I want you to picture yourself on your favorite ride and then I want you to picture yourself not experiencing that favorite ride. So what is it? A particular roller-coaster?"

I shrug again. Here's the thing: I'm not nuts about roller-coasters. I don't have a problem with height and I don't have a problem with speed. I just don't like speed and height as a combination.

"Mr. Zelko, name me a favorite roller-coaster of yours."

I shrug a third time.

"Mr. Zelko, give me a name."

I swallow and then speak: "I don't like roller-coasters. I don't mind the Ferris wheel or the Sky Ride, and I don't mind things that go fast, but I don't like when speed and height is combined, like roller-coasters."

Mr. Cage pulls off his glasses. "So you're saying the Ferris wheel is your favorite ride."

"Maybe."

He slides his glasses back on, leans forward and places his hands on the desk. "Okay. Let's talk more seriously." He pauses for a long moment. "Danny, I know you lost your father last summer so I'm going to assume you're struggling with the read-justment."

I'm shocked. Just shocked that he knows this. How does he even know this? I doubt my mom told him. She couldn't make it to Back to School night so she's never met Mr. Cage or any of my teachers.

I look at Mr. Cage and he doesn't flinch.

"My dad died of cancer," I say, feeling strange just saying it. I know my friends know but I think I've only said it to Tyrell.

Mr. Cage nods. His handlebar mustache twitches.

I don't know what else to say. It was called pancreatic cancer and my father died four months after they told him he had it. The doctors said there was nothing they could do but make him comfortable, which meant they drugged him up and kept him in a spare room at my grandmother's house. She was the caretaker. There was also a nice German nurse who came to the house to administer his pain medication. I didn't even get to really say goodbye. By the time I got to my grandma's the day before he passed away, he was in a coma and there was an awful growling sound coming from his throat. The German nurse called it a "death rattle." I couldn't take it, standing in the room listening to that rattling, feeling haunted. After my father finally passed away and we had the wake, I tried kneeling before the open casket and saying goodbye then, but it wasn't him. It was a stiff, weird version of him. They even had makeup on his face. Not girl makeup like my sister wears but thick, flesh-colored makeup to make him seem better than he really looked when he was dying.

I stare at the floor in Mr. Cage's office. I'm not crying, no-where near crying. My fist still aches from punching Jimmy Horak but I could give two craps about him.

"Are you okay, Danny?"

"Sure."

"Anything else you want to talk about?"

"No." Well, yeah. That I was locked out of the house by the man who is going to marry my mom. That they drink too much. That he calls me Danielle. That I'm afraid when he moves in, it's going to get worse.

I don't say all that. I don't want to cry in front of Mr. Cage, a man who had eighty-four kills in Vietnam. I don't want him to know that my life is the way it is, that my mom is going to marry a gorilla that shouts at her and calls her names. I'll admit, I'm ashamed. Ashamed of the entire situation.

I start to crack my knuckles but stop immediately because that is definitely not presentable. I sit up straight and apologize. "Sorry. For cracking my knuckles."

Mr. Cage takes a deep breath and stands. "All right."

That's it. I go off into in-school suspension and take a seat near a cubby. The door is open and I can hear Mrs. Panelli typing. I take out a piece of paper and start scribbling down Ways #2 and #3.

Kindness
> a. I took a stupid pill and thought that Harry forgave me for the Donald card.
> b. He seemed to like me and I started being nice to him. He gave me money to go roller skating. I thought he liked me.
> c. I was wrong. He locked me out of the house.

I bite on the pen cap and think about how I can get rid of Harry. I go right for the bad stuff, not even caring if someone thinks I'm psycho.

Truck
> a. Tell Harry that a dog has been hit on Route 37.
> b. Harry and I go out to the highway.
> c. When a semi comes rolling by, I push Harry in front of it.

I lean back in my chair, stare at the door, wishing Janine Finn were here. At least it would be someone to talk to.

This truck thing is stupid. I scratch that out, fold up the paper and stick it in my jeans pocket. Soon Richard Plimpton comes in with my literature work.

"To keep you busy because you're missing class," he says.

Even though I'm still pissed about the wedgie situation, I'm in no position to go off on Richard. Besides, I remember I told him to shut up and the memory makes me wince. I take the books and the worksheets and thank him.

"You want a piece of gum?" Richard asks.

I nod. "I'm sorry I told you to shut up. I was in a bad mood."

Richard gives me a piece of gum and walks to the door. He peers over his shoulder then approaches me again and whispers, "I thought it was great that you beat up Jimmy Horak."

I say, "I didn't do it for you, just so you know." Here I go, being nasty to the guy again. What's wrong with me?

Richard stuffs his hands in his pockets. "Yeah, I know. I just liked seeing Jimmy get his butt kicked."

I grin.

Richard leaves.

At home, my mom is really pissed that I got into a fight at school.

"They called me at my job today. Do you know how embarrassing it is to get a call from your son's school? Do you think my boss needs to know that my kid is a troublemaker?"

"No," I say, scuffing my foot along the kitchen floor.

"Danny, I get it. You're having a tough time since your dad died and now with Harry around. But I thought things were better?"

"They're not."

"Why?"

I shrug.

"Will you just spit it out?"

So I tell her. I tell her that Harry locked me out of the house, that I was banging and then I drop the bomb: "When I looked through the window, his eyes were open so he wasn't asleep like he told George across the street—because that's how loud I was—it woke—"

She sighs heavily and cuts me off: "Stop! Harry told me. He told me that he was playing a joke on you."

My mouth drops open. She believed his story. She believes it now. I don't know what to say.

She points her finger in my face. "A little payback for that stunt you played with the card so he would break up with me."

"He was a dickweed! He told me he forgave me and then he went ahead with his evil plan! He just let me bang and scream and it was cold." I'm so frustrated. "It went beyond a real joke."

"Danny, I believe you," my mom says. "I'm sure Harry took it too far. He takes things too far. I'm working on that with him. He had a tough childhood and sometimes he has difficulty being gentle. Knowing boundaries. He's changing."

"Bullshit."

"Watch your mouth."

And then we go our separate ways in the house. Forget my mom. There's no talking sense into her.

The next morning, I report to in-school suspension. Mr. Cage is out and about, meetings and what not, so the secretary keeps her eye on me. I'm good. I do the work Richard Plimpton brings me from my teachers. I cause no problems. At one point, I pretend talk to my dad in my head. I imagine he's sitting next to me. I try to put him in normal clothes but for some reason, he's wearing the light blue hospital nightgown I saw him in when he had the death rattle.

"I see you're trying," my dad says.

"Thanks."

"I saw what Harry did. If I were around, I would beat the you-know-what out of him."

"But you're not around."

"Yeah, I'm aware of that but I can't help it if I had cancer."

"Whatever." And he goes away.

Fourth period, Mr. Cage places a sixth grader in with me. The kid is little and he's crazy, crazier than Janine Finn. As soon as Mr. Cage leaves to do hall duty or something, the kid starts moaning. "I didn't do it. I didn't do it. I hate in-school suspension! Nobody listens to me! I did not do it. I did not do it…"

It goes on and on. I tell him to shut his mouth but he starts crying, blubbering, "I didn't do it. Didn't do it." Snot is dripping from his nose and I call out to Mrs. Panelli that the kid needs a tissue. She comes in, holds out the box but he slaps the box away, and it ricochets like a pinball, bouncing off the wall, then at a chair, and finally at my feet.

"I didn't do it! I didn't!" the kid screams.

"Oh, mother-of-God," Mrs. Panelli says, rubbing her head. "I need a new job."

She leaves the room and calls Mr. Cage on the walkie talkie. Within minutes, Mr. Cage arrives and takes the kid away.

"Peace and quiet," I hear Mrs. Panelli say once the kid is gone. She speaks some more and I tilt back in my chair and peer through the doorway, to where she's sitting. "Huh?" I say.

But I realize she's not talking to me. She's talking to herself. *"I'm on a beach, the waves are crashing, I have my book, my feet are in the warm sand…"*

I fall forward on my chair and say, "O-kay."

Last period, Mr. Holland, one of the science teachers, walks Gordon Urszulak in. Gordon is square, solid, and thick like a refrigerator. He's pretty scary—I overheard the gym teachers saying he could be a linebacker for the New York Giants—and I can tell you I'm not too keen on sharing this small space with him. He has a great round moon face and a large thick nose with wide nostrils big enough to hide bats. Someone told me that he fell down a flight of stairs and smooshed the family cat. I choose not to believe this story.

"Hey, Zelko," Gordon says.

"Hey, Gordon," I say.

"What'd you do?" he asks, scratching his chin.

I go on the offensive and act tough: "I punched Jimmy Horak a few times during the eighth-grade assembly yesterday."

"I heard about that," Gordon says, looking at his dirty fingernails before lifting his eyes to me. "I was absent."

I'm hesitant but I finally ask: "What did you do?"

Gordon studies me for a long moment, as if deciding whether he can trust me or not. Finally, he responds: "I told Mr. Holland his experiment on moldy bread sucks."

"Why?"

This simple one-word question appears to annoy Gordon. He leans forward, closer, so close I can smell his rancid breath, and says, "Why'd you punch Jimmy?"

"'Cause he ticked me off."

Gordon leans back and crinkles up his big, bat cave nose. "Yeah. Mr. Holland didn't like that I said his moldy bread experiment sucks and he said I had to be quiet."

"That's it?" I say. "You got thrown in here for saying a piece of bread sucks?"

Gordon chuckles. His belly shakes. "No. I got thrown in here because I threw my moldy bread across the classroom and it hit Mr. Holland."

"Oh."

"Yeah, hit him in the bald spot." Gordon touches the back of his head.

I smile. Then I have to ask like he asked me: "Why'd you throw the bread at him?"

"Zelko, I don't know why I do half the crap I do."

"NO TALKING!" Mrs. Panelli hollers from her desk.

Gordon shrugs.

I turn back to my private wall in my cubby.

That night, Harry is there with my mom. Lisa is working at

McDonald's so it's just me and the two of them. The night is warm and Harry makes us hamburgers on the grill. They're drinking beer but they're not drunk. We have potato chips and coleslaw and afterwards, brownies my mom made. Once she places the brownies on the table, she leaves the kitchen, stepping out through the back door. I see her wandering around the yard, lightning bugs glowing in the dim light of the evening.

"Your mother wanted me to speak to you about the trouble you got into at school." He talks for a long time, speaking about when he was a boy and how he got into fights and how it didn't do him much good in the long run except that time he was down in Daytona and he had to fight off two bikers and this other time he was in New Brunswick and this guy got out of line…He's talking like he's a big shot but the story is as boring as my literature teacher.

I pick at my brownie. It's on a napkin and I start pulling little pieces off, rolling them between my fingers into balls, pretending they're Jupiter's moons.

"What I'm saying is that I'm not like your mom. I'm not going to get up in your face if you knock some a-hole kid out at school. I told your mom that that's what boys do. They fight, they stand up for themselves, they stand by their friends."

He's got my attention now and I look up at him.

"I get it," he says, sipping his beer.

I don't respond.

"I respect it, in fact."

I look at my moons. I want to trust him, I do.

"Listen, Danny, I'm sorry about locking you out of the house as a joke. I took it too far."

I don't move.

"Hey, look at me."

I don't.

"Look at me."

Be polite, I tell myself. So I do.

"I took it too far. That's on me. And I'm sorry."

"Okay," I say. There's an awkward moment but I finally stand up. I see my mom coming toward the back door.

"Cool. Now get me a beer, boy."

"Is that another one of your jokes?" I snap.

A shadow crosses over Harry's face. "No. That'd be a request."

"Request denied," I say, walking out of the kitchen and toward my room, expecting and fearing he might come after me, but that may be a good thing. If he beats me up, I can call the police.

Nothing happens. I just hear my mom's voice in the kitchen.

I still lock the door behind me.

"Man, you're just itching for Harry to whoop your butt," Tyrell says in lunch.

"I don't care."

"Yes, you do. Just so you know, what you tried to do was entrapment. You tried to lure him into beating you up so you could call the police."

"So?"

"Entrapment doesn't hold up in court."

"Why not?"

"Because..." Tyrell sips his milk and after he sets the container down, he explains. "It works like this: say you have some drugs, like marijuana, and you don't like a person so you plant those drugs in his car. Then you make an anonymous call to the cops saying you know someone has drugs in their vehicle. Then that person gets a mighty good lawyer and they trace the call back to you. You're in big trouble for trying to trap someone."

"Isn't that more like framing?"

"It doesn't matter. It's the same concept."

"How do you know?"

"My uncle is a cop in Jersey City."

"I didn't try to get Harry to come after me," I say. "It just happened. He gives me that big speech about understanding why I got in trouble at school and then how he sometimes goes too far when he plays jokes and how sorry he is…I wanted to believe him but I couldn't. I don't. I think he's still the same psycho, mean dickhead he always was."

"It sounds like you're right," Tyrell says, picking up his ham sandwich. "You have to come up with a better way to get rid of Harry."

"I know."

"You better work quick. You got June, July, and August. When's the wedding date in August?"

I huff. "Like I know."

Tyrell bites into his sandwich and I have to wait until he swallows before he speaks again. "I bet your sister knows."

"August thirteenth," she says. "Why?"

"No reason."

"You still gonna try to get rid of him?"

"Maybe."

We're sitting at the kitchen table eating cereal. It's Saturday morning and the cartoons are playing in the living room. My mom and Harry haven't gotten up yet. Two empty wine bottles and used wine glasses sit on the counter. I stayed in my room all night listening to Pink Floyd, trying to come up with a real third way to get rid of the man. All I did was waste brain energy because everything I thought of was dumb: calling up his job, pretending I'm him and quitting; writing my mom a letter claiming I'm Harry's wife who he hasn't divorced yet (I saw that on a TV movie); taking a bat to his head when he is sleeping.

None of that stuff is feasible. Especially the letter because I already blew that idea with the card. Well, maybe the bat is feasible but I'm not a murderer.

I know I could probably tell someone about what happened, how Harry locked me out of the house. I could call the police but with my reputation, they'll never believe me. All they have to do is call my school and see that I've done in-school suspension and they'll assume I'm lying. I could find Miss Lewis, my literature teacher from last year, but truthfully, I'm not her student anymore and I don't think she even remembers me. I've passed her in the hall and I've said hello, but she just smiles like people do when they can't remember who you are. It sucks because she is my all-time favorite teacher and she doesn't even remember me. I guess, if I wanted, I could go to Mr. Cage and tell him Harry locked me out of the house, that he gets my mom drunk, that he screams at my mom and tells her to shut up.

No. I don't want Mr. Cage or anyone else knowing what's going on. (Except Tyrell because I've already told him.) I don't want Mr. Cage thinking my mom is a loser for dating such a jerk. If I really think about it, what's so bad about Harry? Yeah, he's a dickweed but it's not like he beats us or chains us up in our rooms. So he locked me out of the house, gets my mom drunk, screams at her to shut up. Men have done worse.

"So," Lisa says, slurping her cereal. She peers behind her and lowers her voice. "You tried two different ways: that dumb card and trying to kill him with kindness."

"I didn't try to kill him with kindness."

"Not deliberately. Had you done it deliberately, it might have worked."

I play with my cereal.

"Too bad we don't have a mean dog," Lisa says. "A dog that was protective of you. A dog that would bite him every time he pulled crap."

Just then, we hear the bedroom door open down the hall. Then the stomping. Harry appears in the kitchen, grabs the tea kettle from the stove, and fills it up with water. Harry doesn't drink coffee like my dad did. He drinks tea, like he's British or something.

Lisa and I eat our cereal. The milk gallon is on the table and I remember how Harry doesn't like when we leave the milk out. He doesn't like warm milk in his tea.

And sure enough, he says something about it. "What'd I tell you about the milk?"

I look up and see Harry's narrow eyes are swollen and his face is scruffy and his thin stringy hair is a mess.

"Huh?" he says to me.

"It was my fault, Harry," Lisa says. "I left the milk out. Not Danny."

He scratches his neck. The kettle whistles.

I'm finished with breakfast.

I have three lawns to mow today. I put a box of plastic leaf bags on top of the mower and a broom to sweep the sidewalks and driveway. I do the first two lawns and get my money. It's about three o'clock when I get to the third house. This house is across from Janine Finn's. Her dog Orson is out. That stupid dog does nothing but jump and growl and bark as I mow. I do the front and the back, bag up the lawn clippings and put it at the end of their driveway for the garbage men to take. It's after I get my pay from the owner of the house and when I'm loading up my gear onto the lawn mower when I stop and stare at crazy Orson.

Mean dog.

Okay. This has possibilities. I think for a long moment, watching Orson bark and slobber and jump. If this were my dog, in my house, surely it would hate Harry too. I bet Harry is no good with dogs. I bet every dog he ever encountered sensed his bad character. Animals and kids can sense bad characters—I heard that on a news show once.

I begin to push the mower home, the idea swirling around my head. Maybe I can borrow Orson? Pretend he's my new dog. Teach him to sic Harry. I push the mower faster as the notion begins to take hold in my brain. I know it's a far-fetched idea but it has potential.

I'm sweating when I get home, when I put everything in the garage and get on my bike. I'm dripping wet and excited when I arrive at Janine's house, but I remember to take my comb out of my back pocket and run it through my hair. I go up to the side door next to the garage, the door outside of the chain-linked fence, and bang on it. Orson is right in my face, barking, snarling, jumping, but I keep banging on the door. Soon it opens and I see Janine's older brother, Pete. She has another older brother, Gary, but he's finished with high school already.

"Shut up, Orson!" Pete shouts at the dog. The dog stops but still growls.

"Hey," I say. "Is Janine around?"

"No, dude." Pete has a bunch of dark, wavy hair that hangs in his face and he's wearing a Led Zeppelin T-shirt. People say he sells pot. I heard he smokes it more than he sells it.

"When will she be home?"

"Tomorrow. She's with our cousins in Delaware."

"Delaware? The state?"

Pete shakes his head. "No, man, I mean Bricktown."

Holy cow. He is a real stoner. How do you mix up the state of Delaware and a town fifteen minutes away from our neighborhood? I bet he's high right now.

Orson starts barking again.

"Shut up, dog!" Pete shouts.

Orson grows quiet.

"What time will she be back?" I ask.

"I don't know, dude. Soon. I gotta go."

He shuts the door and sure enough, Orson begins barking. I read that if you put your hand near a dog's nose and let it sniff it, the dog will take a liking to you. I slowly bend down and carefully place my hand near the chain-link fence. Orson stops barking and tries to sniff it. Then he bounds up, snarling, almost leaping over the fence. I fall back onto the driveway, my heart hammering, watching this dog bark and jump. He doesn't get over but I smile. I stand up and point my finger at him. "You'll do." For a second, the dog freezes and gazes at me as if he knows what I'm talking about.

I imagine he does and I imagine he says, "I can't wait to sink my teeth into Harry's ass!"

Yeah, this dog curses.

I get home and I need to take a shower because I'm still sweaty and dirty from mowing the lawns, but Harry is taking one of his baths. He likes to relax and listen to music. He puts my sister's boom box next to the tub on the toilet. (I know this because one time I burst in there and saw him all naked. It was very weird and so gross. The man is very, very hairy.) Harry listens to an oldies station and he sings along. He doesn't have a good voice but it doesn't stop him from crooning all those old songs from the fifties and sixties.

My mom is up and she looks okay for drinking two bottles of wine the night before and she tells me, ever so nicely, that Harry is taking us out to the movies that night.

I decline, saying I have homework, because it's sort of true. I have to write up my plan.

Way to Get Rid of Harry

Mean Dog: Orson

    a. Find Janine Finn and ask to have Orson for a few days.

    b. Pay her money if she demands it.

    c. Get her to tell me how to get Orson to like me. Probably needs food.

    d. Bring dog to the house.

    e. Tell Mom and Harry I found it and it's now mine.

    f. Unleash the dog and let it rip apart Harry.

It's far from perfect—it's actually very stupid—but there's a smidgen of a chance it works. I just don't want Orson to go after my mom or Lisa. There must be some way to keep that from happening.

* * *

I go to sleep early and get up early so I can do more lawns. I run out of gas so I have to take the gas can, pedal eight blocks up to the highway where the gas station is, and fill it up. It isn't easy riding on a bike with a full gas can. I have to hold it with my right hand and steer with my left. Sometimes my mom fills the can for me but she hasn't done that this year.

When the lawns are done, I ride my bike over to Janine's house. Luckily, Orson isn't outside.

She opens the door. "Zelko. What do you want?"

It's about one in the afternoon and she's still wearing her pajamas. Her dark hair is in a ponytail.

"I need to talk to you," I say.

She shuts the door and I have the sinking feeling she's not going to come out but she does, this time dressed in shorts, a T-shirt, and sneakers.

"What?" she says.

I tell her that I want to borrow her dog for a few days.

"Why?"

I thought she might ask this and I decide that I will tell her the truth because A, I can't think of another story and B, Janine is such a good liar that she'll be able to tell if I'm lying if I make up some story. "I want to get rid of my mom's boyfriend. I think if I tell him I have a new dog, Orson, and it tries to bite him, he might just leave for good."

Janine puts her hand on her hip and shifts. "That's the dumbest thing I've ever heard."

My heart sinks. I know it's stupid, dumb, one of the worst plans on the planet. But I have to try, a man has to give every ridiculous idea a shot—great men in history have thought of even more ridiculous ideas. I mean, great ideas must have seemed ludicrous when they were first out in the air. People told Columbus he was going to fall off the edge of the Earth and be eaten by sea monsters; the Wright Brothers must've been told they couldn't get a machine in the air to fly; nobody thought we could make it to the moon. So yeah, my little idea is dumb but it has potential.

Besides, I have to do something. Harry locked me out of the house. He's going to marry my mom. I have to take action.

I stare at Janine and say, "I think it's one of those things that sounds dumb but when put into action, might work. Sort of like Columbus sailing across the ocean when he was supposed to fall off."

"So you're Columbus?"

"No," I say slowly, attempting to stay calm in the wake of her sarcasm. "I just want to get rid of Harry."

She licks her lips. "Is this the guy you're going to murder?"

"I'm not going to murder anyone. I'm not a psycho killer. I just want him to think that Orson might murder him."

"Dogs don't murder people. It's not in their biology."

I'm not so sure that statement is true but I'm growing too frustrated to argue. "Can I just borrow your dog?"

She shrugs. "Sure. Nobody likes him anyhow."

Janine goes inside and returns with Orson on the leash. He's pretty good for her and I write that off to her being a witch and casting a spell on the poor beast—well, not really, but she must have some magic touch or something. He sits by her side, no growling, no barking.

"He's good for you," I say.

She pets him on the back. "Yep."

"Do you stick him with needles or something?"

"No!" She bends down and hugs him. "I just show him love."

Love? She just told me nobody likes him. She lies so much. I watch her hug and pet Orson, and he turns and licks her face.

"That's right, Orson, you just need love," she says, kissing him on the head before she stands.

Maybe I can get the magic touch. Love. Not food. Just love. "So if I'm nice to him, if I show him love, he'll be good for me?"

"Yeah."

I remember my mom. "I don't want him to hurt my mom or my sister."

"He doesn't hurt females."

"Really?" I'm skeptical about this.

"If he tries, he likes bananas. Do you have bananas?"

Strange choice of food for a dog but I think about it. There were bananas on the counter this morning when I was eating breakfast.

"Yes. I have bananas."

Janine bends down again and I bend down too. She tells me to lift my hand to his nose and he sniffs and growls but Janine tells him, no, be a good dog and sure enough, Orson is good. I pet him for a while, even hug him, tell him what a good dog he is, and it's nice, me and Janine and Orson, the three of us together.

Eventually, she stands and hands over the leash. "Good luck. And if Orson kills your mom's boyfriend, I'll deny everything. I'm telling the cops you just took my dog."

I agree to her terms and begin walking Orson down the driveway.

"Oh, and, Zelko—"

"Yeah?"

"Ten bucks. That's how much I'm charging you for renting my dog. You can pay me when you return him."

I agree to this last term, too.

"Bye, Orson!" she calls.

The dog is good as I walk the four blocks to my house. He's good when I go in the house and he's good when I sit on the couch watching TV waiting for Harry and my mom to come home. I don't know where they went but they'll be surprised when they see my new pet.

I watch an entire movie, Orson just sitting by my side, and I even get him a banana. Janine wasn't lying about this. Orson's slobbering as soon as I start peeling it and gobbles the fruit up in fifteen seconds. He looks at me like he wants a second helping so I get him another banana. He wags his tail and I pet him on the head.

"We're buddies now, right?" I say.

Orson barks then settles down on the floor.

My mom's car pulls into my driveway and Harry and my mom get out. I watch them walk up to the front door, my hand on Orson's collar. Like a good dog, Orson stands and starts to growl, deep curdling growls, and my heart batters with excitement. This is gonna work. I am Columbus!

My mom enters first and just like Janine said, he calms down because he likes females.

"What's this?" she asks, halting immediately, clearly annoyed.

"My new dog. Orson."

"I didn't say you could have a dog."

"I didn't say you could marry Harry."

She glares at me and gorilla guy Harry comes in. He stops behind her.

"Danny got a new dog."

Someone up in Heaven, probably my dad, pulls the hand of fate and makes the phone ring. My mom moves slowly by Orson and goes to the kitchen to get the phone. Harry doesn't move.

Orson is standing on all fours now and begins to growl again, then barks—deep, loud, scary barks.

"You get that animal under control," Harry commands.

I release my hand from the collar and Orson charges toward Harry. But the dog stops when he reaches him. Then, to my horror, the dog sinks down to the floor and whimpers. What the hell?

Harry chuckles. "Thought so."

I can hear my mom talking on the phone, saying she has to go. She slams the phone into the receiver and Orson snaps his head around. He barks. She shouts at him. I tell her not to yell at the dog. He barks louder. She yells louder.

"Get that monster out of here!" she hollers.

Then—and this is when I realize the dog is not really mean but just touched in the head like the rest of the Finn family—Orson rushes in circles across the room, my mom goes after him, I yell, "Mom, don't scream at him!" and I try to grab Orson but I can't and he leaps on the couch and starts biting the back cushion.

"Make him stop!" my mom screams. "Danny! Make him stop."

I race across the room and grip the dog's collar. "Orson! Stop!"

But the dog is in full destruction mode, tearing apart the cushion with its teeth. I'm not strong enough to pull the dog away.

Harry pushes me aside, clasps his hand on the dog's collar, and yanks him down from the couch. With an open hand, he beats Orson on the head, does it again, and a third time, each time harder and harder and harder. Orson sinks to the floor on all fours, whimpering, moaning, his ears back, his tail down.

"Get the leash," Harry orders but I'm stunned at what just happened. I look at my mom and she's standing there in a daze.

"Get the damn leash, Danny!" Harry shouts.

I pick the leash up, hand it over, and Harry hooks it to Orson's collar.

"Get rid of this beast before I do."

I take the leash and tug at Orson, who stands and follows me to the door.

Harry walks up to me and whispers, "You're pissing me off, Danielle."

My brain splinters and I could kick Orson for being such a wimp, but I'm not an animal beater like Harry is. I can't believe he hit Orson so hard.

I walk Orson back to Janine's. He's subdued and quiet. He doesn't even bark when a rabbit races across the street.

"Is your mom's boyfriend gone?" Janine asks when I get to her house.

"No. It didn't work. Orson was afraid of Harry."

"Not possible."

"Yeah. Harry hit him."

Janine glares at me. "Your mom's boyfriend hit my dog?" Her face is red. She's irate.

"Now you know why I want to get rid of the idiot," I say,

handing her the leash. "He hit him three times. Really hard."
I'm baffled, frightened, secretly worried that I'll suffer the same
fate.

Janine bends down and hugs Orson. "You poor thing. I'm so
sorry for renting you out to Danny who subjected you to an
animal beater."

"Orson ripped up my mom's couch cushion," I explain quietly. "I didn't know Harry would hit him."

Janine stands up. "I can't believe you let him hit my dog!"

"I didn't let him hit him."

"What did you do when it was happening? Did you try to
help? Rescue him?"

My shoulders slump and I see the stupidity in this dumb
plan. I feel awful. I'm also scared. In my brain, the scene loops
in my head: Harry whacking Orson, Orson sinking to the floor,
me stunned and helpless.

"You're a butthole," Janine says.

Her words snap me back to reality. I want to tell her off but
this is my fault. "I'm sorry," I say.

I start walking down the driveway but Janine shouts after
me: "Zelko, you owe me ten bucks! Twenty! I want twenty
because Orson got hurt!"

Embarrassment, fear, depression—it's overtaking my body
and my mind. I can't even look back at Janine and Orson. I can
barely put one foot in front of the other to go home. I should
run away. Just go into the woods and head out into the un-
known, like an explorer, making my own way in the world.

"Zelko!"

I keep walking. Orson starts barking again.

"Zelko! Twenty bucks! Zelko!"

I continue walking, knowing my fate at home is grim.

* * *

It is grim. I'm punished for the next two weeks. I can't go anywhere after school and I can only leave the house to mow my

lawns. My mother hands down the sentence while Harry sits at the kitchen table, drinking a cup of tea and eating a banana.

I glance at Harry and for the first time, I realize how really downright frightened I am of him. When I walked in the house, I thought he might start hitting me but he didn't. He just stayed out of it and let my mom scream at me. Still, it was the way he stayed out of it, the way he stood back, the way he sat at the table eating a banana. Something is going to happen to me, something bad.

"You better figure out what's wrong with you!" my mom shouts. "Now get out of here! Go to your room."

I do as I'm told.

I pull my list from under my bed.

Under Way Three, I write, *Didn't work. Stupidest idea ever. I'm an idiot. What was I thinking? I subjected an innocent animal to Harry. I feel awful.*

Then I add, *I'm afraid.*

WAY FOUR: ELECTROCUTION

Lisa apologizes to me. "Sorry for putting the idea in your head."

The next two weeks are a drag. I hate sitting in the house and I have the urge to just get on my bike and go out. I could probably get away with it, too. My mom is either working or hanging around Harry, so it's not like she'd know if I went to Tyrell's or got on my bike to ride around.

I don't want to get into anymore bad situations, though. I need to behave. Harry is lurking around and I'm still nervous something is going to happen, but he just ignores me. I stay low at school, even when Jimmy Horak starts with me a couple of times, I keep myself in check and walk away. I know I look like a wimp because I hear kids laughing at me, but I'm not going back to in-school suspension and I don't want to lose my trip to Great Adventure.

June rolls in and so does the deadline for the trip money. My mom says she doesn't have it and Harry doesn't volunteer to give me money.

"The boy is mowing lawns," Harry says. "He can pay for himself."

My mom agrees, muttering about how it's a good lesson, that money doesn't grow on trees. She forgets that I gave her money a couple times to pay the bills.

Tyrell's mom gives him money for the trip and so does Lou and Steve's parents. Bobby Kovacki tells me that his parents don't have the cash so he can't go. "You can hang out at my house," Bobby offers. His voice is quiet. "We can play basketball and stuff."

Screw that. I like Bobby but I'm not going to stay home and play basketball like a loser. I go into my piggy bank and pull out the money. I have enough for the trip, plus extras, like lunch money and cash to buy a souvenir. When the money is due, I pay up.

But luck is not on my side. An hour after I hand in my trip money, Jimmy Horak finds me in the cafeteria, just sitting with Tyrell, and calls us faggots.

"Go away," Tyrell says.

"Do you give each other kisses?" Jimmy says.

My blood starts bubbling and my head is on fire.

Tyrell tells me to ignore him but my brain doesn't hear it. I barrel out of my seat and get in Jimmy's face.

"Say it again," I dare, standing in front of him.

"Faggot. Faggot."

I push him hard, and then charge at him. He comes at me but I'm too pissed and knock him to the floor, me falling with him. We start wrestling and punching each other. I get a good shot to his side and he gets a good hit to the side of my face, which dazes me for a few seconds. Kids are yelling and cheering and before I know it, I'm torn away by Mr. Holland who happens to be on cafeteria duty.

Next thing, I'm in Mr. Cage's office, my face still aching from that punch Jimmy got at me, and Mr. Cage is returning my Great Adventure money, telling me I'm kicked out of school for the next three days. "OSS," he says. Out of school suspension.

"What about Jimmy?" I shout.

"Watch your tone, Mr. Zelko."

I slide down in my seat and lean to the side. "He called me a faggot. He called me and Tyrell Colton faggots."

"I understand Jimmy Horak provoked you, and he's off the trip, too, but you went after him first. This is the second time you started a fight in school in just a couple of weeks. I'm sorry but I gave you a chance and I have to follow protocol."

"So Jimmy's not kicked out of school?"

"That's none of your business, son."

"Right. So he's not kicked out of school."

"Danny, I've called your mother at work. She'll be picking you up soon."

I'm sent out of his office to sit in the chair across from Mrs. Panelli, who ignores me and keeps typing. I don't appear presentable, just slouched in the chair, my legs out, I don't care. It takes a half hour for my mom to show up. She doesn't look at me. She just stands there with her pocketbook on her shoulder, smelling like hair stuff, before Mr. Cage appears and informs us that the principal, Mrs. Rosen, wants to talk to both of us.

My mom's eyes widen and she moves her head slowly toward me.

My gut twists. Now I'm really in trouble.

Mrs. Rosen's office is down the hall and it's a long, frightening walk beside my mom and Mr. Cage. When we arrive, we're escorted into a large office with plants and shelves of photographs of what is probably Mrs. Rosen's family. My principal is sitting in a large chair, behind a very large mahogany desk, but stands and shakes my mom's hand when we arrive and motions for us to take our seats in front of her. I remember my dad's words and I sit straight, my hands in my lap, and I don't speak.

"I'm going to cut right to the chase, Daniel," Mrs. Rosen says, pulling off her glasses. She's got puffy short dark hair, a real shiny face, and she wears small gold earrings, a gold necklace, and a wedding ring with a big diamond. "You've been in three altercations in the past few weeks and if there is one more, we're going to expel you temporarily."

"What?" my mom gasps.

"I'm sorry, Mrs. Zelko." My mom still uses her married name. "But this is protocol. The expulsion would not be forever. It would be for a few months, beginning immediately and carrying over for three months in the fall."

"But he will be a freshman in the high school."

"Correct. But it's the same district so we'd still keep him out of the high school."

"This isn't right. He's only been in two fights."

Mrs. Rosen slides her glasses back on and peers down at the paper in front of her. "No. Three. He was first placed in in-school suspension for an altercation in the locker room. It says here that Mrs. Panelli spoke with you."

"What do you mean? Nobody called." My mom shifts uncomfortably. "I would have remembered that."

That was Lisa covering me. I know this is the locker room incident and I didn't do it so I jump into the conversation and do my best to be respectful. "I didn't do the locker room altercation. You can ask Mr. Cage."

Mrs. Rosen looks at the paper and shakes her head. "There's nothing noted."

My fists begin to clench. "I was cleared. I didn't do that."

"Okay, I will talk to Mr. Cage. But Daniel, back in March it looks like you were involved in a fight in the hallway."

I didn't start that one, either. That fight was with this kid, Kurt Leeds. He pushed me and I pushed him back and then he started pummeling me so I had to defend myself. Mr. Collins broke up that fight and he stuck up for me so I only got spoken to by Mr. Cage. Luckily, Kurt moved away not long afterwards. "I didn't start that fight," I say.

Mrs. Rosen takes off her glasses again and sighs. "Daniel, you're causing too much trouble."

"Wait," my mom says. "You said you spoke to me about the locker room incident? I don't remember that."

My mom is still on this.

"We did," Mrs. Rosen says.

I should come clean about what really happened but I don't want to get my sister in trouble.

"All right, Mrs. Zelko, I realize you're upset. I would be too if my son pulled this nonsense." Mrs. Rosen stares at me.

"This is ridiculous," my mom says. "How do you make a boy stay home for three months?"

"He won't," Mrs. Rosen says. She explains that I would have to go to a special school in Toms River where they send all kids who are expelled.

"How would he get there?" my mom asks.

"You would have to drive him."

My mom smacks the arm on her chair. "I have a job. I can't go and get him in the middle of the day!"

My principal appears irritated at my mom's outburst but she remains calm. "I suggest you lay down some serious consequences at home for the next three days so we don't resort to expulsion. No television, no Atari, no friends, no music. Give Daniel chores. Keep on him. Know what he's doing twenty-four hours a day."

"How am I supposed to do that when I work?"

"I understand your predicament but my hands are tied."

My mom shakes her head and glares at me. "Thanks a lot, Danny."

I look down, feeling terrible.

"Daniel?" Mrs. Rosen says.

I look up.

"Please take these three days to examine your behavior and when you return, you have two weeks until school ends. Do you think you can control yourself for two weeks?"

"Yes."

"Oh, he will," my mom snaps.

"Very good." Mrs. Rosen stands up.

In the car, my mom doesn't speak. It's silent. Her hands grip the steering wheel and I sneak looks at her—her face is red, beads of sweat drip down her face even though the air conditioner is blowing. Finally, once we're on Route 37, she starts screaming: "I don't know what is wrong with you! I had to leave work, leave my clients who pay me, and I'm out money. And now you could get expelled? Just because you couldn't control yourself!"

I say nothing. Just sink down in the seat and stare out the window, watching the trees go by.

"And who did they speak to when they called about the locker room?"

I don't answer.

"Danny, answer me!"

She's driving a little crazy and has to slam on the brakes at a red light. "Answer me!"

"I don't know," I say. "Besides, that locker room thing wasn't me. I was framed."

"Framed?"

The light turns green and she resumes driving but stops screaming. Not until we're in the house does she start in again. "You need to stay in this house for the next three days." She repeats what Mrs. Rosen said about no TV, no Atari, no friends, no music. She also adds, "No bike."

"Fine," I say.

She points at me. "I need to have a life. I know you don't like Harry but he isn't that bad. He's just old fashioned. I'm working on it. But I need him. I need to have an adult around and I need to cut loose once in a while. You don't know how stressful it is raising two kids on your own."

"He hit the dog really hard," I protest. "You saw him! You saw how hard he hit Orson!"

"That dog ripped up my couch! Do you know how much couches cost?"

I plop down on the living room chair.

My mom says, "Did Lisa take that call from the school?"

"I don't know."

"She did, didn't she? She tried to protect you."

I want to cover for my sister but I can't help myself. "You

were passed out from drinking with Harry so she had to."

"Oh, really?"

I keep going, boiling with anger: "You didn't drink when you were married to Dad. He didn't tell you to shut up, either."

My mom bites her lip and slits her eyes. Then she says, "No. He just cheated on me periodically."

"Just once, with Debbie."

"No, Danny. Several times. Your dad wasn't the saint you make him out to be."

The "several times" jars me.

She grabs her pocketbook and tells me she's going back to work. Before she leaves the house, she says, "I deserve a life." She's crying now. "You don't know what I've been through. You don't know what it's like to wake up in the middle of the night and know you're going to lose your house because you can't pay the mortgage because your ex-husband didn't leave any money for his family. You don't know what it's like to be thirty-nine and no man will go out with you because you're old and you have two kids. Harry has a job. He can help us. You're going to have to deal with it. He's not abusing you. He's not beating the hell out of you. So he hit a dog. That dog was out of control and that's how you control dogs. We're not dogs. Harry is not going to hit us. Put things in perspective. Try to think about other people for once!"

She slams the door and leaves.

I don't know what to think about this.

I go into my room and pull out my secret shoebox. I find a picture of my dad sitting in a brown chair, a cup of coffee in his hand. He's wearing an orange Mets T-shirt and cut-offs, white socks, and blue sneakers.

"Why didn't you leave us money?" I pretend ask him.

I look up and see he's leaning against my closet. "I had nothing to leave you. Cancer is expensive."

* * *

That evening, my mom and my sister get into a big fight about Lisa covering for me. Lisa says exactly what I said: "You were drunk, Mom! What was I supposed to do?"

"You tell them I will call them back when I'm available!"

They scream and argue, then Harry shows up from work and Lisa goes into her room. I sneak in to apologize. It feels like all I do is apologize. "I'm sorry for getting into trouble and getting you in trouble."

Lisa looks up from a novel she's reading and I see she's crying. "It's okay, Danny. There's no getting through to Mom. She's brainwashed or something. We've lost her."

I tell her what Mom said, that Harry can bring money in and that Dad cheated on her several times, not just once.

Lisa confirms both. "Yes, Dad used to cheat. And yeah, she's right about the money."

"Harry is here to stay," I mutter.

Lisa gazes out the window near her bed. "I don't know. It still doesn't seem right. I mean, even if she lost the house and we had to live in Florida with Grandma, would that be so bad? Sure, we'd have to leave our friends but it's gotta be better than having Harry around." She turns to me. I notice the makeup on her eyes is smeared, making her look like a raccoon more than a poison dart frog. "Don't you think?"

The thought of moving away is not something I would be happy with but she has a point.

"I just think," Lisa says, "I think Mom is making excuses. That she's really just so in love with Harry that it's messing with her common sense. She's choosing her boyfriend over her kids, simple as that."

For the next three days, I follow all rules, except the music one. When no one is home, I listen to Pink Floyd. Even guys in prison get to listen to the radio—I saw it in a movie.

My mom assigns chores for me to do: rake some leftover

leaves from the back of the house, clean out the refrigerator and wash the shelves, dust the house, mop the kitchen, vacuum the rugs, do the laundry. I even have to wash Harry's laundry, which is gross. It smells like sweat and cigarettes and motorcycle gas.

When the three days are up, I return to school. Mr. Cage gives me another talking to and I sit straight up, nodding, agreeing to behave. I hear from other kids that Great Adventure was fantastic until it rained. I couldn't help but smile on that one.

Tyrell thanks me for sticking up for him against Jimmy Horak. "But don't do it again. Who cares if Jimmy calls us names? Just ignore him. Don't get yourself kicked out of school because of that turd. He isn't worth it."

He's talking like an adult. I almost tell him that but I know it's not a compliment.

That weekend I mow my lawns and see Janine Finn come outside when I'm doing the house across the street from her. I wave but she gives me the middle finger and calls Orson over.

I manage to get to the last day of school without any altercations. Afterwards, I take the bus home. Everyone is excited, including me, knowing we have all of summer ahead of us. Janine is on my bus and she sits in the back and I expect that she'll start tormenting me, but she doesn't. Instead, I don't hear her until we get to her stop. She walks by me and says, "Twenty bucks. I haven't forgotten."

"Get going!" the bus driver says and she huffs and gets off.

I refuse to respond to her because I'm not going to let her ruin my last day of school mood.

I'm off punishment so when I get home, I hop on my bike and head over to Tyrell's neighborhood. He has agreed to go swimming at Baskro Lake. As soon as I'm on the trail toward Route 37, I feel free and fantastic and I'm not thinking about anything except getting to Tyrell's house.

It's a sunny, hot day, and we each have a towel rolled up and shoved between the seat and the back reflector plate of our bikes. We head through the woods, skirting along the path away from the sugar sand. Tyrell gets stuck at one point and we have to stop but then we keep going. There are a pack of kids behind us on bikes, kids from Tyrell's neighborhood, and they race by us, laughing that they're faster and one even, when going by Tyrell, mimics a robot and says, "Nerd alert. Nerd alert."

I'm about to say something but I don't. We don't need any trouble. We keep going, passing three girls from Tyrell's neighborhood and I say, "Hello, ladies," and this girl Beverly Carter says, "How's it going, Rocky?" She's referring to my fights in school, obviously.

I look back at her and grin, then look forward and lift both arms and fists in the air. I hear the girls cackle and I almost lose control of my bike, quickly grabbing the handlebars to stop it from twisting out of control. I hear the girls laugh louder and I feel my face turn red, but I keep going.

Tyrell and I bust out of the woods and into the wide open. Baskro Lake is before our eyes. The dirt is thick, like sandbox sand, and it goes on forever. We have to walk our bikes toward the water, trudging through the small dunes, sweat rolling down our faces. A warm breeze sways the trees in the distance and ripples the water. There are no houses or cars or boats, just a beautiful gigantic turquoise lake before our eyes, unnatural because the other lakes throughout the Pine Barrens are the dark color of tea. I heard Baskro is contaminated, which is why it's turquoise and why they never built houses around it or made it into a lake resort. The story goes that in the sixties or seventies, a mining company dug a colossal hole, maybe as large as the Titanic, in search of some special mineral to use in paint. They dug down in huge steps, down, down, down: that's why you can wade out in the water, just walk a bit, and suddenly the floor will be gone. It's like walking off a shelf. I'm not sure how the hole filled up with water—this lake is wide and monstrous, so I doubt it was just rain—but I'm guessing they dug too deep, hit the water table, and the water just gushed in, along with the special mineral to make paint, which polluted it and made the lake turquoise.

We're not supposed to be here, nobody is, because it's technically private property and there are obviously no lifeguards. If you get hurt, there's no one to call. There's a secret dirt road off of Route 37 that's wide enough for a cop car. If you're on a four-wheeler or dirt bike, you'll get a ticket. If you've come out on your bike, they'll just make you leave.

We spread our towels down on the dirt, only feet away from the water. The boys who passed us earlier are far away from us, jumping in the lake. It's very hot but a breeze off the water cools us.

"Have you come up with another way to get rid of Harry?" Tyrell asks.

I tell him no. I also tell him what my mom said, all the crummy details about my dad cheating and how she needs money and Harry has a job, then I tell him what my sister said, that my mom is just using all of that as an excuse to stay with Harry, that my mom is choosing a man over her kids.

"Yeah, I'd agree with your sister," Tyrell says, lying back, his hands behind his head. He's wearing sunglasses, the aviator kind issued from the military. They're too big for his face.

"Are those your dad's glasses?" I ask him.

"Yep. I have a few things of his. I have a jacket, too. I keep that in my closet."

"Does your mom know?"

"Yeah. She gave me them."

I think about this, how I have nothing from my dad except photographs. I lie back and watch a hawk circling in the sky. I wonder about Tyrell and his dad. I know I shouldn't pry but he's my friend and I think at this point I should be able to ask him something private. "Did you find your dad after he killed himself?" As soon as I say it, I realize it's probably too private, that I went too far.

Tyrell turns to me. The sun gleams against the reflective lenses.

"I'm sorry," I say. "None of my business."

Tyrell answers, though. "No. I didn't find him. I wasn't home. I was at my Grandma's for the night. My mom found him."

He scratches his arm and turns back to the sky.

I figure he's into talking so I ask another private question: "Did he say why he did it? Leave a note or something?"

"No. My mom said Vietnam messed with his head. She said he wasn't the same when he came back. That's why I'm against war. I'm never joining the army or marines or air force. I don't want my head messed with."

"We need soldiers to defend us," I say.

"Yes, but not me. I'm not doing the defending."

I laugh.

Tyrell is quiet so I figure he's done talking but he isn't. "I miss my dad," he says quietly, so quietly, I can barely hear him. "Like you miss yours," he whispers.

I nod.

"He couldn't help dying. It wasn't his fault. He was screwed up from the war. But I still feel like he didn't take me into consideration. That killing himself would hurt me."

I hear my mom's words: *Try to think about other people for once!*

"Maybe his head was that screwed up that he couldn't think about anyone but his own problems," I say.

The sunglasses have slipped down Tyrell's nose and he pushes them up again. "That's what my mom says. She said he loved me, that he was proud of me, that he wanted to see me grow up. But he would go into these spells, like temporary depressions and she couldn't get him out. I remember when those spells would happen. He wouldn't go to work and he'd just stay home, sleeping or hanging out in the..."

Tyrell goes quiet.

I stare at the blue sky, feeling rotten for bringing up the whole thing.

"We didn't know my dad had a gun in the garage," Tyrell explains. "My mom hated guns, still does, and she would've taken it away if she knew about it, especially with his spells, and..."

There are voices in the distance. I look and see Beverly and her friends coming out of the woods. Beverly lives down the street from Tyrell. They're still a while away from us.

Tyrell continues the conversation: "I bet he killed a lot of people in Vietnam like Mr. Cage did. But maybe my dad wasn't like Mr. Cage. Proud that he was a soldier that killed people. I think my dad felt bad about killing folks, even enemy folks, and he just couldn't be happy in life again."

I agree with Tyrell because it sounds like he has it all figured out. I add, "I bet Mr. Cage is messed up, too. He never smiles."

Tyrell laughs. "You're so right."

Soon the girls are standing over us, asking what we're doing.

"What does it look like we're doing?" I say.

Beverly puts her hand up. "Excuse me for living."

They roll their towels out near us and lay back. Besides Beverly, there's Janelle Taylor, and Dawn Rodriguez. Iris Cruz usually hangs out with them and I look at Tyrell and then ask Dawn where Iris is.

"We're not talking to her."

"Why not?"

"Because," Beverly explains, "she thinks she's better than us."

"Yep," Janelle says. "She's all like, I'm sorry, but I have to go with my sister to the mall, and we're like, you're lying because we know that you're hanging out with Michelle Spano."

Michelle Spano lives in the nicest neighborhood in the township, over in Oak Woods, where the houses are brand new and most of the kids think they're rich.

"That's too bad," I hear Tyrell say and all of us look at him because everyone knows that Tyrell never speaks around girls.

Beverly nods. "That's right, Tyrell. It is too bad because

we're gonna have some fun."

The girls get up and step into the water, squealing about how cold it is but then Janelle says it's not so bad when you get used to it. I get up and rush in and they shout at me not to splash and get them wet. Dawn has a Frisbee and for a while, we throw the Frisbee to each other, even Tyrell, who jumps in after I pressure him. White puffy clouds sail in front of the sun and when this happens, I shiver. But it's only for a minute, until the sun is out again. We're all standing in water about waist deep, and we know not to go out too far because a kid drowned in this lake. Still, when Tyrell throws the Frisbee and it goes over my head, I step back and suddenly drop, the lake floor gone. I'm just floating, legs dangling in the abyss, my head just above water.

"Danny!" the girls yell and Tyrell shouts after me, "Don't drown, man!"

I can swim and I make my way out to the Frisbee, grab it, and toss it back to them. I don't like the feeling of not being able to touch the floor—even though the water is bright blue from the outside, it's really a mirage or something. The water is dark blue when you're in it, not like a pool, where you can see how deep it is—and I know I have to get in toward shore. A breeze blows and the water ripples. There's a current in the lake that surprises me, making it hard for me to swim but I do it and before long, I've found the shelf and I'm standing.

We all get out of the water and Dawn says, "Danny, you scared us."

"I didn't mean to," I say.

"I thought you were a goner," Tyrell says.

I pick up my towel and dry myself off. I guess from their view, it appeared like I was in danger.

"Nah, I knew what I was doing," I say, playing it off.

"Like you knew what you were doing when you got into the fight with Jimmy Horak?" Beverly says. "Yeah, I saw that."

"What? Are you my mother?"

"You just think you're all that, don't you?" Beverly says.

"I'm gonna call you Rocky for the rest of your life."

I throw punches in the air.

"Danny," Beverly says, "you're just too much."

Later that afternoon, when I get home, there's a note on the counter from my mom that says she and Harry are out for the evening and there's leftover macaroni and cheese in the fridge. She also hopes I have a good night.

"Yeah, right," I say, and heat up the food in the oven. Lisa isn't home either, probably working at McDonald's, so I sit at the kitchen table, reading the comics from the newspaper, eating my macaroni and cheese. When I'm done, I hear the ice cream man so I go to get money from my baseball bank, but when I look inside, all the money is gone. Instead, there is a note from Harry.

A new couch costs $500.00.

I just lose it. I punch the wall, then drop to the floor because my fist is in so much pain. Dammit! Tears well in my eyes and everything goes blurry. I can't believe he took my money! I had almost a hundred dollars in there.

From the floor, I sidekick my dresser and my baseball bank tumbles onto the floor, but it's carpeted so it doesn't break. I kick the dresser again and again until I just roll on my side and start crying. After a while, I'm quiet and I try to wrap my head around the situation. I understand that the dog tearing up the couch is on me but you just don't go into someone's bank and take their money. You ask, demand that they have to pay for it, give them a bill. You don't just take it. That's not fair.

I remain on my floor for the next three hours. I even take out my Legos and start building a lighthouse, or what I think can be a lighthouse. Focusing on this brings me some peace and takes my mind off of things. When I hear my sister come home, I break up the lighthouse and put the Legos away. I go out into the living room.

"He took my money," I tell her. She's sitting on the couch, watching the news from New York City. More murders. She's not wearing her McDonald's uniform so she wasn't at work.

"For a new couch?" Lisa says.

"Yeah, how'd you know?"

"Because I was here when he did it."

"Did you try to stop him?"

Lisa stares at the TV. "I pulled Mom aside when she got home from work. She told Harry to return the money but he told her to shut up and she told him to shut up and then they started yelling at each other. She went into her room and started crying and he went in after her and then it got quiet. Then I left. When I got home, they were gone."

"He could've asked," I say.

"He could drop dead," Lisa replies.

I sit beside her and admit that it was my fault that the couch got torn up. We both eye the couch across the room and the blanket over the ripped back cushion.

"I just don't like how he treats her," Lisa says. "I know he gets on you but you bring it on yourself a lot."

"Thanks."

"I'm just telling the truth. But I don't like how she does what he says, like her mind is gone. I don't like how they fight."

I say nothing.

My sister looks at me. "You need Number Four."

"I'm staying out of it."

"I'll do it this time."

"How?"

"I don't know." She gets up and goes into the bathroom. When she returns, she points at me. "Kick the boom box into the water when he's taking a bath."

"Umm…"

"Yeah. Electrocute him."

I can hear Tyrell in my head. *Juvie city.*

"I'm not doing that," I tell her.

A car pulls into the driveway. My mom and Harry. Lisa gets up and looks out the window. "They're drunk," she mutters.

"Great."

Lisa swings around. "Whatever you do, don't bring up the money now. For your own safety."

We both rush down the hall into our rooms as the front door opens. I hear Harry talking but I jump into bed and put the pillow over my ears.

In the morning, it's not good. I'm up too late, about eleven, and when I go into the kitchen, Harry is already there, making his tea. My mom is gone, he says, doing a Saturday shift at the salon. Apparently her days changed and now she does Saturdays.

"You get my note?" Harry asks as I'm pouring milk into my cereal bowl.

"Yes."

"You got something to say about it."

I put the milk down and face him. I'm not thinking about how he hit the dog, how dangerous it is for me to talk back to him. My mouth just starts going. "Yeah, I do. You should've asked. You don't go into someone's bank and take their money."

"Yeah, and you don't bring home a monster dog just to get rid of me."

I stare at him and then look away.

"You owe another four hundred."

"Whatever," I say.

That just sets him off. He heaves up, shouting, "You know what your problem is? You're a punk! A rotten kid who has a rotten attitude and if you think I'm gonna take your crap, you got another thing coming!" He grits his teeth and snatches my arm. He's never grabbed me before and now I'm very scared.

"Do you hear me?"

I try to twist away but he just grips me so hard I think my arm is going to come off. "I hear you."

"What?" he shouts.

"I hear you!"

He lets go and I stumble back. I look up and see Lisa standing there. She's not frightened, just angry. She turns and disappears. I don't think Harry sees her.

I'm not hungry anymore so I dump my cereal, put away the milk, and return to my room. I change into shorts and a T-shirt, put on my old sneakers and when I'm tying them, I hear Harry shouting and my sister yelling.

I jump up from the bed and race down the hall to see her screaming. "You don't own this house! You can't talk to me that way!"

Harry stomps toward her and she cowers back, like he's going to hit her but his hand isn't raised. "You watch your tone."

He marches by me, down to the bedroom where he slams the door so hard, the framed school photos of me and Lisa rattle.

Lisa's face is red, her eyes watery and her lip is trembling.

"What was that about?" I ask her.

"I told him he needed to leave," she says, "but he told me to shut up. He told me to shut the hell up." She brings her hand to her mouth and starts chewing on her thumbnail. She hasn't done that in a long time—bite her nails. "He actually told *me* to shut up. He's not my father."

We hear Harry go into the bathroom and the water start running. My heart is thrumming because I know what's going on in Lisa's head. "Don't. Lisa don't."

She steps forward. I jump in front of her. "Don't. I'll do it."

Because I'm not going to do anything. I want him gone, too, but we're not murderers.

As soon as I hear the water stop and his stupid doo-wop music playing, I begin creeping down the hall. I stand in front of the door, glancing back at my sister. I take three deep breaths and burst into the bathroom. I catch a glimpse of his hairy naked body but I quickly avert my eyes. Harry yells and I move to the boom box on the toilet. Yes, I can throw it in the tub, electrocute him, but I don't. I grab the handle and put it on the floor. Harry pulls the shower curtain forward—thank God!—and I lift the toilet lid. I'm supposed to pee but I can't.

"Do your business!" Harry shouts but I'm too nervous to do anything. The oldies music is blaring and all I can hear is *Come go with me…*

I give up and yell, "False alarm."

"You better be good and gone when I get out," Harry warns from behind the curtain.

My eyes fix on the boom box and I see myself throwing it in the tub, but I don't. I just walk out of the bathroom, shutting the door behind me.

Lisa is standing in the hall, wiping her eyes. "I'm gonna go to work." She rushes into her bedroom, and when she comes out in her blue McDonald's uniform, I tell her we can't just electrocute a man.

"I know," she says. "I'm not an idiot."

I shake my head—this was her idea and I saved her from it. You'd think she'd thank me.

For the rest of the day, I keep far from Harry, mowing my lawns and even taking a break at the park to play ball with Bobby Kovacki. It's hot and I'm thirsty and Bobby gives me some of his water in a canteen.

About five-thirty, I head home, knowing my mom will be there. She isn't but neither is Harry. I put the money I made in the back of my drawer, take a shower, eyeing the boom box, grateful I didn't do anything terrible. I make myself three hot dogs in the toaster oven, eat half a bag of chips, a banana, an orange, and a bowl of cereal. I didn't eat anything all day so I'm ravenous. Lisa isn't home and at seven o'clock, she calls and tells me she's staying at Robin's for the night. I ask her to come home but she says she just needs a night away from the house, that she was glad I didn't go through with the fourth way and because she was so angry, she scared herself thinking she would actually kill Harry or put me up to it. She whispers the kill part.

Later, I find my list and write:

4. Electrocution:
    a. Burst in bathroom and kick boom box into the tub.

MISSION ABORTED. CONSEQUENCES DIRE. JUVIE
DEFINITELY. MAYBE LIFE IN PRISON FOR ME. I'M
NOT GOING TO PRISON FOR HARRY.

That last part is true. Even if he nearly broke off my arm today, I can't kill the guy.

The next morning, something fantastic, fabulous, wonderful
happens! After I wake up and hit the bathroom, I hear my mom
crying in her bedroom. At first I think she and Harry are
fighting again, but I check outside I don't see either of Harry's
vehicles—not his motorcycle or his car. I check the garage but
still, no vehicles. He's nowhere and she's really crying, bawling.
I can hear her from the living room. I tiptoe down the dark hall
to her bedroom.
    "Mom, you okay?" I ask after knocking on her door.
    I hear her get up. She cracks the door open. "It's over."
    "What's over?"
    "Harry and me. We broke up. So if you don't mind, let me
cry in peace."
    What? I can't believe it! I want scream with joy but I hold it
together. "That's terrible," I say, doing my best to sound glum
and concerned.
    "You know what, Danny?" my mom says.
    "What?"
    She opens the door a bit more. Her face is wet and pink. "Let
me cry in peace."
    Still, I can't help myself: "Who dumped who?"
    "Jesus!"

"I'm sorry."

"Leave me alone!" She slams the door shut and calls me an a-hole, but she uses the real word.

I don't care. I throw my arms up in the air like Rocky and do a silent boxer dance. I poke my head in Lisa's room but she isn't home. I race down the hallway, into the living room. I bop around, quietly cheering, "Yes! Yes!"

I burst out of the house, doing my Rocky dance on the front lawn, my hands in the air, not caring if George across the street is watering his flowers. He looks at me and stares but it I don't care. I jump and cheer and I do something I never knew I could do: A cartwheel. I do a friggin' cartwheel on my front lawn!

BREAK

My mom goes into a little depression for a few days. She goes to work grim, comes home grim. Doesn't talk to us. Doesn't eat much. Tells us to get our own dinner. Spends her free time in her bedroom crying. I try to help, cheer her up. I tap on her door and say, "Hey Mom, you wanna play Atari?" or "Hey Mom, you wanna do a puzzle? Play Monopoly?" All I hear is sniffles and "No, thank you, Danny." Lisa, who is as overjoyed as I am, orders me to back off and give her time. "She'll get over it."

By the last week in June, life returns to the old days. My mom is home, making us dinner, sitting at the table with us. She's quiet and jumps for the phone when it rings, but other than that, she's her old self. She takes on another shift at the salon, sits Lisa and I down to tell us that money is tight, that we have to really keep to a budget in order to hold onto the house. "We can't do anything extra. No pizza nights or fun stuff. I can't buy you guys anything. I can't afford to get any desserts. I may have to shut off the cable."

"That's okay, Mom," Lisa says. "I have some money saved. If you need to borrow anything..."

"Well, that's the problem, Lisa," my mom says. "I can't borrow any money from you because I can't pay it back."

"Can you ask Grandma for money?" Lisa asks.

"Grandma can't afford to send money. Besides, I'm not asking her."

"What about Dad's family?" I suggest. My other grandmother, my dad's mother, Grandma Zelko, might be able to help.

"You can't ask your ex-mother-in-law for money," she says.

I think about this for a second and remember we haven't seen Grandma Zelko in a long time, since my dad died. "How come she doesn't come see us?"

My mother shrugs, presses her lips together. "She and I had a falling out."

We were never very close with my father's mom. She's mean and she never seemed to like us and she never liked my mom. If I search my memory, I can recall my mom breaking into tears a few times at Grandma Zelko's house. She's a round woman with broken teeth who lives up in Bloomfield on a street with a bunch of old houses squished together. Her house is an ugly peach color and it's very stuffy inside because she won't open the windows. She's afraid of burglars.

"Grandma Zelko is a strict Catholic. Strict Catholics don't believe in divorce," my mom explains. "Because I asked for the divorce from your father, she disowned me. When your dad got sick, she let up a bit so you guys could see your father but after he died, she told me I was dead to her." My mom picks at her nails. "She's a nasty woman that I don't want you guys around."

"Wow," is all I can say. I quickly bring up my dad's brother, Uncle Rick, but my sister reminds me that he has a gambling problem.

"What does he bet on?"

My mom smirks. "Everything. Mostly horses."

The three of us are silent for a bit.

"The goal is to not fall behind on the mortgage payments," my mom finally explains. "That's the most important part. Even if we have to shut off the electric—"

"Mom..." Lisa says.

"I know it's harsh but one of my friends at work told me that you can turn off the electric in the spring and the fall to save money. We don't need the air conditioner or fans to stay cool or the heat to stay warm during that time."

"It gets pretty cold in November," Lisa says.

My mom puts her head in her hands. "I just can't lose this house. If I lose this house, I'll never be able to buy anything again. Not a car, not another house, nothing."

"Why?" I say.

"Because my credit will be ruined. I'll never get a loan again. It's hard enough for a single woman to get a bank loan. With bad credit, forget it."

Miss Lewis explained this to us once. If you default on a loan—meaning you don't pay the money you borrowed back— you get a bad reputation with the banks and they won't loan you money anymore. For the rest of your life.

"I'll try to get more lawns," I offer.

My mom smiles sadly.

A few nights later, I hear Lisa and my mom talking outside while they're sitting on the patio. We can't use the air conditioner anymore because the electric it uses costs too much money, so we have to keep the windows open. I don't mind. I'm okay with the heat at night—I'll take this over air conditioning and Harry in the house. Besides, I like the way the crickets sing when I'm falling asleep. It really feels like summer.

Anyhow, I'm sitting at the table, eating a peanut butter sandwich and flipping through my sister's teen magazine— there's nothing else to read—when I hear them speaking.

"You can go out on dates with other guys," Lisa says.

"I know," my mom says. "Some of the girls at work tell me the same thing."

"Then do it."

I want to yell through the window, "Don't do it!" because I think my mom needs to take a break from dating any men, but peanut butter and bread is stuck in my mouth. I have to jump to the refrigerator and drink milk right from the container, but by the time the peanut butter and bread is gone down my throat, I decide to just stay out of it. I go into my room and listen to Pink Floyd and think how cool it was to drink milk from the container. Harry would've lost it.

My mom does go on a date. One of her coworkers hooks her up with this guy named Doug. He comes to the door on a Saturday night, wearing jeans and a striped polo shirt. Even though I'm not happy my mom is going out with another guy, he looks okay. He's thin and tall. His hair is curly, he has a small mustache, and he wears a gold necklace with an Italian horn hanging from it. Before she went to work, Lisa told me Doug sells cars, but not used cars, fancy cars, like Cadillacs. "He sounds promising," Lisa added.

My mom is in the bedroom getting ready. It's just Doug and me in the living room.

Doug shakes my hand. I shake it back, really hard, because I remember my dad telling me that a firm handshake is essential to people respecting you.

"You like baseball?" Doug asks.

"Yeah," I answer.

"I got a customer who sends me Yankee tickets."

"So?"

Doug blinks, and I see him swallow. He has a really big Adam's apple. "Well, maybe, if your mom and me get along, me and you can go to a game."

I cross my arms over my chest. "Maybe."

My mom appears. She looks nice. She's wearing a black flowery sundress and those wedge cork sandals she likes. They leave the house and go out to his car. I stare through living room window and check out the car he is driving. It's a long, sharp, cream-colored Cadillac Coup de Ville! It has white-wall tires and the chrome is gleaming in the evening sun. Doug opens the door for my mom and I notice George across the street is standing on his porch watching. *Yeah, aren't you jealous,* I think. *Wouldn't you like to have a vehicle like that?* My head starts blowing up and my thoughts go happy and suddenly I'm seeing myself driving a car just like that. Because if my mom and Doug hit it off, not only will I be going up to Yankee Stadium, when I'm seventeen, I'll be getting a sharp, fierce Cadillac that will make me the coolest guy in the school. Hell, I even might have it painted—like in the movie *Grease*—with flames on the side. I'm gonna get a convertible, too. I'll drive around real slow, my music blasting just to tick off the people I don't like. *Yeah, look at me,* I'll be saying. Might drive around Jimmy Horak's block a few times. Tyrell will be beside me. I might even let Bobby Kovacki in the back because he doesn't talk much and won't annoy me. Yeah, the tunes will be playing—Pink Floyd, Van Halen, and something Tyrell likes. And there we go, rolling by Jimmy's house. Hell, I might give him the finger.

I spend the evening riding my bike, thinking about my future convertible Coupe de Ville with the flames on the sides. The night is warm and high school kids are on the corners, some smoking, some hanging out, some lighting off mini firecrackers since July fourth is only a day away.

"Zelko! Where's my damn money?"

Janine.

I swing around and barely make her out hanging with her brother, Pete Finn, and what I think are some of his buddies. Even though they're all standing under a cone of fluorescent street lamp light, it's still hard to make them out. I don't like hanging out under streetlamps. First, if you look up, all you'll see is a swarm of bugs. Second—and this is the worst thing—bats! They swoop and dive all around you, feasting on the smorgasbord of insects. I know I'm a guy and I'm not supposed to be afraid of bugs or bats, and I'm not, but that doesn't mean

I want to risk some bat landing in my hair. I have longish hair and I heard that bats like long hair. I don't believe that crap but still, there's a lot out there in the world I don't believe but that doesn't mean it isn't true.

"Zelko!"

Crap. She just isn't going to let up. I have to confront this money situation so she stops harassing me. Hell, I hired her dog to do a job and it didn't do the job, so that means justice is on my side. What if I stopped mowing people's lawns but demanded the money? Same thing. I won't back down to her, even if her older brother and their friends are around. They're probably stoned anyhow.

I cruise up to Janine and stop short in front of her. "What?" I say.

"I want my money."

I say my piece: "I hired your dog to do a job and it didn't do it. So I'm not paying you."

Janine puts her hands on her hips.

I grip my handle bars.

"Janine, man," her brother Pete says, lighting a cigarette.

"What?" she snaps, turning and facing them.

Pete's friends go "Whoa!" and one says, "Feisty," and then they snicker and giggle. Pete sucks on his cigarette and slowly says, "What's your problem, girl?"

"Don't call me 'girl.'"

The friends cackle and mock her. One guy mimics a female voice, "Don't call me girl," and the other goes, "Just call me bitch."

"Shut the hell up!" Janine shouts, dropping her arms at her side.

"Yo…" Pete says, stepping in front of her. He's got a real slow, spacey way of talking. "Chill, dude. I was just gonna tell you we're taking off."

The light is so shadowy, it makes it difficult to make out Janine's face well. Pete's face is hard to see, too, but that's more because his messy wavy hair is hanging in his face. Only when he sucks on his cigarette do I get a glimpse of the guy—his long nose glows and I notice his fingers are really fat.

Janine shifts her weight. "So take off. I got my own stuff to do."

The two guys laugh and mimic her again. *"I got my own stuff to do. My own stuff."*

Janine flips out and charges at them but Pete drops his smoke, steps on it, and with both hands, holds her back.

The guys are now bent over howling in laughter. They're making fun of Janine, using a lady voice. *"I got my own stuff to do! I'm a bitch, not a girl!"* It's really getting out of hand and the only thing Pete is doing is holding Janine back. In the dim light, I can see he is trying not to laugh.

Janine is really upset. She's screaming and threatening to beat their butts which makes them howl even louder. It's getting pathetic because they're just being mean and her stupid brother is just giggling along with them. I step away from my bike, letting it drop to the street, and get in these high schoolers' faces.

"Knock it off! You're being dickheads!"

And—no surprise here—these two jerks turn their attention to me. "Here comes Superman!" one says.

"He's kinda short for Superman."

"Yeah. He's R2-D2!"

Okay, that makes no sense.

They make funny beep-beep computer noises that the Star Wars robot makes and laugh even harder. They're obviously stoned—how do you move from Superman to R2-D2? I remain steadfast, my feet planted on the ground, my blood boiling, my fists clenched and I realize it's just me out here, no Mr. Cage and if I want, I can ram right into one of the wasted morons and start punching, even if they both are bigger than me.

Finally, Pete decides to man up and take control of the situation. He lets his sister go and signals to his buddies to leave. "Let's jet, dudes," he says and like a pair of dimwitted dogs, the guys mumble, "Yeah, good idea," and "Yeah, man," and off they trot into the night.

"Assholes," Janine says.

"Dickheads," I add.

Janine shoves her hands in her shorts pockets and looks up at the streetlight. I peer up, too, and see three bats swooping at the swarm of insects. We read each other's mind and I pick up my bike, and we begin walking down the street side by side. We're quiet and I don't know where we're going but it's in the opposite direction of Janine's brother and his friends. We walk for two blocks without speaking, me looking in the windows of the houses that are lit up. Most people are inside, the air conditioners buzzing. A few people sit on their porches and talk and at one house, four little kids are on the front lawn playing tag. At another house, I can hear people in a pool in the backyard. It's a nice evening and the sky is bright with stars and the moon.

Eventually, Janine says, "I don't smoke no more."

"That's good," I say. "Cigarettes will kill you."

"Yeah. I just started looking at older people who smoke and listening to their gravelly voices and noticing their bad teeth. Totally gross."

"Yeah," I say. "My mom's ex-boyfriend smoked."

"You mean the guy you tried to scare with my dog? You still owe me money."

Not this crap again.

Janine glances at me. "What do you mean, *ex*-boyfriend? They broke up?"

I can't help but grin. "Yep."

"When?"

"A couple weeks ago."

"Well that's cool. So Orson did do his job. I might charge you extra."

I roll my eyes and ignore this. "Yeah, and now she has a new boyfriend. Doug. He sells Cadillacs and other fine cars and if he and my mom stay together, he's gonna take me to see the Yankees and buy me a new car." I know that last part is a lie right now but it will eventually be true.

"I'm tired of walking," Janine says and I follow her over to the curb, dropping my bike to the side. We sit in front of someone's house I don't really know. It's a small ranch and the front window is lit up. I see a big cat sitting inside on the window sill.

"So you like Doug?" she says, exaggerating the word Doug to Do-*ug*.

"Yeah."

Janine glances at me. She smirks. "How many dates they been on?"

I shrug.

"I bet it's only one, right?"

Caught. I really don't know how she sees through stuff. "Okay," I admit. "Their first date was tonight. But he had this beautiful Cadillac and my mom has to be real stupid to turn down a guy like Doug. I bet he makes good money and she needs money."

Janine scoffs. "Everyone needs money."

I pick up a small stick and draw in the dirt on the side of the street. The moon is so bright, we can see each other a little. "My mom is pretty broke. We can lose the house. We can't even use the air conditioner because it costs too much money to run and we might turn off the heat in the fall and spring. We're probably gonna get rid of cable. I gotta find more lawns to mow to help out."

Janine is wearing old sneakers and she pushes her foot along the ground. "That sucks."

"I know."

She lets out a heavy breath. "All right. I won't bug you for the money. You know, renting Orson and never paying me."

I thank her.

"If things get better, I want my money."

"Sure."

"Cool."

After a minute, I tell her that Harry went into my piggy bank and took a hundred dollars out of it. "To pay for the couch that Orson tore up."

"Are you kidding?" Janine says.

I stretch back against the lawn, put my hands behind my head, and look at the starry sky. "But old Harry is gone now. I'd rather be poor than have him around."

Janine lies back too, but she turns on her side, propping her head up with her hand. "I don't mean to rain on your parade here, but if I were you, I wouldn't get too happy about this breakup."

I turn to her. "Why?"

"Come on, Danny. You're not stupid. You know romance is a spider web of emotions."

I laugh out loud. "What?"

She smiles—something she never does and it makes her even prettier than ever. Even in the low light of the moon.

"I heard that on a soap opera," she says. "My brother—not Pete, but my oldest brother, Gary, you know the one with the truck."

I don't know Gary. I see him sometimes, riding around in his messed-up, rusted white pickup.

"Well, anyhow, Gary and his girlfriend have gotten into many fights and they break up, get back together. I mean, he's sworn her off to Hell and even gotten with other girls he's met and then Leanne calls and boom, they're back together, all kissy face. Then a few weeks later, they're fighting again. My point is, people break up all the time and then get back together."

I can feel my stomach clenching. "My mom is smart. She knows Harry is a jerk. She won't bring him back."

Janine sits up and looks down at me. "Who broke up with who?"

I tell her I don't know, that my mom won't tell me.

"Is she crying a lot? Hiding in her room?"

"She was. But now she's out with Doug."

Janine laughs. "Then Harry broke up with her."

"It doesn't matter. He's gone."

"Danny, all it takes is a moment of weakness. All she has to do is call him and he'll be back. Especially if Doug didn't make her heart flutter tonight."

I sit up now.

"When you go home, check out how you're mom is acting. If she's like, Oh, the date was nice, then you know you're in trouble."

I'm starting to get angry. "Doug seems like a cool dude."

"He probably is. But the heart wants what the heart wants. And your mom's heart wants Harry."

"You don't know that!"

Janine stands up. "Zelko, I'm just trying to help you out here."

I get up too, picking up my bike.

"Nice talking to you," she says, and I let her walk off. I turn and go the other way, back to my house.

My mom isn't home but I wait in the living room, trying to watch TV. There's nothing good on because apparently my mom cancelled the cable already so we have to resort to antenna TV. We haven't used it in a year and I'm obviously gonna have to get on the roof to fix it to get a better signal. With antenna TV, all you get is thirteen channels, three are repeats because channels two and ten are the same, one is from New York City, the other from Philadelphia. Same goes for three and four, six and seven. But most of the channels are fuzz because the antenna on the roof is messed up.

About ten-thirty, the Cadillac pulls into the driveway and Doug and my mom walk up to the door. The front windows are open so I can hear them talking—he's saying he had a nice time and she's saying, Yes, me too, and then he is saying, I'll call you later this week, and she's saying, That would be nice. I listen for a kiss but I don't hear anything and I see his shadow walk down the sidewalk to the car and my mom walks in the door.

She smiles at me.

"How was it?" I ask.

"Oh, it was nice," she says blandly, walking by me, down to her room.

My heart sinks. Janine might be right.

"Is Harry coming back?" I pretend talk to my dad. He's wearing the black tuxedo he wore the day he married my mom.

"I don't know, Danny."

"If he does, will they get married?"

"I don't know."

I'm in my room, staring up at my Pink Floyd poster on the ceiling. I turn on my side and look at the wall. I fall asleep with the light on.

Nothing happens. I do my lawns and give my mom half the money. I do our lawn too, like I always do—my mom is lucky. I do that for free. I ride my bike over to Tyrell's house and hang out with him. We go to Baskro Lake and swim. I go down to the park and shoot basketball with Bobby Kovacki. I see Shawn Stinson and Lou Barth playing baseball and I tell them I might go see the Yankees and they say, Who cares? The Mets are better anyhow. My mom goes out with Doug again. Lisa thinks this is a good sign but I tell her what Janine said.

"Janine Finn is crazy," Lisa says. "She was dropped on her head. Twice."

On July thirteenth, I'm invited to Tyrell's house to eat dinner. His mom cooks us cheeseburgers on the barbecue but she also serves carrots and peas instead of oven fries or potato chips or corn on the cob. Who serves carrots and peas with cheeseburgers?

"I don't eat carrots and peas with cheeseburgers," I inform Mrs. Colton as kindly as I can.

She puts down her fork. "In my house, you do."

I sigh and begin eating the vegetables.

"So," Mrs. Colton says. "Tyrell tells me you mow lawns and earn money that way." She eyes Tyrell who looks away.

"Yes," I say with my mouthful but I remember to swallow and take a swig of my lemonade before I continue speaking. I'm trying to be as presentable as possible here. "It's my own business."

"I like that," she says. "Your own business."

Tyrell shoots me the evil eye because he's probably thinking she's hinting that he should do the same thing in his development. He'd never do it. Tyrell takes a lot of crap from the neighborhood kids and I'm sure people would make fun of him. I hope she understands that.

She seems to. She smiles at me. I finish all the vegetables while Tyrell tells us about another book he is reading, *The Hobbit*. This one isn't science fiction, he says. It's fantasy. It's about this little guy who goes on a "quest." I ask questions but Mrs. Colton doesn't seem interested. Although she does mention that Tyrell's father liked the book.

"Really?" Tyrell asks, his face lighting up.

"Yes," she says sadly.

The room suddenly goes bleak and I say, "I don't think my father liked books."

Mrs. Colton nods and then smiles at us.

Later, I help Tyrell clear and clean the dishes. Mrs. Colton remains seated at the table drinking her lemonade. "It sure is nice to have the men taking care of me."

Before I get on my bike to go home, she pats me on the shoulder. "You're a nice boy, Danny."

I nod deeply, embarrassed, and mumble, "Thank you."

She smiles again. She has a bright, wide smile. "Be careful going home."

I hop on my bike and wave to Tyrell and Mrs. Colton.

It's almost dark when I go through the woods and it's kind of hard to see where I'm going. But I'm used to the terrain and I know where to direct my bike to stay out of the sugar sand. When I get out of the woods and onto the road, I pass Janine walking with this girl, Maria Trezza.

"Hey, Zelko," Janine says.

She and Maria giggle. Girls are weird.

I maneuver around the corner and down my block. It's just about dark and at first I think it's Doug's car in my driveway, but it's not. It's Harry's old lime green piece of junk.

I stop short and just stare at my house. My fists ball up into tight knots but my stomach goes sick. I think I might throw up.

WAY FIVE: PSYCHOLOGY

Here's what goes down: I take my time opening the garage and putting my bike away. I wander around the front yard, just looking up at the stars, trying to keep myself from getting sick. I don't want to throw up. I steal glances through the front window. My mom and Harry are sitting at the kitchen table. Eventually the mosquitoes are so bad that I'm forced to go inside.

I head to my room but I don't get far, because my mom calls me into the kitchen.

And there he is: ugly hairy Harry. Just sitting at our table, drinking a cup of tea, wisps of dark gorilla hair sticking out of the top of his dark T-shirt. He says, "Hello, Danny."

My skin is tight and my stomach is sick and I feel like I'm going to lose my dinner.

I finally manage to choke out: "Where's Doug?"

My mom's mouth drops and I see Harry smirk a bit.

She says, "Doug and I went out on a date. We weren't serious at all. Now stop that."

"You went on two dates," I correct her.

"Stop it."

"Danny," Harry says, "Your mother told me that she went out with this Doug person."

"She seemed to like him."

"Danny!" my mother yells.

I scratch a mosquito bite on the back of my neck.

"Sit down, Danny," Harry orders.

I stare at him and sit down.

"We're going to try this again," he says. "Your mother and I have decided to get back together. But we need you on board. We need you to accept that I'm going to be in your mother's life."

In my chair, I slouch to the side and look at the floor.

"I know you and I didn't get off to a good start," he says.

My lip curls. "Maybe if you didn't lock me out of the house and steal my money, we'd be off to a better start." I lift my eyes to him.

He just stares at me.

Then he says, "Fair enough."

"But," he says, "You needed to pay for that couch. That's why I took your money."

I look at my mother. She says, "I told Harry he just can't take your money."

"I won't do that again," Harry concedes. "And I won't lock you out of the house again."

I'm not sure how to respond. It really isn't about my money or being locked out. It's about how I know deep in my gut this guy is bad news. That I've heard these promises before and that he always breaks them. That he and my mom drink too much when they're together. That she's better without him. That's what this is all about. She's stronger without him. I like her better without him.

I don't say any of this, though. I wish Lisa were around but she's obviously working or at a friend's house.

Anyhow, I say, "Fair enough," and get up and go to my room. I lock the door and put in my Pink Floyd tape cassette, *Wish You Were Here*. I like all the songs on this tape. Especially, "Shine on You Crazy Diamond," which was written as a tribute to their former bandmate, Syd Barrett. He took too much LSD and had a mental breakdown and had to leave the band. He never recovered.

I like this line:

Remember when you were young,
You shone like the sun.

It's melancholy and lonely and even though the band is singing about their friend, I feel like he's singing about my father.

I pull out my Legos and try to build a plane. A plane that would take me far away, maybe to England where Pink Floyd is from.

After a while, I notice the air conditioner is back on.

The next few days, I keep to myself, doing my lawns, riding my bike, trying to stay in a decent mood even though I feel like screaming and punching the walls. Harry seems to be at my house all the time. The cable gets hooked up again and he hogs the TV.

One afternoon, I happen to ride by Richard Plimpton's house and see him outside, standing at the edge of his yard near the acre of woods next to his house. He's got a stick in his hand, pointing at something on the ground. I keep riding, but I look back until curiosity gets me. I swerve around, rolling slowly by his house, Richard still standing, pointing at the ground with his stick. I stop and get off my bike, letting it drop to the ground.

I approach slowly because I have a feeling Richard is pointing at something scary. And sure enough, when I'm just feet behind him, I see a snake, gray with lighter gray strips, nestled in low brush and pine needles. It's not long and huge, actually kind of small, but bigger than a garter snake. The thing is curled up on itself, but it moves and coils and rolls. Richard inches closer and touches the snake with the stick. The snake lifts its head, hisses, attempts to strike like a cobra, then retreats.

"Dude!" I say, jumping back.

Richard keeps poking, not hard jabs, but enough to make it hiss loudly. The snake puffs its neck out.

"Watch," Richard says, poking the snake again, this time harder. It suddenly rolls on its back and stops moving.

"I've scared it," Richard explains, stepping closer to the snake. I edge forward and look over Richard's shoulder. I'm waiting for the snake to lift its head up and strike.

Richard pokes it again but the snake doesn't move.

"Did you kill it?" I ask.

"No." Richard steps back a bit, and I follow. We still have a clear view of the snake.

"It's an eastern hognose snake," Richard says. "All bark and no bite."

"What do you mean?"

"A hognose isn't venomous to humans. I mean, if you tease it enough, it will bite you, but you won't drop dead or anything."

I stare at the snake. "Why isn't it moving?"

"It's playing dead. All that hissing and inflating of his neck is a defense mechanism to scare but it can't do much. Well, if you're a toad or a rodent, you're out of luck. Hognose snakes eat those guys."

"They eat toads?" I ask.

"And mice," Richard says.

We watch the "dead" snake. Out of nowhere, it flops over, wiggles and slips away into brush and pine needles of the woods.

I'm really impressed. "Wow. How cool."

"Yeah." Richard drops his head and stuffs his hands into the pockets of his shorts. "Well, I'll see ya."

I look into the afternoon sky, listening to the insects in the summer heat. I was going to head over to Tyrell's house but I remember he's up at his grandmother's for a few days. I'm really not into playing ball with Bobby Kovacki. I was thinking about going to see Shawn and Lou, but I just don't feel like hanging around them, especially after I told them I was going to see the Yankees. Harry is at my house because he has the day off from work. So what else am I going to do? Richard did give me that Milky Way and he did apologize and I'd really like to find more snakes.

"Do you know about snakes?" I call out to Richard who has walked up to his porch.

He swings around and nods. "Yeah. I know a lot about nature." He lopes over to me, still with his head down and his hands in his pockets. "I'd like be a forest ranger some day or nature conservationist but my dad and mom said I have to be an accountant or engineer."

"What's a nature conservationist?"

"It's like a biologist who cares for the environment, making sure endangered species are cared for, watching out for companies who pollute the land and kill the habitats."

"Sounds boring compared to a train engineer. I think it would be fun to ride trains," I say.

Richard smirks, lifting up his head. "Not a train engineer. They want me to be a different type of engineer. The kind that designs machines. Sort of like architects who build machines that are used in factories."

Now that sounds sort of interesting—I like building things—but if Richard wants to work with snakes and habitats, why would his parents try to make him an accountant or someone who designs machines when he clearly wants to work in the outside? I ask him this.

"Because they think I won't make enough money doing what I want to do."

I can understand that. Money is important. You need it to survive.

I ask Richard to go through the woods with me on our bikes so we can check out more snakes.

"My bike chain is broken."

"Fix it," I tell him.

"I can't."

We go into the garage and sure enough, his bike chain is

broken but I hook it back on. Richard claims he knows how to hook his own bike chain on but it keeps falling off.

His mom opens the door and steps into the garage. I haven't seen her up close since the third grade. She's got a pale white face with big blue eyes and when she smiles, you can see her gums.

"It's been a long time since we've seen you around," she says. "Do you want some iced tea or something? It's hot out."

The door to the house is open and I can feel the cool air. Richard looks uncomfortable, like he wants to get away from her, so I decline the iced tea. "Maybe later."

We take off, heading down some roads and then onto the trail I take when I go to Tyrell's. There's a path that shoots off this trail and I follow Richard's lead. We ride and ride, skirting on the sides, the insect noises growing louder and louder. You can still hear the cars from Route 37 so we aren't too far from civilization.

We arrive upon an almost-dried-up creek bed. "I like to come here because nobody knows about it." Richard rests his bike on the ground and finds a piece of old concrete with enough room for both of us. "If you sit here long enough, you'll see something. I've seen a few foxes, deer, ground hogs, skunks, snakes..."

I see a red cardinal, a few squirrels, a couple of toads, but no snakes. It's buggy by this little dry creek—the gnats keep floating into my ears and my nose—but they don't seem to bother Richard. We stay here for what seems like an hour and when my stomach starts grumbling, I suggest we leave.

"Wait," Richard says, signaling with his chin across the mini-creek. It takes a second but soon I make out the big bird— a wild turkey!

"Holy crap!" I shout and the turkey stops still.

It eventually moves, the head jarring forward. It steps across the cracked dry creek and passes right by us. I get a front-row view of its white head, red gobble neck, shiny brownish coat, fleshy skinny legs, and webbed feet. Its eyes are small and the beak a little yellow. It even makes turkey noises and I have to bite my lip to stop myself from laughing. We watch it make its way up the small incline and disappear into the brown woods.

"Fantastic!" I shout when the turkey is gone.

Richard beams. "I was a little nervous when it went by."

"Why?"

"Turkeys are pretty unpredictable. We were lucky it didn't attack us."

"They attack people?"

"The toms. Those are the male turkeys. They're pretty territorial."

We climb back on our bikes but Richard's chain is off again. He puts it on and it seems okay. We decide to go get a slice of pizza at Luigi's. Luigi's has the best pizza in the world, even if there's no air conditioning. Both Richard and I sweat while we eat our slices. Luigi and his guys know me because I'm a long-time customer. They refill our sodas three times without charging us.

On the way home, we pass the neighborhood park. It's not like it's a nice park. The tarmac is broken up on the basketball court. The swing set area is busted. Graffiti is spray-painted on the slide. The picnic tables are dug in with people's names, bands, symbols. There are drawings on the tables of stuff you wouldn't want a little kid to see—naked body parts. Lots of bad words, too, along with Satan stuff. Richard and me are just rolling by talking about snakes again when Jimmy Horak comes hulking out of nowhere. His buddies, Ryan and Brian, are with him along with his brother, Mark.

Mark has reddish-blond hair and a pink face, but he lifts weights and plays football. He's a sadistic monster, the worst of the worst. Two years ago, when he was in eighth grade, I saw him throw this little chubby kid into a fence over and over again. He cackled and everyone laughed and called the chubby kid "bubble butt" and other cruel things. It got worse, too. Mark has a thing about accusing kids, especially smaller boys, of doing it with their fathers or their pet dogs. It's weird and when I saw this happening, when the boy was pleading and crying for it to stop, I wanted to do something but I was only in sixth grade and smaller than I am now.

I try to swing my bike around but it's a direct hit: Mark charges me and I go flying to the ground, hitting it hard, my bike landing on me. The peddle digs into my calf and when I get my bearings, my bike is gone. Mark has it hiked over his shoulder and I watch him throw it up at the basketball net.

"Stop!" I shout, getting up and noticing blood dripping down my leg. It doesn't stop me. I'm so friggin' angry that I start racing toward Mark. Richard grabs my upper arm—he's sort of strong—and holds me back.

"Danny. It's no use."

I see that Richard's got dirt on his arm and he's pretty scraped up. His bike is gone, too. Jimmy is on it, cruising around the basketball court. The other two guys are laughing and Mark keeps throwing my bike up at the basketball net until it gets wedged between the backboard and rim. Mark howls and the other guys double over and Jimmy keeps rolling around the court on Richard's bike. My heart is jamming and I'm about to go kill one of them but again, Richard holds me back.

"Let's just go," Richard says. "The chain is gonna fall off my bike soon so it won't be useful to Jimmy."

"I'm not going," I growl. "I'm not a coward." I stand in the dirt, the late afternoon sun glowing over me, my arms across my chest. Screw them. They can take my bike and hang it from a basketball net, but they're not gonna chase me off.

I watch them. Ryan and Brian try getting my bike down by jumping up and hitting the tire, an attempt to pop it off the ring. They think the entire situation is hilarious.

"They need a ladder," Richard mutters.

A ladder. Great idea. "Let's go," I tell him.

"I thought you said you didn't want to leave?"

"We're not leaving for good. We're coming back."

I march toward my house, Richard beside me. He's still loping, his head down and this pisses me off. "Richard, you gotta lift your head up. Take your hands out of your pockets. Stop looking like you're waiting to get your butt kicked!"

Richard appears hurt. "Danny, maybe I should go home."

"You'll be fine." Jesus Christ. How'd I get stuck with such a wimp? "Confidence, Richard." I pick up our walking pace. "Always look like you have confidence in your ability to kick butt. Even if you know you're going to get killed." This is something my dad used to say.

Richard just eyeballs me. But he lifts his head up and takes his hands out of his pockets and walks faster.

"There you go," I say.

We reach my house and in the garage I locate the ladder. It's a good ladder, not a step ladder or one you use inside to paint. It's a construction ladder, double paned so it should reach the rim fine. I also grab a baseball bat and hand it to Richard. He takes it like I handed him a shotgun, all nervous and confused.

"We need some protection against those dickheads," I say.

"I'd rather forget the whole thing and go home." He's lost his confidence.

I sigh and shake my head. "So you'd go without a bike all summer?"

Richard shrugs. "The chain keeps falling off anyhow."

I'm starting to seethe. "It doesn't matter if you don't want your bike or not. It's the fact that they took it!" I grip the bat in his hands and shove it toward his chest. "We may have to take a beating but we're getting our damn bikes back."

"What if they grab the bat and use it against me?"

"Then you'll die with some honor!" I can't deal with this weakness. I grab another bat, this one aluminum. With my other hand, I pick up the ladder, loop my arm through the panes, and hike it on my shoulder.

We're just about to leave when the house door to the garage opens. It's Harry. He notices the ladder. "What the hell are you doing?"

"We have a problem," I say. "I'll bring the ladder back." It's not his ladder anyhow. It was my dad's so that means it was willed to me. I'm sure he didn't leave it for my mom after the divorce.

Harry grimaces and pulls out his cigarettes, lights one. I ignore him and start walking but Harry tells us to stop what we're doing. I put the ladder down and face him. Harry demands to know what our plans are.

I don't want to tell Harry because it's none of his business and I don't know how he's going to react. He doesn't seem drunk so I have that on my side, but I'm still unsure what he's going to think of me when he learns that some dickbrain took my bike and threw it like a basketball and got it caught on the rim.

It's Richard who spills. He tells Harry what happened and I gotta tell you, it makes me super crazy mad, so bad, I could swing the bat at him. I should've just kept riding when I saw him staring at that stupid snake.

Harry chuckles and snickers. He starts laughing, coughing, and laughing more.

Jerk.

I turn and begin walking. Screw him.

Harry stops me again. "Put the damn ladder away."

"It's my ladder."

Harry steps into the garage, closing the door behind him. He walks slowly toward me and I have the awful feeling I'm going to get smacked.

It doesn't happen. "Put the ladder back. I'll get your bikes."

I hesitate. "How?"

"Put the damn ladder back!" he shouts and Richard's eyes go wide.

I return the ladder to the hook on the wall. Harry grabs a street broom, the one with the hard bristles, and swipes the bat from Richard. He begins stalking down the street, one hand gripping the bat at his side and the other on the broom. Richard and I trail behind him, me with the aluminum bat in my hand.

When we get to the park, Jimmy is still spinning around the court on Richard's bike. My bike remains hooked on the back of the basketball rim and now Jimmy's buddies are chucking rocks at it. Mark is sitting on the top of one of the picnic tables, his legs stretched out. He sees us and immediately stands up.

Harry doesn't miss a beat. He stomps up to Mark and shouts, "Get that damn bike down now!"

Mark doesn't move but Harry hurls the broom at Mark's feet and lifts the baseball bat like he's going to whack him with it.

"Get it down!"

"Okay," Mark mumbles, picking up the broom. He goes over to the basketball net and attempts to lift the bike off the rim but it's caught. He calls his brother over.

Jimmy, who has stopped riding, steps away from Richard's bike, letting it drop to the ground on the broken asphalt. He runs over to the basketball pole and unbelievably, scurries up it like a monkey, and somehow lifts the bike up with one hand and drops it to the ground. It bounces on the tires once and then tips over, smashing on the court.

"Get your bikes," Harry tells us. Richard goes for his and I go for mine. I test it out, making sure it isn't bent, and miraculously, it's still in good shape.

Harry grabs the broom from Mark and takes the bat from me. He marches down the street, a broom in one hand, two baseball bats tucked under his arm. Richard and I follow him, but we stay behind him.

I don't know what to say. Richard keeps looking at me and all I can do is shrug. When we reach my driveway, Harry is already in the garage, putting the bats and broom away. Richard stops because his chain has fallen off again.

Harry notices. "Did they do that?"

"No," Richard says quietly. "It happens all the time."

"Bring it here."

In the garage, Harry reattaches the chain. He produces a

Phillips head from his tool box and shows us the trouble. He points to the derailer, the piece near the back of the chain, and tells Richard he needs to tighten the screws. He gives Richard the Phillips head and shows him which way to move it. "Your bike is old so you might want to invest in a new one. But for now, if it happens again, this is a quick fix."

"Thank you," Richard says.

"Yep."

Harry goes inside.

Now I feel like the jerk. I've been hating Harry for so long I feel bad now that he's done something good. Two things good. Helping us and helping Richard with his bike.

Richard claims he has to get home and I can tell he's had enough of his day with me, so I let him off easily. He wasn't so bad to hang around so I call out to him, "Whenever you wanna go find snakes or turkeys, stop by!"

Richard waves and rides quickly away. I probably gave him the most excitement he's had all summer.

Inside, Harry is sitting on the couch, watching television. I know I need to say something so I take Richard's lead and say, "Thank you for helping us."

"You gotta be tougher," Harry says. "You can't let idiots take your bike and hang it from a basketball net. Stupidest thing I've ever seen."

"I didn't let them. They shoved me off my bike and just took it."

"And what did you do? Just watch them?"

I avert my eyes, look at the floor. My head is beginning to flare with anger.

"In my day, no kid took my bike," Harry brags, leaning back on the couch, stretching his legs out. He's wearing jeans because he never wears shorts. I look around for my mom but I remember she's working. Harry points at me. "You never let nobody take your bike."

"I didn't let them take it!" Now I'm desperate to plead my

side. "I didn't!"

"You did." He stands up and walks by me, into the kitchen. For a split second, I think I smell a faint whiff of alcohol. Not beer, but whiskey or gin. Something strong.

I remain in the living room confused until I go out the front door and back into the garage. I stare at my bike, feeling really angry. I said thank you. I did. I was nice.

After a while, I pretend talk to my dad in my mind. He's leaning against the garage refrigerator.

"Harry drinks whiskey, right?" I ask.

My dad, wearing jean shorts, flip-flops, and a red T-shirt with Coca-Cola on it, nods. I have a photo of him in this outfit. We were camping and my sister snapped the picture.

"Why did he help us and then chew me out for letting them take my bike?"

"Because he's a dick, Danny. You know that."

I sit on the floor and examine the derailer part on my bike. "It was really cool that he helped us. Did you see Mark's face when Harry showed up? It was great! I thought he was gonna poop his pants."

"He was gonna poop his pants," my dad says. "I'm dead, so I know these things."

I grin and study the derailer. I think for a second and wonder, if you're dead and you know things, then why can't you tell me what's going to happen? Is Harry going to marry my mom? Is this asshole going to live with us forever?

Soon my dad is gone. Of course he doesn't know things. He's a ghost I made up in my head.

A day later, Tyrell comes home from his grandmother's and we head off to Baskro. While we're wading in the crystal blue water, I tell Tyrell about the snake. Tyrell doesn't like snakes but I explain to him about eastern hognose snakes and how they're all bark and no bite. Tyrell doesn't buy it and tells me that he's never gonna touch any snake.

"Why don't we go look for one and I'll show you."

"Nope."

It's a hot day and the water feels cool on my skin. We stand in the water by ourselves, kind of bored, and I keep hoping the girls will show up. It was fun with them last time. After a while, I see a huge figure stomping out of the trail and before long recognize it's Gordon Urszulak. He's by himself, no shirt, just trunks and flip flops and a pink towel draped over his shoulder. Tyrell and I watch him stomp nearer and nearer until he's finally at the shoreline.

"Hello, boys," Gordon says, dropping his towel next to my towel. He lumbers into the water, crouches down, cools himself off, then floats on his back, his inflated white tummy and his bulbous moon head and his big pale toes sticking up. He looks like a cartoon character. Fred Flintstone.

Tyrell shakes his head.

"I heard you got your ass handed to you the other day, Zelko," Gordon shouts up at the sky.

I didn't tell Tyrell this part. I know we're best friends but sometimes you don't want your best friend knowing the embarrassing stuff.

Gordon stands up, his big pale body dripping with water. "Heard Mark Horak tossed you off your bike and threw it up on the basketball net."

Tyrell eyes me but I ignore him.

"Yeah," I say. "And I came back with a bat and Jimmy took it down."

"You scared the Horak brothers with a baseball bat?" Gordon says.

"I did." I say it tough. You can twist a story around to your advantage, leave out certain parts and act like you had everything in control.

Gordon nods, flicks a bug off his thick shoulder. "I heard different."

"Well you heard wrong."

I get out of the water and grab my towel, shaking the sand off of it. "I gotta go," I say to Tyrell.

Tyrell follows and Gordon lifts up his left arm and smells his armpit. "Do I smell?"

"Definitely," I say, marching off. I know Gordon can come shooting out of the water and tackle me like he's a Dallas Cowboy or something, but I don't care. I'm too pissed off.

I don't know why I'm mad. I guess when Gordon said, *I heard different,* means that he probably heard most of the truth. He might've even heard Harry came to the rescue but what nobody knows is the part where Harry was a jerk and smelled like whiskey. It means he'll never stop drinking and neither will my mom. That's why I'm mad, I realize, as I struggle to walk through the sand, Tyrell behind me.

The good thing about Tyrell is he doesn't pressure me to tell the story. He just keeps quiet until he brings up the snake. "Why doesn't the snake have any venom? I thought all snakes had venom."

"It does have venom but it only works on toads and rodents."

We discuss snakes, which calms me down. At his house, Tyrell pulls out an old book he has in his room about snakes. We find the hognose snake and read about it. Everything Richard told me about the hognose snake is in the book.

Later we ride over to my house, but Tyrell has to leave his mom a note first. I know Harry isn't there and my mom is at work. Lisa is home and she's plopped on the couch, her shoes and socks off but still in her dark blue McDonald's uniform, her poison dart frog makeup smudged.

"What's with you?" I ask her.

"I did a morning shift but nobody could drive me home so I had to walk. It's hot out there. Try walking two miles in this heat wearing polyester."

Tyrell laughs and she lets out a small smile.

"Did you call Mom?" I ask.

"Yeah, but she's working."

I feel bad for my sister. "If Mom kept dating Doug, he could've gotten you a nice car for free and you wouldn't have had to walk home in your ugly uniform."

Lisa stretches out. "You're so helpful."

Tyrell and I decide to play Atari—Space Invaders—and Lisa drifts off to sleep on the couch, her McDonald's visor in her hand. We keep it down so we don't wake her.

About five o'clock, both Harry and my mom pull up—my mom in her car, Harry on his motorcycle. Tyrell has never met Harry and when we look through the window, Tyrell remarks that he has a fine bike.

"That thing is a piece of junk," I grumble, even though I know it isn't.

They're both very happy and my mom says hello to Tyrell. Lisa wakes up and Harry takes a seat at the kitchen table. He announces that we're all going down to the boardwalk tonight.

I don't want to go anywhere with Harry and it looks like Lisa feels the same, but Tyrell is all bright and hopeful. Like we're going to take him.

Harry picks up on this and says to Tyrell, "You can come too."

Tyrell beams. "Really?"

"Of course," my mom says.

I'm not sure about this. They seem sober but that doesn't mean they're going to stay sober. The boardwalk has a bunch of bars. I don't know if Mrs. Colton wants her son hanging out with drunks. I want to stop this rock racing down the hill but Tyrell is so excited I just can't take away his happiness.

Tyrell calls and gets permission from his mother. He doesn't have any cash on him so he gives her directions to our house and within fifteen minutes, she pulls up in her brown Nova, still wearing her white nurse uniform. My mom steps outside, along with me and Tyrell. My mom puts on her customer face, the one she uses at the salon. She and Mrs. Colton chat for a minute about which boardwalk we're going to—Point Pleasant or Seaside—it's Seaside—and Mrs. Colton frowns because everyone knows that Point Pleasant is the family boardwalk and Seaside is the wild boardwalk with lots of bars. It's at this moment I debate whether I should jump in and say, *Just so you know, they might stop off at a bar and they might have too much,* but I don't. My mom assures Tyrell's mother that she won't take her eyes off us. Mrs. Colton reminds her that kids get snatched up at places like Seaside and my mom tilts her head and says, "Really? When did that happen?"

Mrs. Colton can't come up with a specific example but she says that kids are getting grabbed in all sorts of places, even the mall, that hasn't she ever seen the milk carton pictures? My mother says she has but who would want two thirteen-year-old boys? Mrs. Colton chuckles and hands Tyrell a sweat jacket, which he takes reluctantly. "It gets cold down by the ocean," she says and hands him a crisp ten-dollar bill.

"Have fun!" she says, walking back to her Nova and once she's inside the car, she delays backing up. Her hands are on the wheel and she's just staring at us, probably my mom. I can tell she doesn't have trust in this situation. I wouldn't have trust either.

Off we go, me and Tyrell in the back seat of my mom's car, Harry driving. It bugs me that she lets him drive her car. Lisa bailed at the last minute claiming she had cramps. She has cramps all the time and we all know that women only get cramps once a month so that claim was bull crap. Besides, I share a bathroom with her and my mom so I know when they're really at that time because Tampax wrappers fill up the bathroom trash can.

Harry slides his seat back so Tyrell, who is sitting behind him, is squished. He doesn't seem to be bothered by it though. He just angles his legs and sits up straight. It's a Friday night so

142

the highway out to Seaside is crowded with vehicles, especially sporty cars like Camaros and Firebirds. There are jeeps with the tops off and in the setting sun, I can see people with tanned bodies, their hair blowing back in the wind, their music blaring. Lots of Journey and Bruce Springsteen and Van Halen. Harry allows these wild cars to blow by him, not saying a word. He keeps to the middle and right lanes and when we ride over the bay bridge to the ocean, I look out at the glimmering water, studying the boxy white houses that line the enormous bay. I'd like to live in one of those houses one day. I can see myself, just getting up in the morning and sitting on one of the docks, catching crabs. When I was a little kid, my dad used to take me crabbing down here. We never kept the crabs because neither of us liked eating shellfish. We'd just toss them back in the bay.

From the top of the bridge, you can see the amusement rides of the boardwalk. It's almost dark so the colored lights flash and glow. We roll into town and park our car in a sandlot which Harry has to pay for. The four of us walk up to the boardwalk and begin strolling through the crowds, both Tyrell and me eager to play one of the games at the stands. Harry and my mom stay behind us, Harry smoking, my mom leaning into him. Tyrell and I do a spinner game, then we do another spinner game and another, and before we know it, we're both down three bucks. I look in my pocket and I only have another ten because that's all I brought. My mom suggests we go get a slice of pizza.

A slice of pizza from the boardwalk is huge so you can only eat one slice. We all sit squished in a booth and eat. Everyone drinks soda so I'm hoping there will be no alcohol tonight and all will be good. Then, when my mom gets up to go to the women's bathroom and Tyrell gets up to go to the men's bathroom, Harry pushes a ten-dollar bill across the table at me. He says that my mom and he are going off by themselves and we should meet in two hours, near the big yellow cheesesteak stand, not far from where we came in.

I stare at the ten for a quick second and then slide it back to Harry, reminding him that we're supposed to stick together. Harry shifts in his seat and places his fingers on the bill. He shoves the ten back across the table and tells me not to be such an f-ing girl.

He uses the entire word.

I glare at the ten on the dirty table.

"You're not supposed to drink tonight," I say. "You gotta drive us all home."

"Are you my goddamned father?"

I lift my eyes to him.

"Are you?"

"No."

"Then shut the hell up."

I almost say, *You shut the hell up,* but I can't. I'm so angry. I know I need to hold myself together so I slide to the side in my seat and my mouth curls. I focus on a little boy across the aisle. His legs are swinging as he happily chomps on his slice of pizza. He's with his grandparents who look tired. The boy makes a face at me.

Within minutes, my mom and Tyrell are out of the bathroom and my mom explains to us that we're teenagers now, so we can have two hours of independence. "Have fun. Meet some girls," she chimes and she and Harry walk away.

"Sorry about that, dude," I say to Tyrell.

"What?"

"My mom told your mom that she'd stay with us."

Tyrell shrugs. "It's not like they left us in Seaside. Technically, they're still with us."

Boy, has he changed his tune.

"Let's go!" Tyrell flicks his head. "Come on!"

He's ecstatic.

We buy a bunch of tickets and start hitting the rides. We do the Ferris wheel, walk through the fun house, and watch a few guys throw a mallet down and test their strength on the High

Striker. On the line for the Tilt-A-Whirl, I pull my comb out of my back pocket, run it through my hair, then strike up a conversation with some cute girls from New York City. They're from Queens and they have thick, old-time accents like mobsters chewing gum. Denise and Donna are their names and I start telling them about the hognose snake I found the other day only I embellish a bit, explaining that I actually lifted it up and it flopped out of my hands and played dead.

"You did not!" Denise hollers and I say I did, "Didn't I, Tyrell?"

"He sure did," Tyrell says, backing me up even though he wasn't there.

"Then what'd you do?" Donna asks Tyrell.

Tyrell, who never has any game seems to have it tonight. Must be the salty air. Even though he's not dressed to the nines like he usually is, he has a nice gray T-shirt on and clean black shorts and blue Nikes. He looks better than me—I'm in a Pink Floyd shirt and my cut-off jeans are a bit dirty and so are my white sneakers. Still, I know my blond hair is blowing in this nice sea wind and I know these girls from Queens are digging both of us.

"So, what did you doooo?" Donna says in her New York mobster accent. "Ty-*rell*?"

Tyrell says, "I grabbed that dead-playing snake up from the ground and it hissed at me and even tried to bite my hand. It works like a cobra, you see, dips its head up and down, strikes at you, but the venom doesn't work on humans so you don't need to be scared of it. Anyhow, I put it on the ground and it suddenly flopped over and scooted away."

"*Scooted?*" Denise says, mocking him. The girls start giggling and babbling, "Scooted, scooted."

I'm as stumped as Tyrell until I realize these girls are making fun of us. Soon it's time to load onto the ride. The girls are gone and soon we take our own seats.

"Those girls are idiots," I say to Tyrell.

He says, "Yeah." But I can tell he's embarrassed.

After that, we're low on money and it's time to meet my mom and Harry. We go to the designated spot and wait. We sit on a bench and watch a group of crazy teenagers laughing and joking.

Tyrell asks me about my bike, about what Gordon said, so I tell him the truth. That Mark knocked me off my bike and tossed it up on the net, that Jimmy took Richard's bike, that Harry defended us, then later, Harry yelled at me for getting my bike taken in the first place.

"That stinks," Tyrell says. "I guess it's good that you had Harry to go get the bikes."

"So you don't think he's a jerk?" I say.

"He seemed okay to me."

Great. Even my best friend doesn't believe me when I say Harry sucks.

We sit for another ten minutes and soon I see Harry's ugly face and my mom walking beside him. He's got a cigarette in his hand. She looks trashed because she keeps stumbling and he doesn't look too sober either.

"Great," I mutter. "Now they're drunk."

"What?" Tyrell says.

Harry and my mom approach us. "Let's go," Harry says, leading my drunk mom down the boardwalk.

I don't want to go. I don't move.

"We'll call Tyrell's mom," I yell out.

Harry jerks around, dragging my mom in a half circle, then leaves her to stand drunkenly by herself.

He marches up to me and points his cigarette at my face, inches before my eyes. He wants me to step back but I'm no coward.

"You ain't calling no one," he says.

I eyeball him and after a second, move back, glancing at that pack of teenagers from before. Most of them are still joking with each other, but a couple of them see us. They seem concerned but don't say anything.

"Danny," Tyrell whispers. He's clutching his sweat jacket in his hand. "It's fine. My mom is probably sleeping."

I start walking. I can barely look at my mom who seems to stumble every five feet. Harry doesn't get upset with her, which is good, he just laughs. Soon we're at the car and Harry helps my mom inside. When Harry walks by me, I can smell the beer and whiskey. I watch him fiddle with his keys and I know he's drunk too. I take a deep breath and ask my dad and Tyrell's dad in Heaven to make sure we don't get in an accident.

Harry drives carefully out of Seaside and he even drives very slowly over the bridge. I sneak looks at Tyrell and I can see he's got his hands braced on the seat like he's ready to get into a crash. My mom is passed out and Harry has the window open while he smokes. The radio is playing but it's that old music from the fifties and early sixties, the doo-wop. He sings along and I clench my fists as we go.

We travel through Toms River, past diners and fast-food places and closed strip malls. Soon the road goes darker and narrows into a two-lane highway. You have to pass the entrance into my neighborhood and drive another two minutes down the road to Tyrell's development. I remind Harry that we need to drop off Tyrell but Harry turns into our neighborhood.

"Hey!" I say. "We gotta drop off Tyrell. My mom told his mom that we'd bring him home."

Harry doesn't answer. I say it again, that we have to drop off Tyrell, but the jerkass doesn't answer. That is, not until we roll to the first stop sign. Then Harry sucks on his cigarette, peers into the rearview mirror and simply says, "I don't drive into spook neighborhoods at night."

I feel my skull crack. I look at Tyrell and through the dim light of a streetlight, I can see Tyrell is suddenly not scared but really angry or frustrated or maybe a mixture of it all. Shocked. His mouth is tight and he's breathing through his nose and his chest is going up and down.

My mom's boyfriend will not drive my friend home because he doesn't drive in black neighborhoods at night.

Information we could have used five hours ago. So I could have told his mother.

Harry drives us to our house and helps my mom inside.

I stand in the driveway with Tyrell. I know how upset he is but I'm so embarrassed I can't even speak. There is only a crescent moon tonight and a haze has covered the stars. I start pacing the driveway, kicking the tires on my mom's car. Tyrell does nothing. Just stands there, holding his sweat jacket.

"I'm friggin' so sorry," I say to him. "You can sleep over."

"I'm not sleeping here."

"Okay," I say, not knowing what to do. "You wanna come inside and call your mom?"

"No, I want my damn bike."

Wow. Tyrell cursed. "Okay. I'll get it."

The front garage door is locked so I have to go in through the house. I switch on the garage light and eye the ax. I'm so enraged I could chop that dickhead into pieces and I almost go for it, but I look up and see my dad. It's just a flash, he's in his coffin suit, a weird reminder for me not to become a murderer. I walk by Harry's motorcycle and I want to knock it over, but I stop myself.

When I lift the garage door open, Tyrell walks right in and grabs his bike. He's got his sweat jacket on and the hood up.

"You gonna take the trail or the main roads?" I ask.

Tyrell has his back to me and he shrugs.

"Wait," I say, going into Harry's tool bag and grabbing two things: a screwdriver and a small flashlight. "If you go through the trail, use the flashlight to see where you're going. The screwdriver is for defense in case a zombie or alien comes at you." I laugh a little but Tyrell keeps his back to me and just takes both, putting them in his sweat jacket pockets.

"No need to return them," I say and Tyrell nods. He pedals off.

After shutting the garage door, I go inside and find Lisa at the kitchen table, picking at her nails, wearing sweatpants and a Rolling Stones T-shirt.

"Where are they?" I say.

"Harry's in the backyard, smoking and drinking a bottle of scotch."

I'm not really sure what scotch is.

"It's whiskey only it's made in Scotland," she tells me. "Hence, 'scotch.'"

"So that's what I smelled," I say.

"He didn't drive Tyrell home?" she says. She's got no makeup on. Her face looks swollen like she's been crying, but not recently crying. Like she was crying a couple hours ago.

I think about poor Tyrell, riding through my neighborhood at this time of night. It's after midnight! I hope he doesn't run into the Horak brothers or some weirdo who captures kids, even thirteen-year-old kids, and does awful things to them in a basement. I wish I would have told Tyrell to call me when he got home and let me know he was okay. Do the ring twice thing. When I was a kid and we used to visit my grandmother's house in Sayreville—before she moved to Florida—right before we'd leave, she'd always say, "Ring twice." When we arrived home, my mom or dad would dial her house and let it ring two times and hang up. That was the signal for saying all was okay.

I'll have to wait until the morning. I'll ride over there and check that he's not chopped up in the woods.

"Why wouldn't he drive him home?" Lisa asks, her legs curled up on the chair.

Just her asking me infuriates every nerve in my body. Everything goes squirrelly and I just lose it and punch the wall. Right near the phone, shaking it and making it chime.

The pain is instant and I shake my fist, pacing the kitchen, wanting to cry out but Lisa puts her finger to her mouth and points to the backyard. "You don't want him inside."

She gets up and makes me a bag of ice. There are tears dripping down my face and she says again, "Why wouldn't he drive him home?"

"Because," I say, "he doesn't go into 'spook' neighborhoods at night."

Lisa's mouth twists up into a disgusted sneer. Then she does something she hasn't done since we were little kids: she hugs me. I begin to shake and cry. I feel so awful. I keep seeing Tyrell riding his bike alone in the dark, so late at night. I hope his chain doesn't fall off like it does on Richard's bike. Lisa holds me and pulls away. "Go into your room," she says. "Just go to sleep."

"I hate him," I say, tears and snot running down my face. "I hate him."

She pushes me to my room. I shut the door, switch my music on low, and flop on my bed. I don't even brush my teeth or get out of my clothes. I just lie there in the dark, listening to my band, Pink Floyd.

The wall was too high as you can see
No matter how he tried he could not break free
The only people who understand me are Pink Floyd.

In the morning, my mouth is grimy and my face is sticky from all that wimpy crying. I sit up and see that I'm in the same clothes as the night before.

I take a shower, brush my teeth for forever because I don't want to end up with rotten teeth—I brush my teeth three and four times a day—and put on a fresh T-shirt and shorts. I'm the only one up and so it's nice to be in the kitchen alone, eating my cereal and banana and drinking my orange juice and reading the morning newspaper. I eat quickly because I want to get over to Tyrell's but then about 9:00 a.m., I hear a car pull up. I look outside the front window and see a brown Nova and Mrs. Colton, wearing shorts and a hot pink T-shirt, slamming the door. She charges up the driveway and our sidewalk. Tyrell is in the car, too, but he's slouched down.

"Good morning, Danny," Mrs. Colton says when I open the front door. "Where is your mother?" She has her hands on her hips just like Janine Finn does when she's ticked off and I can tell Mrs. Colton's is doing her best to hide her anger. But she's as mad as mad can get and then ten times over.

I open the door wide. "Come in," I say. I want to see her tell off Harry.

"No," Mrs. Colton says, lifting her eyebrows and crossing her arms over her chest. "Just bring me your mother."

"Okay." I'm so excited. Finally, another woman is going to tell my mom to get her act together and not get drunk and let your stupid jerk of a boyfriend control things. Way Five! I bet I can get Mrs. Colton to convince my mother that she needs to kick him out. Use mother-to-mother psychology. I mean, once my mom hears what Harry did—leaving my best friend to ride his bike home after midnight—then surely she'll see the light.

I have to write Way Five in my head:

WAY FIVE: PSYCHOLOGY
   a. I'll tell Mrs. Colton exactly what went down.
   b. Then I'll ask her to talk to my mom, like really talk to her, make her see that she's putting her own children and other children at risk.
   c. Mrs. Colton will convince my mom to have Harry leave and then my mom can go out with Doug again.

"Did Tyrell tell you what happened last night?" I ask Mrs. Colton.

"Yes, he did and I'm very upset."

"Good," I say, taking a deep breath because here's the part where I have to get her to help: "Listen, me and my sister, Lisa, don't think Harry is good for my mom but it's like no one is telling her but me and my sister. She needs a friend to talk to, someone to make her see that he drinks too much and he's not cool. Maybe you can do that?"

Mrs. Colton opens her mouth, then closes it. She seems surprised.

"You can tell her how bad he is for us."

"I don't know if I can convince her of that."

"Last night she was passed out so she doesn't know what Harry did, so if *you* tell her what Harry did, it might make her see the light. You know?"

"Just go get your mom, please."

I'm not happy that Mrs. Colton isn't completely on board with my plan, but she seems mad enough. Maybe she will say something to my mom. I tell Mrs. Colton I'll be right back and march down to my mom's room, banging on the door. I try the knob but it's locked. "Mom!" I shout. "Someone's here!" I bang again.

Lisa comes out of her room.

I whisper, "Tyrell's mom is outside and she's pissed!"

Lisa grins. "Oh, shit."

"Mom!" I shout again, pounding on the door. "Get up!"

My mother finally cracks open the door, her mouth stinking like a rotten ham. "You gotta brush your teeth," I tell her when she slips out of the room with her robe on. "Your breath smells."

She glares at me but does as I say. A minute later, she's dressed in a T-shirt and shorts. She follows me to the front door.

"Can I speak to you outside?" Mrs. Colton asks.

And then there we are, out on the sidewalk, Mrs. Colton going off on my mom about letting Tyrell ride home on his bike in the middle of the night.

"What is wrong with you, Mrs. Zelko? I mean, honestly?"

I have to hold my smile but I think this plan is working!

Mrs. Colton's eyes flick to me and then back to my mom. "Listen, I don't mean to be intrusive, but do you really want that type of man in your life? A man who leaves your son's friend to fend for themselves in the middle of the night?"

This statement backfires, though. I can see my mom's mouth

tighten and her eyes go thin. "Thank you for your concern but I can make my own decisions about what type of man I want in my life."

Mrs. Colton frowns and my mother apologizes for the night before and swears it won't happen again.

"I know it won't happen again," Mrs. Colton snaps, "because you aren't allowed to take my son anywhere ever again."

My mom glances at Tyrell who is still slumped in the car seat.

Mrs. Colton shakes her head. "I would really like to speak to your—" she stops for a second and then says, "boyfriend."

"Harry?"

"Yeah, him."

My mom tells her that he's sleeping but he isn't because a second later, he steps outside. "I'm Harry." He stands on the small concrete porch so he towers over us.

Tyrell's mother takes a deep breath. "I was explaining to Danny's mom that I didn't appreciate the fact that you let my boy ride home in the middle of the night when she told me that you would drop him off. And I was also telling her that I didn't appreciate the fact that you two went to the bar when you were supposed to be watching the boys." Actually, she didn't tell my mom that she was upset about the bar part but now she's telling her. I'm doing cartwheels in my head! This is fantastic!

Harry pulls a cigarette from the pack in his T-shirt pocket and lights it. "The boys are old enough to take care of themselves. Not good to baby them."

"Is that what you're calling it? A good deed?"

Harry coughs. "No. I'm just telling you that they were fine on their own. Thirteen is old enough to walk around the boardwalk with a friend."

"All right, I'll accept that but I don't accept the fact that you both went to the bar and then drove the boys home drunk."

"I was not drunk."

"Apparently you were something."

Harry sucks on his cigarette. "I was not nothing."

Mrs. Colton isn't finished. "Liquor makes us say and do cruel things."

Now she's referring to the "spook" comment and the not driving him home.

Harry licks his lips and pins his eyes hard on her. Finally, he says, "I apologize about that one."

He doesn't mean a word of it.

Mrs. Colton blinks, wrings her hands, like she's trying to stay focused. She's trying to be tough but I can tell he's making her nervous. It's like she's throwing the words out like punches, and they're good solid hits, but Harry is just too tough of an opponent for her.

Mrs. Colton looks at my mother, then at Harry, then at me. "Danny, you are welcome at my house any time."

"Thanks," I say quietly.

Tyrell's mom stands for an awkward moment while she stares up at Harry again. He smokes and says nothing. Just watches her. Soon Mrs. Colton's facial expression goes dismal, no—frightened, and she turns and walks quietly away.

"Have a nice day," Harry calls out.

She gets in the car and backs it out of our driveway. Tyrell's eyes are down. Mrs. Colton avoids looking at us.

My mom is clearly upset, which is a surprise. "I can't believe you did that, Harry!" She begins to cry. Harry steps aside and lets her go in the house.

I follow her but just head to my room. I thought it would be fun to watch someone tell off my mom and Harry but now I'm just embarrassed.

Later, I'll write Way Five down and say just like I did with Orson: DID NOT WORK.

WAY SIX: POISON

Tyrell suggests I should try poison. "Just enough to make him sick. Not dead."

This is a change. "What about juvie?" I say.

"If you do it right, you should be able to scare him so he just leaves."

I tell him I tried that with the dog. It didn't work.

Tyrell nods. He's different since the incident with Harry. Gloomy, serious. Depressed. It took me four days to get the nerve to ride my bike over to his house and tell him that I was sorry for getting him into the situation. "I knew something could go bad," I said. "You were so excited to go to the boardwalk that I didn't want to burst your bubble."

Tyrell said nothing and now here we are, discussing poisoning my mom's boyfriend.

"I could put a hognose snake in the bedroom, or something," I suggest.

"Nah," Tyrell says. We're sitting in his backyard, facing the small detached garage. The door is open because we were going to ride bikes but we just sat down in the sun and started talking. Or not talking. I feel like such an idiot for being associated with Harry. I haven't said two words to the creep although he's got double shifts at his job or something so he really hasn't been around. My mom hasn't said anything.

Tyrell stands up and walks into the garage. He's looking through the cabinets but most of them are empty.

I follow him. The garage is cool and the faint smell of kerosene seeps into the air. I'm nervous being here, in a place where someone killed themselves. It doesn't seem to bother Tyrell. He just looks around the place and sighs. I feel like I should say something about his dad killing himself in here but I don't know what to say.

"You can buy rat poison at the hardware store," Tyrell finally says.

"How do you know?"

"I'm guessing that's where you get it. I mean, where else?"

We decide to just buy the poison. It's strange. I know this is evil and wrong but I'm so angry, and obviously so is Tyrell, that it propels us to go. We ride our bikes along Route 37, all the way down to Toms River, which is where the nearest hardware store is. The summer heat is oppressive and humid. The woods along the highways scream with insects and toads. Sweat pours down my face and my T-shirt is soaked by the time we get to the store. Tyrell puts the small canister of poison on the counter. The man at the register looks at us sideways, more so at Tyrell. "You got a problem with rats at your house?"

Tyrell doesn't answer so I do. "We made a fort and there's a couple of rats that keep getting in it."

"Oh yeah? You sure they're rats? Could be possums."

"Maybe," I say. "No, they looked like rats."

The man pauses, puckers up his lips. Then he places his hands on the counter. "I don't believe this story, boys."

"Why not?" I say. Who is he to tell me whether or not he believes my story? Besides, we're paying customers. It's not his business to ask us what we're doing.

"You don't have rats," he says.

"Yeah, we do."

"I will not sell you this poison."

"Why not?" Tyrell asks.

The man straightens up, his head snapping back like that hognose snake. "Because I don't sell rat poison to juveniles. That's why." He snatches the poison up and puts it behind the counter. "Get going. Now."

"Dickweed," I mutter as we leave.

Tyrell and I return to the heat. We're in a strip mall area and a few stores down, there's an ice cream place. We use our money and buy ice cream cones.

Strangely, the ice cream place isn't cold inside. We have to stand because the one table is taken up by a senior citizen couple slowly eating sundaes and staring. The old man has a light blue button-up shirt and I see a blurry greenish tattoo on his right forearm. WWII, I bet. Could be WWI. He's old enough.

My ice cream starts melting so I do my best to lick all the chocolate sprinkles as fast as I can but I can't do it and half of them drop to the floor. They look like ants. I laugh about it but Tyrell doesn't. Neither does the woman behind the counter. I would offer to clean it up but she looks so mean, I don't want to talk to her.

"What do you want to do now?" I say to him when we get outside.

He shrugs. He seems even more depressed. Me, I'm secretly okay with the poison thing not working out.

We ride back to his house. The sky has grown dark with heavy gray clouds and in the distance, I can hear thunder and even see lightning. When we turn into his neighborhood, a huge streak splinters across the sky.

"Holy crap!" I scream.

We ride as fast as we can down his street. Those little kids who call me booger head go flying in their house, yelling their heads off. When we get to Tyrell's house, we ride our bikes into the garage but the lightning is so close and scary, we can't make a run for it inside his house. So we stand in the open garage and watch the rain smash down. I try talking to Tyrell but he has nothing to add to the conversation.

When the storm is over, Tyrell tells me that he was thinking a lot about his father lately. "I think my dad would have gone over and beat the hell out of Harry."

Tyrell said another curse word!

"Like really punched him."

"That would've been cool to see," I say, throwing punches in the air.

He scuffs the concrete floor. "My mom was really angry. She kept saying, 'He had no right. No right.' She kept saying, 'Your father would have beat his butt into the ground.' That's what she kept saying. She doesn't like violence."

I nod.

"But the thing is, I don't think my dad would've done anything. He wasn't like that. I don't remember him ever getting mad or wanting to beat anyone up. He just liked to read and watch TV and come out here."

I steal a look at Tyrell, who is staring at the sky. The storm is fading, the rain now little drips, the hot smell of dampness filling the air. I can even hear birds chirping again.

"So I think it was good my dad wasn't here for all of that. I think I would've been embarrassed if my dad did nothing."

I don't know what to say. I think of Bobby Kovacki and even Richard Plimpton and wish I was hanging out with them, shooting basketball or searching for snakes.

I look behind me, around the garage. "What did your dad do when he came out here? You said he used to hang out here."

"He built birdhouses."

"Birdhouses?" I thought old men only did that. I scan the empty place. "Where are they?"

"My relatives took them. Everyone put a birdhouse up in their yard. To remember him."

This makes me smile. "Do you guys have one?"

Tyrell steps out from the garage and points up into the one

tree in his yard. It's one of those ugly scrub pines and I don't know why I never saw it before but now that Tyrell points to it, I see it nailed to a branch. It's worn and it was once bright green because a splash of paint is still visible.

"My uncle put it up there. He used my dad's ladder and then took the ladder home with him. Boy was my mom mad."

Beyond the tree and birdhouse, the clouds have almost cleared and a partial rainbow shines in the sky.

Tyrell says, "Just so you know, my mom was really angry with your mom."

"You said."

"Then she was sad for her," Tyrell says.

"Sad?"

"Yeah."

"Why?"

"My mom said because she obviously can't see Harry's character."

"Yeah, well, I know that. Nothing new."

"Right. So that's sad."

Tyrell tells me he's gonna read, that he's not into hanging out. I watch him go into the house through the back door.

There's a sting in my chest. I can tell Tyrell doesn't want to read, he just wants to get away from me. I'm connected to Harry. So that makes me guilty by association. It should make me angry, and it does, and after the back door is shut, I flip Tyrell the middle finger.

Screw him. You can't blame me for Harry and if you do, then you're a no-good friend.

I get on my bike but I don't close the garage door for Tyrell. I have my own stuff to do. I don't need him.

The moron kids are out, buzzing like bees, calling me booger brain and other stupid second grade names. I plan to ignore them but the more they scream at me the more my brain starts cracking. I swing around on my bike and begin circling them like an Indian in a western movie. "Shut up! Just shut up!"

"You shut up, you booger idiot."

I circle around another time and listen to them now call me idiot and suddenly all sense in my brain just crashes. I halt on my bike, grip the handlebars hard, and snarl, "Shut the..." Yeah. I use the F-word on these little kids. I know it's wrong and I watch their heads jerk back, their eyes widen and mouths open. I ride away.

When I reach the highway, the traffic is pretty heavy so it takes a bit before I'm able to cross. On the other side, I conjure up my dad for a minute. He's in the same clothes as he was the last time I talked to him—jeans, Coca-Cola T-shirt—standing on the side of the trail I'm about to take.

"That was wrong," I tell him. "Using the F-word on little kids."

My dad smiles. "Yeah, but it was funny as hell."

At home, I run into Lisa wearing her McDonald's uniform. She's waiting for her friend to pick her up for a night shift. "Hey, good news," she says. "Mom told me they put off the wedding until October."

It doesn't make me happy.

"Hey," she says, "it's better than August." And since it is August 1st, she's right about that.

I decide not to tell her about the poison failure.

I don't bother with Tyrell for the rest of the week. I do my lawns, ride my bike, listen to Pink Floyd, although Pink Floyd can be depressing, so sometimes I put on my Van Halen or Queen tape. I go over to Richard Plimpton's house twice and his mom lets me inside and we play his new Atari game called *Frogger*. Basically, you're a frog and you have to cross a busy highway and then jump on turtles and logs, avoiding snakes. Richard loves it—of course he does. His mom even makes us lunch—ham and cheese sandwiches on rye with mayo and mustard. Best sandwich ever and after I gobble it up, she offers to make me another and I eat that too.

"Do you eat much at your house, Danny?" she asks on the second day, after she hands me another sandwich.

"Sure," I say, vaguely realizing that she's after something here. Like I'm without a dad and I'm poor and she's feeling sorry for me. "We get lots of food at my house." Which is not true but we have enough. "Besides, I make good money with my lawn business so I go and eat at Luigi's a lot."

"You can't live off pizza."

"Sure you can," I answer.

My lawn business has grown. I just took on two more customers. One of them is this new girl's house. She's real prissy—white sneakers, pretty shirts with pink and sky blue shorts. Her hair is dark blond and wavy. She looks like she should be on a commercial that sells acne medicine or girl products. Her mom got my name from the woman across the street with the husband in a wheelchair. I just landed them a week earlier because their son who used to do the lawn joined the navy. So I do their lawn and now I'm doing the new girl's lawn. The first time I go to her house to mow, she sits outside on her front concrete porch and reads a magazine or examines her nails. I can tell when she gets to school, the girls are gonna go after her for being so prissy. I mean, Iris Cruz is a little prissy but for some reason, she doesn't get kicked around. This new girl looks like she's gonna have her butt handed to her. I bet Janine Finn would be first in line.

After I finish the front and backyard, I walk up to her. "Is your mom home? 'Cause I get paid as soon as I finish a job."

"I'm supposed to pay you."

She goes inside and returns with an envelope. "Here."

"Thanks," I say. Then, "What's your name?"

"Erin."

"Danny. Zelko. You going into the high school this year?"

"Yes. Ninth."

"Me too."

I study her for a minute and I know most guys would like her look but it's too much of a selling-girl-products look for me.

"Are the people nice around here?" she asks.

I chuckle. "Not really."

She nods sadly. Suddenly, it hits me: Richard Plimpton would like her. So that's what I do. The next day, I go over and get her and we walk to Richard's house and we all play *Frogger* and his mom makes us ham sandwiches. Even though the two of them barely talk, I see him stealing looks at her and I know he likes this girl. So does his mom. I do it the following day—go get her, and eat ham sandwiches and play Atari at Richard's house. I find out Erin has a bike and on the third day, we ride up to Luigi's to get pizza. It's ninety degrees outside and Luigi still hasn't gotten an air conditioner. "Why don't you have air conditioner, Luigi?" I call over to him from our seat.

"Are you gonna pay my electric bills?"

Luigi does have a new boom box and he's got the *Thriller* cassette playing and he's singing along, going, *"Billie Jean, not my lover…"* Luigi is probably about thirty-five and he's almost bald. A gold chain hangs around his neck with a cross and he has a small tummy that sticks out and a thick Italian accent from Italy. I can't help laughing at him.

Anyhow, things are going good. Erin isn't so bad. She's cool. She's from Pennsylvania and she and her parents moved here because her dad's job was transferred. She misses her friends and I get it, I say. But I don't say that I miss hanging out with Tyrell because frankly, Richard is all right. We don't have too much in common except that I like looking for animal life and he can locate it. Luigi gives us free refills again and I'm up at the counter getting mine when my nemesis enters: Jimmy Horak.

He's with his jerkbutt friends, Ryan Gumlek and Brian Donnelly.

They shoot evil death looks at me and I shoot them right back, which is pretty dumb because it's not like my buddy Richard is gonna be my wingman here. Still, I heard that because the pizza joint is open late, Luigi keeps a gun underneath his register. Luigi likes me so I know if things go bad, he will come to my aid.

The three boneheads don't say anything to us. They don't say anything at all and for a moment, I'm thinking Harry scared them with the bike thing so I might roll scot-free out of this situation. The tension is thick but all is civilized. No words are exchanged. After we finish our pizza, we step outside into the blazing sun and Erin finds her back tire flat. Richard's front tire is also flat. And both my tires are flat. I see the slash marks. One of those criminal dickbrains slashed our tires.

"Danny, don't bother," Richard says.

"Why?"

"'Cause."

Erin seems confused. "Why would they do that?"

"Because they're dickheads!" I answer. My arms go stiff and my mouth clenches and I'm about to just lose it. The F-word comes flying out of my mouth and Erin sort of smiles and Richard looks concerned and I say to him: "Are you gonna help or are you gonna hang out here like a loser?"

Richard drops his head. "I have to stop hanging out with you."

I order him to follow me.

We march into the pizza parlor and I head right for their table. I can't stop my body from doing what I do: I flip their pizza tray over, slices go flying, and I grab Jimmy by the shirt and punch him in the face. He's stunned for two seconds but recovers like a champ. Soon we're both knocked to the floor punching each other, wrestling, banging into the chair legs, his idiot sidekicks going, "Get 'em, Jim!" We roll and hit and the back of my head bangs hard against the wall. I can faintly hear Michael Jackson singing, *Beat it, Beat it*…which gives me more power and I get Jimmy underneath me and I punch and punch until Luigi is pulling me off and Richard—Richard!—is dragging Jimmy across the room and props him up against the garbage can.

"What is wrong with you?" Luigi hollers, then starts going off in Italian. His coworker is in front of us, hollering at me in

Italian, then a third coworker is cheering, but he's hollering in English, going to me, "Great fight! I'm gonna lay money on you next time!"

Luigi tells him to shut up and I start yelling, telling Luigi that Jimmy slashed our tires but Luigi says to get the hell out, all of us kids, "Just get the hell out of my establishment!" He yells some more in Italian and Jimmy and his dudes leave first, racing away on their bikes. We are left to walk our bikes home.

It isn't a good walk. First, it's gross hot, difficult-to-breath hot. Second, my right hand is killing me from all the punches I threw and the back of my head hurts from smashing into the wall and there's blood at the top of my forehead—Erin pointed that out. The three of us don't speak much until it's time for Richard to go his way, Erin to go hers, and me to go mine. When I get to my house, I see Harry's green tank car and my stomach just drops. I should've just gone to the bike store to get my tire replaced—there's a shop near the hardware store in Toms River—but it would've taken me over an hour to walk there. Probably an hour and a half. I need my bike so I'll ask my mom to take me on her next day off.

Harry steps outside from the front door as I'm walking my bike up the driveway.

"Flat tire?" he says, lighting up his cigarette.

I don't answer him. The way he treated Tyrell, I don't have to answer him. I have the right to ignore him.

"Hey! I asked you a question?"

I keep walking until I get to the garage. I'm thinking maybe I might be able to patch up my tires like the mechanics patch up car tires.

"Hey Danielle!"

I swing around. "What?"

Harry sucks on his cigarette. "What happened?"

"Flat tire."

164

"How'd you get that?"

The words *Jimmy Horak* are on my tongue but I know that's a bad move. He'll just make fun of me even if I tell him I beat Jimmy's butt.

"I rode over some glass and it sliced up my tires."

Harry walks closer and examines them. Then he examines me. "You're bleeding."

"So? What's it to you?"

"You're such a friggin' mouthy punk," he says. "I was gonna help you get new tires but now you're on your own."

"Whatever."

I watch as he turns away from me but I see his right fist clench up. I catch my breath because this time, I think he might punch me.

He doesn't.

Lisa gets her "guy friend" Tim to take me over to the bike shop. He uses his dad's van to drive us. The shop is just about to close because it's seven o'clock but they put two new tires on my bike. I use my own money to pay for it. When it's done, we go over and get ice cream, which the three of us eat outside, sitting on a curb of the parking lot. Tim seems okay. He's got blond hair like me but his is more yellow blond, not dirty blond like mine. He's tall and very skinny. He and my sister talk about McDonald's mostly. He works the grill—meaning, he cooks all the burgers. My sister works the drive-thru because you have to be smart to work the drive-thru she says. "People get pissed if they have to wait in their car too long. So you gotta get those orders fast and you can't mess up. Nobody likes driving back to McDonald's and coming in with a wrong order."

Tim goes to St. Joseph's, not my sister's high school, so when someone he knows sees him, he gets up to talk to them. My sister is eating a sundae and I'm eating another soft chocolate ice cream cone with sprinkles.

Lisa eats ice cream fast. She scrapes the side of the paper cup, sighs, and says, "October twenty-second."

I know exactly what she's talking about.

"Mom says it's a nice time to get married."

I close my eyes and let the depression fall over me. I get up and throw the rest of my ice cream cone out.

There's a pool party at Tommy Wicky's house. This dude isn't one of my favorite guys—he thinks he's a big shot because he lives in a very nice two-story house with an in-ground pool, cabana, and tiki bar in the backyard. I go to his pool party every year, something he's been having since second grade. You're supposed to get an invitation to attend but for the past couple of years, some kids who aren't invited just show up. I received an invitation in the mail which was obviously written by his mom because the cursive is perfect and pretty and I'm sure Tom doesn't write like that. I also believe I'm only invited because his mom hasn't updated the party list—me and Tommy haven't really talked much since fifth grade. Tommy lives in Oak Woods, the same neighborhood Beverly Carter said Iris Cruz is hanging out in these days. I would bring Tyrell with me but he's not taking my phone calls—I've tried twice. The phone just rings and rings. No answering machine. I would ask Richard to go but he doesn't seem like the party type. Anyhow, Bobby Kovacki gets an invite too and his dad drives us over to Tommy's house. He tells us to get a ride home because he's working the grave-yard shift at his job. Bobby's father works at the chemical plant in Toms River. He doesn't speak one bit on the way over to the party. Just smokes a cigarette. Bobby doesn't speak either. Must be a family trait.

It's mostly the popular kids at the party. Iris Cruz is there and she's in a pink bikini and I make a note in my head to shove this tidbit in Tyrell's face. If he answered my calls like a good friend maybe he'd be here. Friggin' blaming me for Harry acting like he did. I understand why Tyrell's angry but that doesn't mean he has to stop talking to me. I've been trying to get rid of Harry! You would think Tyrell would give me points for that. He's a no-good friend.

Anyhow, Iris is hanging out with the popular girls in my grade and they're wearing bikinis, too. They look hot but they act like they know they look hot and they don't talk to anyone else until Tommy's older cousin and his buddies show up. Soon they're all sitting by them and talking all sweet and nice. Tommy gets in on the whole thing and so do a few of his friends like Paul Mazziotti and Kevin Cortland. Even my old buddy, Shawn Stinson, is here and he's standing with that crew, trying to be in on the scene. That guy doesn't even wave to me when I go, "Hey, Shawn." So, me and the other outcasts just hang in the pool. Bobby wants to toss the football so I do that with him for a while.

Around nine-thirty, Janine Finn arrives with that girl Maria Trezza.

"Zelko!" Janine yells and soon she and Maria are in the pool with us. We start playing Marco Polo but it gets rowdy because we're splashing all over the place. This oddball kid Kenny Griffin splashes really hard—he makes a wave splash—and then does it again—and because everyone who is cool is sitting by the pool, they all get hit with Kenny's wave wall of water. The girls scream and scatter, Tommy's cousin gets ticked off and his friends shout, "Yo! What's your problem, morons!" Shawn Stinson is right behind them copying what they say, "Yo, what's your problem!" because he's trying to fit in. And because there's so much outrage—which is completely ridiculous and dramatic— Tommy takes charge. He stands at the edge of the pool like some water god, his hands placed firmly on his sides, and bellows: "That's it! You guys get out!"

Kenny Griffin says, "No, it's a free country," and Tommy goes, "It's my house, idiot!" and they start yelling back and forth. Finally, Tommy's mom comes out and orders all the kids in the pool to get out, call our parents, and go home. Kenny lives in Oak Woods, too, so he just grabs his towel, slips into his sneakers and stomps out, but not before swinging around and throwing both hands up, giving the party the middle finger in stereo. Maria goes into the house with Janine and they call their parents. Bobby reveals that there's no one at home to come get us so we both go inside and I try my house. Nobody answers so Bobby and I are stuck. I tell Mrs. Wicky that.

"Well, one of these girls can drive you home," she says.

Maria explains that she can't do it because her mother has a small car.

Janine gets back on the phone and locates her brother who will pick us up. At first I'm thinking it's Pete and I say, "I'm not letting stoner Pete drive me home," and she says, "Pete doesn't have a car, moron. My oldest brother, Gary."

Mrs. Wicky allows us to wait at the kitchen table. She puts a bowl of chips in front of us and pours each of us a glass of soda. Maria's mom is there in ten minutes but Janine's brother takes forever. We sit quietly and eat and listen to noise from the party— lots of yelling and splashing. Finally, after ten o'clock, we hear a honk and Janine says, "That's Gary."

Gary drives up in his dirty white pickup. His girlfriend, Leanne, sits in the front and Gary says there's no room for us so we have to sit in the back, in the bed of the truck. This is cool with me because I love sitting in the back of a pickup. Shawn Stinson's dad used to have a pickup and would take us around the neighborhood in it.

Janine, Bobby, and me climb in and sit along the sides. This is going to be the best part of the night, I can just feel it.

We roll out of the neighborhood and before he pulls out on the highway, Gary slides open the small window behind his head and tells us to lie down. "The cops don't like people in the back." We lie down, bunching up our towels for pillows, looking up at the starry sky. Bobby is on one side of me, Janine on the other. "Isn't this fantastic?" Janine cheers as we race down the highway, back to our neighborhood. I say, "Yeah!" and so does Bobby. We ride and ride and it doesn't feel like we're going to our neighborhood. Gary makes a sharp turn and when I sit up, we're on a dirt road. He's driving us to Baskro. I yell out, "We can sit up!" Janine and Bobby do but we have to sit pressed at the front end of the bed because the trees slap at us when we sit at the sides. Gary turns the music up and now we're in the woods, the music blasting—AC/DC—and the stars shining in the sky. Within minutes we're in front of the lake, jumping out, the pickup's headlights illuminating our space. We stand by the shore feeling the refreshing coolness of the water but Gary's girlfriend tells us not to go swimming.

"Why not?" Janine asks and Leanne explains about the lake. She tells us it's an old mining pit and that they dug too deep and hit the water table, which is why it's always filled up.

"Yeah, we all know that," I say and in the hazy light of the headlights, I see she gives me a nasty look, like how dare I speak.

"Anyhow," she says, "if you go out too far, you'll hit the current from below and you won't be able to swim back in. That's how people die."

"People die because they're lousy swimmers," I correct her.

Leanne isn't happy with me. "Will you shut the hell up and let me talk?"

"Say you're sorry," Janine says.

I apologize.

The music goes off.

"So," Leanne continues, dropping her voice. We're all quiet as she explains. "There's all sorts of bad stuff down there. Old cars, mining equipment, probably bodies. Who knows? It's also polluted so you shouldn't be swimming in it anyhow. Still, it's more about being sucked down. Remember—the hole is so deep in the earth, it hit the water table. So that suction is strong. When you swim at night, especially with no moon, you can't see the shore clearly so you don't know how far out you are. You get disoriented. So don't swim."

"How do you know all this?" Janine asks.

"Because I do."

"But how?"

Leanne is quiet for a long moment and then says sadly, "Because one of my neighbors died in here. About seven years ago."

We all go quiet.

The story scares me enough to hang back, and Bobby too, but Janine, being the crazy chick that she is, says, "Well, I think you're wrong." She rips off her T-shirt and shorts (she's got a bathing suit underneath) and goes racing into the dark water. You'd think Gary would yell after her but he just says to his girlfriend, "My sister don't listen to nobody."

Leanne says, "You need to make her listen," and screams after Janine but all we hear is her laughing. Leanne goes to the truck and switches on the high beams and we see Janine swimming around, not far from the shoreline.

Bobby calls out, "Janine! Stop fooling around!" It's always odd to hear him put more than two words together, and yell loudly, for that matter.

She doesn't come out and Gary goes back to the truck, finds two beers, one for his girlfriend and one for him. They stand there, sipping their drinks, while we watch Janine swim a bit further until she moves to the left, out of sight in the high beams.

"Christ," Gary says, putting his beer down in the sand.

But it's me who does something. I take off my shirt, slip off my sneakers, and wade into the water. It's lukewarm but the more I wade out, the colder it feels. I don't feel the current but it's not long before the floor vanishes and I'm dangling in the dark water. I look around, searching for Janine, then I yell for her. She calls back but I can't see her and then it's quiet. I quickly swim in, to where I can touch the floor and stand. The water is at my waist—it's so strange how it just drops off—and I'm looking and suddenly, bam! There's a splash and Janine is standing in front of me, shouting, "Marco!"

I laugh and smile and she hugs me and then steps away. Gary

and Leanne are screaming at us but Janine is cackling, like it's the funniest thing in the world. I grab her arm and drag her out of the water. It's not hard because she's not really fighting me. Gary and Leanne curse her out and Gary tells her this is why he doesn't want to take her anywhere and soon we're back in the pickup, driving out of the woods.

Bobby lies down and so do I, and Janine lies next to me. We're both wet but it's warm, so it doesn't bother me. When we get out of the woods and onto the highway, Bobby seems dead asleep. Gary tells us that he's going to stop at the liquor store so soon we're parked in front of a strip mall while he goes in. I look over at Bobby and shake him but he doesn't move really. He's out.

Janine gently kicks me and says, "Thanks for saving me, Zelko."

"You're crazy," I tell her, looking up at the sky.

A man walks by us and peeks into the back and says, "Stowaways, huh?"

When we're on the road, Janine turns on her side to face me. "Really, thanks for saving me."

"I didn't save you," I say. "You were fine the whole time." I catch glimpses of her when we ride under streetlights. She has a big crazy grin on her face but she's still pretty. I've never kissed a girl but I turn on my side and she says, "You can kiss me."

I swallow because I'm not sure how to do this but it sort of comes naturally when I lean forward and bring my lips to hers. It's only lasts like three seconds because I pull away. She smiles and says, "You've never done that before, huh?"

This insults me and I want to tell her to shut up but I'm happy, really happy, like I haven't been since before my dad died, before he left and divorced my mom, when I was little and he'd grab me and hug me and tell me I was the best kid in the world. I like being happy and I lean forward and kiss Janine again, this time for seven seconds. Then I answer her question: "Now I have."

She laughs and turns on her back and so do I. We can see the night sky because we're off the highway with the streetlights and I feel her take my hand in hers. We lie there, watching the sky, holding hands. Gary knows where Bobby lives so he takes him home first and Janine and I have to let go holding hands to wake him up. He crawls out of the back of the truck, waves, and goes up his driveway. On the way to my house, Janine and I sit up, holding hands. I want to kiss her again but we're at my house and Gary and Leanne can see us. I let my hand slip out of hers and leap out of the truck.

"Hey!" Gary calls.

I swing around.

"Thanks for going after my loony sister!"

Janine waves to me and I say, "No problem," and soon they're gone.

My mom and Harry aren't home but Lisa is, asleep on the couch, still in her McDonald's uniform, HBO playing on the television. I nudge her and we both go to our rooms.

About three in the morning, I hear my mom and Harry come in. They're laughing and slurring their words so I know they're drunk. Then, as quickly as they're happy, something turns and Harry is shouting at her. "I told you to shut up about it!"

I put the pillow over my head and force myself to think of my happy night, not what's going on outside my door. It's difficult but eventually I don't hear anything from them and I'm able to return to sleep.

The next day I wake up early and get two lawns done and bring home forty-five dollars because one of them is Erin's lawn and her mom gives me an extra five dollars for being nice to her daughter. "She's had a hard time all summer but when you came around, she found a friend."

This is news to me because I haven't been hanging around Erin but then her mom clarifies: "She met that nice boy Richard and the two of them have been spending time together and it's made her life so much easier."

I can't help but say, "Are they boyfriend and girlfriend?"

She says, "No, of course not. She's too young for a boyfriend."

Later, after I bring my lawn mower home, I ride my bike over to Richard's house. He comes outside and I tell him about Erin's mom giving me an extra five dollars because I introduced the two of them. He looks at the ground and says, "Yeah, she's nice."

"Are you going out together?"

Richard turns as red as red can get and mumbles, "No. We're just friends."

"You're lying," I say, laughing, and he turns even more red and says he has to go inside.

Their love connection inspires me to move forward with my own love connection. I go home, take a shower, put on some nice clean clothes and hop on my bike. I ride over to Janine's house.

Gary's truck is in the driveway, and he answers the door. "My dad took her to my aunt's house in Delaware. She's gonna spend the rest of the summer there."

My stomach knots. "Why?"

"Because she's crazy. I told my parents that she just disappeared and almost drowned in Baskro and they decided she needed to go to Aunt Barbara's house. Aunt Barbara doesn't take any crap from Janine so she'll be holed up there until school starts."

"That's two weeks away," I protest.

"If you ask me, definitely not enough time to rehabilitate my crazy dropped-on-the-head-twice sister."

So it is a true story!

"Listen, dude," Gary says. "Janine has been getting into trouble, hanging out with Maria and they are up to no good. They got caught shoplifting at the drug store last week. Stealing some lipstick or something."

"Really?"

"Yeah. And then she was caught with one of my brother's friends and my mom didn't like that one bit. Apparently she's been kissing lots of boys." Gary looks at me sideways. "Lots of boys."

It's a punch to the gut.

"My sis is bad news, loverboy," Gary continues. "You should find another girl to get all worked up about." He shrugs and shuts the door, leaving me standing outside in the sun. Orson quietly wanders up to the fence and jumps up, his tail wagging. I pet him on the head and then wander down the driveway.

At home, Harry is at the kitchen table. It's one in the afternoon but obviously he just got up. He's drinking a bottle of beer. This ticks me off so I go into the garage and open the fridge. There must be twenty bottles in there.

I go back inside, even more angry.

"Hey," he says, looking up from his beer. "I still want some money for the couch."

I'm so upset about Janine, about the beer in the fridge, I don't even think for a second to keep my mouth in check. "You're not getting any."

"What'd you say?"

I swing around and say, "I said, you're not getting any. We said we'd forget the whole thing."

Harry bounds up and pushes me with both his hands. I go flying back but I don't lose my balance. I stand forward, my mind going red with fury. I'm shocked he did this but I knew it was coming.

Harry sticks his finger in my face. "I want fifty bucks now. I know you got it because you've been mowing lawns like a mule. Go get it."

"I'm not giving you my money!" I shout.

He moves closer, so close I can smell his rancid breath. I take a step back.

Harry growls like dog. "You're a no-good nothing. Just a future loser in life. Mowing lawns for a living, that's your future."

"Shut up!" My head is exploding and I can feel myself wanting to cry but I don't. He's the friggin' loser. Drunk. Picking on me because he can't take on a man his own size.

My breathing is ragged as we stare each other down. "You're the loser," I say, but my voice is feeble. Not strong.

Doesn't matter. The words hit a nerve. Harry's arm swings back and for a second I know I'm going to get punched.

He doesn't hit me. A quick, guttural laugh comes from his throat as he drops his arm. Harry returns to the table. "So sensitive. You're like a woman."

The F-word rolls up my throat, like I'm going to tell him F off—which even in my rage state, I know will get me killed. I look by the stove and see my dad. He's wearing that ugly mustard yellow shirt he wore at my fifth birthday party.

"Go to your room," my dad tells me in my head.

I do. I walk away from Harry. Just march down to my room and slam the door, locking it behind me. I turn on my Pink Floyd and pull out my Legos. But I'm too old for Legos—I just kissed a girl, even if she's a jerk—and I can't be playing with Legos. I shove them back into the box and sit on my bed, trying to get my dad to come back. But he's gone.

I drift off to sleep and when I wake up, it's late afternoon. I get up and find the house empty so I pick up the phone and call Tyrell again. This time he answers and when I ask him to hang out, he tells me he can't.

"Why not?"

"Because I'm busy."

"Doing what?"

He sighs and then he says, "Danny, I'm busy. I'll talk to you later." He hangs up on me and I'm so pissed off because my life sucks and it's so friggin' unfair.

I kick the wall and kick it again and again and again. The last kick puts a small hole right through the sheetrock.

Crap. No. No.

I'm gonna get blamed for this.

I did do this.

My brain is fuzzy, sandpaper head. My chest is stiff.

I sit on the kitchen floor, listening to the sounds of the house. The central air conditioner going on. The whoosh of cool wind through the vents. A distant lawn mower running. A crow calling.

This comes out of nowhere but it knocks on my brain: *Check your hidden cash.*

My legs are jelly when I finally stand up. In my room, in my drawer where my cash is secretly stashed in a sock—it's all there: three hundred twenty dollars. I'd go to a bank but I heard you have to be over eighteen to get a savings account without a cosigner. I don't trust my mom to cosign, not with old Harry around.

I take a ten and head out. The day is overcast and not so hot, so it makes it easier to ride up to the hardware store in Toms River. Like I hoped, that mean cashier isn't working, just some other guy, and I buy the canister of rat poison. He doesn't ask me why I'm buying it and I get back on my bike and head home, where I sit in my room with the rat poison. It comes in pellets so I don't know what I'm going to do and I think for a minute. Then it comes to me: I can put two of the pellets in water make them dissolve.

Then I take out my list:

WAY SIX: POISON
    a. Dissolve the pellets in water.
    b. Take the poison water and put it in Harry's beer.
    c. How? Go out to the fridge in the garage, open one of the beers, dump half of it out and put the rat poison water in it.
    d. Put the poison beer behind a fresh beer so that he has one in him so he doesn't notice the poison beer tastes funny.
    e. Doesn't matter if he gets sick or dies. Don't care.

I sit back against my bed because I'm writing this on the floor. I know I can go to juvie for this, especially if he dies. But at this point, I don't care.

I carry out the plan. The pellets don't dissolve very well so I only get a little bit of poison water. I use four pellets because I figure I need all the poison I can get. In the garage, I take a bottled beer from the fridge, open it, pour some out on the side of the house, and dribble the poison in it. I place the cap back on but it doesn't go on well because it's a metal, serrated cap on glass, so this plan might not work.

It's worth a shot.

I slide the poison beer behind another and close the fridge.

I wait. Harry is working and in the evening, he'll probably come home and drink like he's been doing. I sit on the couch, watching game shows on TV because it's raining outside now. About five, my mom comes home. She starts dinner and I don't talk to her. Lisa arrives about six and about seven, Harry walks through the door.

"Hi, Danny," he says but I don't answer. When his back is turned to me, I give him the middle finger.

I remain on the couch.

My mom is making tacos and the house smells of sizzling meat.

I wait.

Harry takes a shower and I switch the channel to MTV. It's the same old videos: Michael Jackson, Cindy Lauper, Duran Duran.

Twenty minutes later, Harry is out of the shower and walking into the garage. He returns with a beer, opens the cap and starts drinking.

"Can you get me one?" my mom says.

I freeze. Oh no.

I didn't consider my mom drinking.

Harry gets another bottle and I have a terrible feeling it's the poison one. Horrible thoughts shoot through my brain and I know I can't poison my mom. I'm terrified and I jump up and slip into the garage. I shut the door behind me and open the fridge, the cold air chilling my heated face. I can barely breathe as I try all the caps because I can't remember where I put the bottle with the poison. Finally I find the right one because the cap comes off easily. I take this away, open the front garage door, and in the rain, on the side of the house, I pour out the poison beer, tucking the empty bottle underneath the large leaves of a hosta plant. I'm so sick that I almost killed my mom I can't even eat.

"I'll eat later," I announce when I go back inside and Harry says, "There might not be anything for you."

Shut up.

In my room, I lock the door and lie on my bed. The room is dim because it's still rainy out. I stare at the prism in the Pink Floyd poster.

"You can't kill Mom," my dad says when I conjure him up. He's wearing that dark blue suit he was buried in. I remember at the wake, when I went up to the coffin, he looked strange— so thin, his hair gone, his neck choked with a red tie.

He's not thin now and he still has his hair because I don't want to remember him how he looked in the coffin.

"I know I can't kill my mom," I say in my brain. I feel a terrible sense of myself. I'm so evil, I shouldn't be alive.

"You can't get rid of Harry," my dad says. "He's here to stay."

"He's such a dickweed."

I imagine my father sits next to me on the bed.

"Why can't you help me?" I ask. I know it's futile to talk to an imaginary person.

I pull out my list and write: *Plan is too dangerous. Almost killed my mom.*

My dad is gone.

WAY SEVEN

The next week is boring. I don't bother going out unless I have to mow a lawn. When I do Erin's lawn, I see Richard loping up her driveway. I stop the mower.

"When I'm finished with this, you wanna go look for snakes?"

He says he and Erin are going for a walk.

"A walk?"

"Yeah."

It's obviously some goofy lovers' walk so I say, "Don't let Jimmy Horak catch you. You don't want to be embarrassed in front of your girlfriend."

Richard goes red again but says, "Yeah, you're right."

I let out a heavy breath. "I'm just kidding."

"No, you're right." He pauses, head down. "Maybe we'll just stay here."

I shake my head. "If Jimmy starts with you, just sucker punch him." I give him a pointer. "If you hit him first, right in the face, you'll stun him. He'll probably try to hit back but at least you'll show him you're not a wimp. Erin will like that."

"Danny, I'm not like you. I'm not angry and violent."

"Who says I'm angry and violent?"

179

Richard doesn't answer right away but then says, "Everyone."

I start the mower again, finish the job, and head back home. I pass Janine's house and Orson comes charging around the front, barking and slobbering, sticking his nose through the chain fence, trying to leap over it.

I guess we're not friends either anymore.

My mom informs me that we're going to Great Adventure on Saturday night.

"I'm not going."

She makes me sit down at the kitchen table. "Harry and I are going to get married in October."

"So I heard."

"Lisa told you?"

"Yes."

"I know you and Harry don't get along. I know he's old fashioned with you, but you need a tough hand. You're not easy to deal with."

I slouch to the side, shaking my head. So this is my fault.

"You always feel sorry for yourself," my mom adds.

"I do not!"

"Yes, you do. You don't think about the overall situation. How we need Harry."

"To keep the air conditioner and cable on?"

My mom's mouth tightens.

"Doug could keep the bills paid," I say.

"I don't love Doug."

"Right. You love Harry."

She ignores that comment and says that she understands he's been too tough, that he's been drinking too much. "I'm on him about that. I told him he has to back off, try a little harder." She takes a deep breath. "I told him if he doesn't shape up, if he doesn't work it out with you, he and I can't get married."

Sure thing, Mom. We all know that Harry isn't going anywhere. My mother will never get rid of him because my mom doesn't get it. She doesn't understand that it's not really me. I know I'm not the best kid on the planet but I'm not sick in the brain like Harry. He's got a demented mean streak. He does stuff, he starts stuff. It's the way he talks to me, like I'm something on the bottom of his shoe, that no matter what I do, that no matter how good I am, he will always try to get one over on me. Me, I'm not that bad. I have my own business. I make my own dinner. I try to be cool. I have tried to be nice to Harry.

"Do you understand me?" my mom asks.

I have no response. I get up and glare at my mom, who is now gazing out the kitchen window. I feel sorry for her. She's no use to anyone anymore. Harry has brainwashed her and Lisa and I are on our own.

I ride over to Baskro. There's another deep depression coming over me. What's the point in all of this? My life is useless. Harry might be right. What if I grow up to be like him? Tormenting my kid or step-kid. I don't want to be like that but I feel so angry and grim that nobody will like me. Nobody does. Tyrell. Richard. My mom. Everyone thinks I'm a trouble maker.

I take the long way around to Baskro. I travel through the same dirt road Gary went through so I can avoid riding by Tyrell's house. The bugs are loud and the sand is thick but I keep riding until I'm alone in front of the turquoise lake. I take my sneakers and socks off, my T-shirt, even my shorts off, so I'm standing in my underwear. I walk into the water, wading out, until the bottom floor is gone. I swim far and feel the water grow cold. I remember what Gary's girlfriend said and I look up into the sky, the sun shining, everything beautiful. I hear a dirt bike but it's far away. I tread water for a bit, waiting for the current to take me out more, for the underwater suction to grab hold of me and pull me down. I wonder if I'll see the old cars and mining gear when I go down. I wonder if I'll see dead bodies, skeletons. Finally I let myself slip under the water, let myself sink and sink. I go down, feeling the chill and seeing darkness, waiting to disappear. I want to see my dad again. I want to get away from my life. I hate everyone.

But I don't sink far. I need air. I want to breathe. My limbs won't let me drown. My legs automatically kick and my arms move. I go up, up, above water, and take a deep gulp of air. I don't have any answers for my shitty life but I know I don't want to die alone in this lake. I start swimming again and quickly make it to the floor of the lake, and wade back to shore. There I sit at the edge in my underwear, listening to the lapping of the miniscule waves. I still hear the dirt bike and even see it across the lake—someone just riding by themselves. I wonder if they see me. In my underwear. Why did I take my shorts off? I get up and pull my shorts on, my shirt, and as I'm tying up my sneakers, I hear a bunch of girls in the distance—Beverly, Dawn, and Janelle, and even Iris.

"Zelko! You swimming?" Beverly asks when they reach me.

"Just finished," I answer.

They place their boom box on a towel, turn it on, and Prince is singing "Little Red Corvette."

Iris seems happy hanging around her friends. At Tommy Wicky's pool party, now that I think of it, she appeared nervous, out of place.

"Where's Tyrell?" Janelle asks me.

I shrug. "We don't hang out much anymore."

"Why not?"

I want to tell them the truth but it seems too complicated. "He's busy."

Iris lies back on her towel. She doesn't seem interested in hearing about Tyrell.

"I heard you guys got kicked out of Tommy's party," Beverly says.

"You tell them that, Iris?" I say to her.

Iris lifts her head. "Maybe."

"Tommy is a fool," Janelle says to Iris. "I don't know why you like him."

"Be quiet," Iris mutters.

Janelle shrugs and sings along with Prince on the radio.

"I heard you liked Tommy in fifth grade," Dawn says to Janelle.

"I heard you liked Gordon Urszulak last week," Janelle retorts and continues to sing.

The other girls laugh and when the Prince song segues into "She Blinded Me with Science," Janelle and Dawn get up and do a dance routine they've been working on.

I leave the girls and take the dirt road back to the highway. I'm hungry so I go up to Luigi's. Speak of the Devil, Gordon Urszulak is sitting by himself eating an entire pizza. He's wearing a blue Giants T-shirt and bright red shorts and his face is all shiny with sweat.

Luigi points his finger at me. "I'll let you stay here but that's because I'm a nice guy."

"Fine," I answer.

Luigi isn't satisfied. "Danny, this is when you say, 'Thank you, Luigi, for being a wonderful man and letting me eat in your establishment after I caused so much trouble.'"

I say what he tells me to say.

Gordon invites me to sit and eat pizza with him. "I'm not gonna eat all this."

"Yes, you are."

"Yeah, probably. But you can have a slice."

I take one and Luigi brings me a soda.

We chow. Gordon lets me eat another slice. He's gross when he eats. He chews with his mouth open and sauce dribbles on his shiny, sweaty face and I think this poor guy is never going to land a girlfriend.

I'm almost done when who comes into the pizza parlor? Mr.

Cage! He's not even wearing a tie and collared shirt. He's wearing really short white shorts that show off his pale hairy legs and a yellow Mountain Dew T-shirt

He orders a sub and when he sees us, he takes a seat across from our table.

"Having a nice summer boys?"

"Yes, Mr. Cage," Gordon says after swallowing.

I don't say anything.

"What have you been doing, Danny?" Mr. Cage asks.

I want to say, *Well, I just almost killed myself because my mom is going to marry a psycho idiot and I almost killed her last night with rat poison and the girl I like apparently kisses a lot of boys and my best friend won't hang out with me...but I got to see a hognose snake and now I'm having free pizza with Gordon so my life is just great.*

I say, "I'm working a lot. I'm mowing lawns."

Mr. Cage seems surprised. Why is everyone surprised when I tell them I mow lawns?

"Yeah," Gordon says, taking a bite out of his pizza. "Danny's got a lawn business."

I wonder how Gordon knows this.

"I'd mow lawns," Gordon says, "but Danny took all the business."

This almost makes me laugh. "You would never mow a lawn."

Gordon sips his soda. "You don't know that."

Mr. Cage nods. "I'm glad to hear that." Luigi brings over his sub and we all eat in uncomfortable silence. Well, maybe not Gordon. He seems happy as a clam just eating his pizza.

When Mr. Cage is done (he wolfs down his sub in five minutes) he stands up and tells us he'll be seeing us soon, when school starts in another week.

"We're in the high school now," I say, hoping this is true, that Mr. Cage doesn't know something I don't know, and me and Gordon haven't been left back. "So we won't be seeing you."

"Yes, you will. I've been transferred to the high school."

I look at Gordon and see he's stopped eating. A wad of chewed-up pizza sits in his open mouth.

"I'll see you boys. Enjoy the end of your summer."

When he leaves, Gordon goes, "Damn. Now high school is gonna suck."

I'm thinking the same thing.

I find seventy-five dollars missing from my sock in the drawer.

At first, I count it. Count it again. Again. Each time the fury inside my body surges like bubbling lava. It seeps in my bones. I'm gonna lose it.

"You put a hole in that wall," Harry explains, getting up from the kitchen table and pushing the red phone cord away so I can see the evidence. The hole is gone, patched up poorly. "I had to fix this," Harry says, pointing to it. "But I wasn't about to pay for the supplies."

"So you just went into my drawer and took my money?"

"Yep." Harry returns to his spot at the kitchen table.

I clench my teeth, ball up my fists. I try to block the anger flaring from my nostrils.

Harry says, "You need to learn to pay your debts."

Rage busts out of my mouth. "God, I hate you!"

Harry scratches his ear, grimaces. Then he says, "Shut the hell up."

My mom is working so she's not around to see this, of course. I hadn't noticed, but Lisa is standing in the kitchen, by the sink. Harry steps outside to smoke a cigarette.

"You kicked the wall," Lisa says.

"Yeah, but you just can't go in and take someone's money. He took seventy-five dollars from me!" I know damn well it didn't cost that much to patch up a stupid hole.

"You should've offered to pay for it," Lisa says.

"Now you're on his side?"

My sister leans against the sink. "I'm not on his side. I hate him too. But you gotta figure out a way to deal with him. Like I am. I stay out of the way." I notice she's got her poison dart frog makeup on again.

"He doesn't pick on you like he does me."

"That's true." She walks by me and then stops. "Think of a better hiding place for your money. Try a decoy spot. Keep a little in one place and put the rest somewhere else. Be clever. Don't use your stupid pills."

I'm so angry I can't see clearly. I go into my room and slam the door. Turn up my music and punch my bed. I can't take this anymore.

Lisa's advice is smart, though. So I do it. I shove forty dollars back in a sock in my drawer. That's the decoy. The real spot has to be smart. I stand in my room, searching, my eyes finally settling on my closet. I stick the cash in an old shoe. I place a pair of old sneakers that I grew out of on top of them. This spot is temporary. When school starts, I plan to keep it in my locker, stuffed in a secret bag and locked up.

It's unreal that I have to hide my money. My dad would never have taken my money. I bet Doug the Cadillac dude wouldn't have stolen money from a kid either. Because like I said before, there's no way that hole in the wall cost seventy-five dollars to fix.

I take out my list and look what I've written. I go back to the ax.

I wait a few hours, after my mom has come home and gone to bed, then I open my door. Just as I thought, Harry is sitting on the couch, a beer in hand, watching the television.

He says nothing to me as I walk by, into the garage.

I see the ax. I take it off the wall.

I see myself going inside. Standing over him. Lifting the ax. Putting it into his head.

But I don't. I'm not a murderer.

I stare at his motorcycle. I envision myself hacking it to pieces with the ax. Whack, smack, crush. That'll teach him.

I don't do this either. I lift open the garage door and with the ax in hand, walk around the house and into the backyard, to the end. We have a chain-link fence and I hop over it and move into the woods. The moon is almost full and it's high in the sky and bright. I can't go too far because it will lead me to the next street so I stop. In the middle of the woods, I find a tree and start hacking away. It's a stupid ugly pine tree but I swing and swing. The ax gets stuck a few times but I'm strong enough to pull it out of the trunk. I don't make much damage but it feels good to hack at something. I swing and swing and it's in those swings that all my anger, the storm inside me swirls and busts open. Finally I end up sinking to the ground, overcome by frustration.

I miss my dad. I miss my mom. The way she used to be. I miss my old self, as a kid, before my dad died, before the divorce. When it was simple.

I stay out in the woods for over an hour, sitting on the ground, with the leaves and brush and night animals that I can't see. I can hear an owl but I can't see it. Richard shows up in my mind and I make a note in my head to ask him what type of owl it might be.

Eventually I pick up the ax and go home.

Harry is asleep on the couch. The ax is safely in the garage. I want to find his wallet and take my money back but the wallet is in his jeans' pocket and I'm too afraid to go after it.

I lie in bed, staring at my Pink Floyd poster on the ceiling, remembering what Richard said to me. He's right. I am angry and violent. I don't want to be angry and violent. Like I said, I miss my old self. I just want to be happy.

I don't know how to do that.

Saturday arrives. Time for Great Adventure. It's my mom, Harry, me, and Lisa in the car. Lisa doesn't want to go either but my mom insisted we have one last summer excursion. Lisa muttered, "Like we've had a bunch of wonderful excursions."

The ride is about twenty, twenty-five minutes long, through swirling roads in Jackson. I sit in the back, the open window blowing hot summer air at me, and I feel depressed. In another life, I'd be fidgeting and smiling and so happy to be going to Great Adventure. In the past when I've gone, my stomach was knotted up with excitement.

It's not now.

Harry smokes as he drives. The windows are open but the cigarette smoke still blows in my face. I glance at Lisa and she's staring through her open window. My mom is leaning back against the seat, a new gold necklace hanging around her neck.

We slow down at one point because there's an accident—a box truck and a motorcycle. The bike is smashed on the side of the road and the biker is a few feet away, sitting up, holding his left leg. His face is scrunched up as if he's in serious pain. There is no ambulance or police.

"Must've just happened," my mom says.

I sit up and say, "We should stop and help."

Harry doesn't do this. He just maneuvers around the truck in the middle of the road.

"You should stop," I say to him.

Harry peers in the rearview mirror. "Cops will be here soon enough. We'll be in the way."

I look back and I don't see any sign of a police car. "You should stop at a house. We can run in and call and maybe we can sit with the biker."

"I said," Harry repeats, "the cops will be there soon."

"Yeah, I heard you, but the guy is hurt."

"Who's driving here? You or me?"

I don't respond.

"Right. So I make the decision about whether we stop or not."

His tone is bossy and my eyes flick to my mom, who doesn't

say a word. Lisa shifts in her seat and keeps her eyes averted from me.

A minute later, a police car flies past us with its lights swirling, siren screaming.

"Told ya," Harry says.

I slouch against the window.

Harry chuckles meanly and I see my mom touch his arm but he shakes it off.

The afternoon heat is heavy, humid. It's ninety-four degrees, one of the hottest days on record. We trudge across the massive parking lot and because the sun is blazing against the asphalt, the air stinks of burning tar and gasoline puddles from leaky vehicles. We follow other people, threading through parked cars, toward the entrance gates. The sounds of the park echo, roller-coasters rolling like trains, faraway screams piercing in the air. Lisa points to Rolling Thunder, the largest coaster in the park. It's wooden with a monster hill followed by other hills. I've been on it once before, when I was between sixth and seventh grade. My mom took Lisa and me and I thought I was a big shot, so I sat in the front seat all by myself because my mom and Lisa were too scared to do the front seat. It was terrifying because I was smaller than I am now and I think I was too little to ride it. Even though the bar was down, I kept popping out and at one point, right at the second hill, as we were going down, the bar gave way a bit and I swear I almost slipped out of the roller-coaster. The only thing that held me in was my grip on the bar. Like a month later, this guy fell forty-two feet from Rolling Thunder and was killed. They said he didn't have the safety bar fastened but I bet it malfunctioned. In my situation, I don't know if my bar malfunctioned or almost malfunctioned or I was too small to ride the roller-coaster, but that's when I developed my philosophy about amusement rides—I like them fast and I like them high—but I don't like height and speed combined. Which is why I don't ride big roller-coasters. Rolling Thunder is too high and too fast.

Harry pays for our tickets and my mom makes Lisa and me thank him.

"It's not like he's shelling out full price," Lisa whispers as we walk behind them.

I don't understand what she means.

"We got the after four tickets," she says impatiently, shooting me the *Duh, don't you know anything?* look. It takes five seconds before I remember that if you come to Great Adventure after four o'clock, you get a discount price.

"Let's make a bet," Lisa whispers. "How long will it take before they dump us and head over to the beer garden?"

"Mom promised me she and Harry would cut back on the drinking," I say, smirking because I'm being sarcastic.

Lisa doesn't catch it. "You take a lot of stupid pills, dipshit."

"I was joking."

"Oh." She pauses because she feels bad. "Sorry."

We walk by the fountain, toward the swings. I like this ride because you sit in a swing all secure, and then it goes around like a merry-go-round. It goes a bit high but not super fast. I worry when I look up at the chains connected to the top of the ride that they're going to come undone and I'm going to go flying and smashing into one of the tall trees in the park, but I know that's just my brain screwing with my head. I have no idea why I'm okay with the swings and not roller coasters. Why can't I get over that time I almost fell out of Rolling Thunder? I don't know. When you have a fear, you have a fear.

"How long you think?" Lisa whispers as we stand in line for the swings. She means, *How long will it take Mom and Harry to dump us?*

I shrug. I hope they do dump us. That way I don't have to spend time with Harry.

All four of us go on the swings. I sit far away from my mom and Harry and when the ride starts going round and round, I close my eyes and enjoy the coolness of the wind, a break from the heat. Round and round. My feet dangle and for a minute I think I'm going to lose my sneaker, but I don't. The ride lasts about a minute and a half.

When we get off, I pull out my comb and run it through my hair. The wind on these rides always messes up my hair.

Next, we head over to Lightnin' Loops, another tall roller-coaster but this one goes upside down. We stand in front of it for a few minutes, watching the two monster coasters loop through one another. It is a short ride—down the hill, around the loop, up to the end. Then the coaster moves backwards—down the hill, through the loop, up the hill, halting where it began. There's no way I'm going on this one. I haven't heard of any deaths, but one is definitely in its future.

"Come on, Danny," my mom says. "It'll be fun. Don't be scared."

"It's nothing," Lisa says, elbowing me. "Be brave."

"No thanks."

My mom and my sister shrug at each other, then have a quick discussion about how they have to pee first. Before I know it, I'm standing next to Harry. Alone.

He lights a cigarette and stares at me.

"What?" I say.

Harry scowls, nods toward Lightnin' Loops and says, "Don't be scared, *Danielle*."

I try to ignore him.

"What? You gonna say, *I hate you*?" He uses a high girl voice on the last part.

I say nothing. I decide I'm going to continue to ignore him. Like Lisa said.

It's impossible. Out of nowhere, Harry clamps his hand onto the back of my neck and presses down at the sides, hitting the pressure points. The pain is immediate and strong and I twist away, crying out. "What is your problem?"

A few people look but no one intervenes. I move far away

from him, doing my best to concentrate on Lightnin' Loops so I don't tear up and start crying like a baby. I focus on the sound. The noise is loud, like a mini-train with loose cargo.

My mom and Lisa return and my mom wants to know why I'm standing a mile away from Harry.

I ignore her. Just keep my hands crossed over my chest, my eyes fixed on Lightnin' Loops.

"What's wrong now?" my mom says. She sounds exasperated.

"Your psycho boyfriend tried to choke me."

Her face twists into disbelief. "What do you mean?"

I point to the sides of my neck.

Harry and Lisa approach and my mom wants to hear Harry's side of the story. "I was teaching him a trick," Harry says, holding out his hand on display. "If you press the sides of someone's neck…" He places his hand on the back of my mom's sweaty neck. "And squeeze, you can bring someone down. It's a way to protect yourself."

He squeezes my mom gently and she rolls her eyes. "Oh, this is ridiculous. Let's have a nice time, today." She says we all need to go on Lightnin' Loops.

"I'm staying here," I say.

"Fine," my mom answers, grabbing Harry's hand. Lisa trails after them.

I find a bench underneath a large oak tree and sit, watching people walk by. The trees are old and tall here. None of them are pine trees. It's as if when they built the park, they kept all the good trees and got rid of the ugly ones.

Sure enough, when they get off the roller-coaster, my mom announces that she's going to let Lisa and me spend the next couple hours on our own.

"Why?" Lisa says, her hand on her hip.

"We'll meet you at seven-thirty, by the fountain." Harry hands us both five dollars each. "If you guys want a snack or something."

Neither Lisa nor I thank him.

"There they go," Lisa says as they walk away. I watch my sister lift her right hand up and give them the bird.

I grin.

"I wish Tim were here," Lisa says after a while, as we walk aimlessly.

"Is he your boyfriend, like for real?" I ask. "Are you in looove?"

She clucks her tongue at me and is quiet for a few minutes. The air is still heavy with heat and every person in the park is so sweaty and stinky, they need a shower and deodorant. Lisa wants to go to the haunted house so we make our way to that area. It's right next to the beer garden so I know that's the real reason Lisa wants to go into the haunted house. I like the haunted house because I like horror stuff. I like ghosts and skeletons and knives sticking out of people's heads. There's nothing better than a good scare. And, it's air conditioned.

When we reach the haunted house, Lisa tells me to hold on a second, and just as I predicted, she jogs over to the beer garden. I stand in front of the spooky building, watching as people wander up the walkway, into the entrance. It's probably the best haunted house I've been in. The place is not set up with creepy living rooms but with dark, twisting catacombs, so dark that you have to feel your way through. Ghouls and vampires pop out of the smoky shadows, making me jump every time.

Lisa returns, nodding, signaling that she has confirmation: my mom and Harry are in the beer garden. "Maybe I'll call Tim," Lisa says and I notice sweat beads on her nose. "Maybe he can come get us."

"Can you call him from here?"

"Probably. There are pay phones by the front, where we came in."

Eerie music spills from hidden speakers. Lisa and I enter the haunted house, passing a witch who curls her finger at us.

It gets dark immediately and the witch disappears behind a curtain. Up ahead of us, you can hear people screaming. We get around the corner and a ghoul jumps out. Lisa screams and I shout, laugh a bit, then we're down another corridor, walking by a cemetery display with white smoke that smells chemical-like, pouring out from the sides.

It's cool in this place, though. A relief from the heat.

We linger for a while, moving down the dark corridors, then finding ourselves in front of another creepy display. Strobe lights flicker and black lights illuminate the place a little, but it really is dark. Someone can get murdered in here and with all the screaming and yelling and darkness, no one would ever know until the body starts to rot and it gets that dead smell.

I tell this to Lisa.

"How do you know what a dead smell smells like?"

I'm sure my dad smelled when he died but before you get shoved in a coffin and displayed at the wake, so everyone can come up to you and say goodbye, they embalm you. I found the entire process of the wake weird and sad. You just sit around for a day and a half in a room with a dead body and talk to relatives and people you don't even know that well. I'd never been to a wake before my dad died so the experience was new to me. I kept looking up from my chair, seeing my dad across the room, dead in the open casket, like a vampire or something. I didn't cry at the wake or the funeral. I was tough. It wasn't until I got home, when I was in my room with Pink Floyd play-ing, did the tears come. Guys aren't supposed to cry in public, so I didn't.

I follow Lisa outside, the humid air knocking into us. The sun is sinking somewhere beyond the tall trees but it's still disgust-ingly hot.

"Sky Ride?" she suggests.

The Sky Ride is over by the swings. It takes you across the park. We stand in line for over twenty minutes behind a group of people who obviously just came off Roaring Rapids. They're soaked, even their sneakers are wet, which is gonna suck later for them. They stink like chlorine and sweat and they talk loudly with heavy New York accents.

"When you gotta go, you gotta go," one dude is saying and I figure he's talking about how he peed when he was on the water ride.

"Gross," Lisa mutters. She figured it out too.

"Yeah!" I say loudly and the group looks at me. It's mostly people in their twenties, guys and girls. I look away, pretending I know nothing.

When it's our turn, we board a small brown metal car attached to a cable. We step inside and within seconds, we're moving, sliding above and across the park over the confectionary-colored rides, passing other cars moving in the opposite direction. Kids call to us, mimicking the Grey Poupon commercial. "Pardon me. Would you have any Grey Poupon?"

I play along, saying, "But of course," and lean over the side to hand over an imaginary jar of mustard. A few cars later, a group of girls are singing "Beat It."

I don't know what it is about the Sky Ride, but when you're over the trees, the land stretched out as far as you can see—nothing but more trees—when you're in the safety of your Sky Ride car, rolling quietly above in the evening air, where's it's cooler than down below, it makes it easy to say whatever you want. "Michael Jackson sucks!" I shout at the Beat It girls.

"No, he doesn't!" screams a girl's voice.

"Yes, he does!" Lisa yells back. I laugh and give my sister a high five and then ask myself why we even said that. I don't think Michael Jackson sucks. Lisa loves Michael Jackson.

Three cars later, when we're at the highest point of the Sky Ride, we pass two guys and a big white butt. We're being mooned.

"Oh my God!" Lisa squeals, hiding her face in her hands.

I can't help it. I explode with a great cackle and full body shake. It's the funniest thing I've ever seen!

"Let's do that to the next car," I suggest, touching the button on my shorts.

"Hell no!" Lisa yells. "I do not want to see my little brother's butt. That is completely disgusting."

I laugh even harder. I'm not going to moon anyone but it's hilarious how Lisa keeps looking at me sideways, shaking her head for the rest of the trip across the park. "You're demented," she says over and over again.

We finally slide downward, to the end of the ride. We're now on the other side of the park, in the Wild West section. There's an old wagon wheel near the wimpy Runaway Train roller-coaster, which Lisa and I jump on quickly because it's basically for people who don't like big hills like me, and when we get off, we wander into the huge teepee that sells T-shirts and souvenirs. There's nothing I want to buy but the air conditioner is blasting. Lisa asks the woman at the counter if there's a pay phone nearby. There is, by the restrooms behind the teepee. We head that way.

I stand off to the side, watching people go down the log flume, another water ride. It's like a roller-coaster on water. I wouldn't mind going on the log flume because it's sort of small but you need to do water rides in the beginning of the day so you can dry off. And you definitely need to leave your shoes in the cubbies before your get on. Something those wet people who were on the other water ride, Roaring Rapids, didn't know.

Lisa returns from the phone. Tim isn't home. "He'll be back later," she says.

We start walking and I ask her how long she's been going out with him.

"Since March. Sort of." She explains that he just quit McDonald's to work at his uncle's gas station. It pays more. "That's why he has a car. His uncle also has a garage and he got a discount on an old car that needed work."

We leave the Wild West and walk slowly toward the arcade where I'm going to spend my five dollars.

"I only have one more year of school," Lisa says. "And then

I'm going to move out."

"You are?" I say, stopping short.

"Yes. Next summer." She opens up her palms, like there is nothing she can do about it. "Tim graduates, too, and we're planning to move out of state."

"Where?" I'm feeling sick.

"California."

"That's across the country!"

"Yeah."

I start walking. I don't want my sister to leave me and she knows it. She follows me into the arcade. A blast of very cold air conditioning and a Styx song hits us.

I get change from the change dude and go to the Pac-Man machine.

Lisa follows and after I've started the game, she says, "I'm sorry, Danny. But I have to live my life."

I keep playing.

"It's a year away, so it's not something you have to get all worked up about now."

I continue to play but I'm worked up and it makes me play bad. I lose. I reach in my pocket for another quarter.

"Danny, don't be a jerk."

Before I start the game, I say, "What if loverboy breaks up with you?" I'm thinking of Janine suddenly, how she made me think we were starting a relationship or something, then I find out she's made a lot of guys think they were starting a relationship. "Things don't always work out. What are you gonna do then?"

Lisa shakes her head.

"It can happen. He can meet another girl and take her to California."

"Shut up."

I'm being mean but I don't care.

I play another game of Pac-Man, then another. I switch over to the pinball machine, the one with the woman with big boobs on the front, but I actually don't like pinball machines. I try other video games but they're just boring and when I use up the five bucks, I look around and can't find Lisa. Panic sets in as I move through the aisles but she's nowhere. The arcade is made of glass windows and when I look outside, I see Lisa sitting on a bench across the pavement. She's surrounded by pink and white flowers. Great Adventure is covered with flowers. They're in flower beds, in gigantic pots, in huge baskets hanging from posts.

"We need to get to the fountain," Lisa says when I reach her.

"Okay," I say quietly.

She doesn't move so I sit next to her.

"What number are you on now?" she asks. "Your ways to get rid of Harry?"

"I should be on seven," I answer. "What do you care? You're not gonna be here."

"Danny, don't be like that."

I scuff my sneaker on the concrete and decide to talk. "I've given up. He's never going away. He's like dog poop on your shoe. No matter how you try to brush it off in the grass, your shoe always smells like poop. But you won't have to worry about it. Will you?"

Lisa stands up. "Let's go."

They're not at the fountain. It's quarter to eight and the late sun washes over us in golden hues. The fountain water gushes out behind us and I feel the cool touches of wet spray on the back of my neck and arms. Some kids are in the water and they're being chased out by a worker. Moms with baby strollers sit around, their heads drooping, like they just want to crawl in the strollers themselves. Across the crowd, I see Iris Cruz and what looks like her parents and little sister and brother. She stands by the candy shop about twenty feet from the fountain. I wonder what Tyrell is doing. I'd make him go up and talk to her.

Lisa announces she's going to get them and marches off to

the beer garden.

Fifteen minutes later, way after Iris has drifted into the crowd with her family, the sun has set, casting a peach-orange blaze overhead. Lisa comes walking up with Harry and my mom. My mom looks smashed. She leans against Harry who glows with drunkenness himself. My mom laughs and laughs, then mumbles how hungry she is. An older man stares at my mother and shakes his head. It's so embarrassing and I'm so glad Iris Cruz is gone. Lisa suggests we get pizza and we follow her to a stand near the Rotor.

The Rotor is the cruelest ride in the park. I love it but I don't recommend the ride to everyone. You need a strong stomach. People step inside a cylinder and are advised to stand against the wall. The cylinder rotates, faster and faster, until you're stuck to the wall by the pressure. Then the floor drops. You can barely move, people's mouths and cheeks rippling from the wind, their bodies plastered to the curved wall like dead bugs. Eventually the torture ends. The floor comes up, the spinning slows, then stops. People always stagger out of the cylinder and down the gangplank like drunks, hooting and laughing at each other.

After we finish our pizza, my mom decides everyone is going on the Rotor.

"I don't think that's a good idea," Lisa says, collecting the paper plates littered with pizza crusts.

Nobody takes Lisa's advice. We head over to the ride. Immediately, the guy running the Rotor says my mom shouldn't go on. She's still visibly drunk and he says if she throws up while they're spinning, it will splash back in her face and could choke her to death.

My mom grimaces and asks Harry to sit the Rotor out with her. "That might happen to you, too."

"No, it won't," Harry says. "'Cause I ain't half-gone, like your drunk ass."

My mom frowns, then tilts her head. "Babe," she says gently, "I'm just trying to help."

"Go lay down."

I think of a dog when he says this.

My mom clearly thinks the same thing because she appears insulted, hurt. She doesn't respond. She shuffles away and heads toward a bench.

I'm disgusted that she actually listens to him. I want to hate her.

"Let's go," Harry grunts.

There is no line because most people don't like the Rotor. I like the ride and along with a few other people, the three of us walk into the cylinder. "Stand by the wall," the guy running the Rotor announces through a loudspeaker. He's speaking to Harry who's near the center. Harry nods and backs up. The rotation begins. Round and round and round, faster, faster, faster. People begin to stick to the walls. The floor drops. I catch sight of Harry, his long face rippling in the spinning, his eyes wide and sick. I gaze across the cylinder at my sister, who has also seen Harry. With her hands up against the wall like she's in a holdup, she shows seven fingers. Number Seven. I get it. Harry will vomit and choke to death. It's brilliant. I grin.

But he doesn't choke to death. The floor rises up, the spinning stops.

Outside, as we stumble down the gangplank, Harry is quiet. My mom is lying on a bench. Suddenly, Harry lunges toward a garbage can and begins to throw up. People walk by and chuckle. Lisa giggles. And I cannot resist. I make a beeline for him. While he's bent over the garbage can, hurling up pizza and beer, I whisper, "Are you okay, *Harriet*?"

I expect to be smacked, punched, so I snap back, preparing to run, but there's no retaliation. Harry finishes vomiting, wipes his mouth, doesn't even look my way. He staggers to the bench, pushes my mom up into a sitting position and slides next to her. He orders us to go away for an hour. "See you at ten. Here."

The sky has gone completely dark but the park is lit up with fabulous colored lights that flash and glitter. Lisa and I ride the giant Ferris wheel, then head back to the haunted house and walk through it again. Nothing scares me or Lisa, not even the ghouls who jump out of the corner.

"You guys are lame," one ghoul mutters.

"I can't believe you called him Harriet," Lisa says after we leave. She's shaking her head but smiling. "My way was good, wasn't it? It almost worked."

"It didn't," I mumble, remembering not to be nice to her because she's moving to California. The hour is up and my stomach is beginning to knot. I'm actually afraid of what Harry might do. I'm trying not to get frightened. I even pretend talk to my dad in my head, but he doesn't answer.

We find them on the bench. My mom is sitting up now, more alert. "One more ride," she says. "Let's try Rolling Thunder."

Lisa pushes me to take a chance, ride the roller-coaster. She talks on and on as we walk toward the ride, promising it's better to ride Rolling Thunder at night because I won't see how high I am.

"I don't have a problem with heights," I explain. "Just speed and heights."

I keep turning around, checking on my mom and Harry, who trail behind us. They're not holding hands and my mom isn't leaning against him. They're just following us.

When we reach the roller-coaster entrance, I plop on a bench, refusing to go on the ride. "I'll wait for you."

Harry announces he's not going on either.

My gut contracts and I feel the pizza rise in my throat. Harry lights a cigarette. It's dark in this area and I can tell by the way Lisa stiffens, that she's hesitating. My mom grabs Lisa's arm and they disappear into the dark wooden tunnel that leads to the ride. Anxiety rips through my bones. Harry and I are in a corner, alone, and nobody can see us. I realize I have to get out of there, get to the gift shop across the way where there are people.

201

Again, Harry seems to know my thoughts. Within seconds, Harry leans over and grabs me by the back of the neck, much worse than before, with a grip so fierce, so dangerous, so meant for a man and not a kid like me, that I know I'm as good as dead.

"You're a little wise ass, aren't you?" Harry growls. His voice is low, sizzling like burning meat, and the words come out clipped because the cigarette is in his mouth. With his hand still on my neck, Harry pulls me up from the bench, squeezing, squeezing. I'm bent over, trying to twist away.

"Huh, you little shit?"

I can't speak. Feeble squeaks of pain rattle from my throat.

"Stop moving," Harry orders and I do. There is some let up in the grip and I'm thankful, hopeful I might survive after all. But a moment later, my body goes weak. I see the orange glow of the cigarette near my left eye.

"I'll do it, you shit." His voice is guttural, demonic. "I will."

The cigarette is so close, the heat and smoke burn my eyes and I clamp them shut.

Then, suddenly, I hear another man's voice. "What's your problem?"

Harry's grip and the cigarette are immediately gone. I stumble forward, tripping and landing on the concrete. The pain is hard but gone in a few seconds. When I roll over, I see a man push Harry against the wall.

There is a second man and also a woman.

"What's wrong with you?" the woman screams. "He's just a kid!"

The second man stands behind the first guy.

Because it's shadowy, dim, their faces aren't really visible. But I can see the men are strong, muscular, built. They spit curses at Harry, telling him off, call him names, threatening. Harry threatens back, has his arms tightened, his chest puffed out, but it's two against one and the men are as big as him, if not bigger.

The woman lifts me up, places her hands on my face and asks if I'm okay. I can see her a little more clearly because she moves me into some light, away from the men. The whites of her eyes are glassy and she has a lot of teeth.

In the end, there is no fighting. Just words. The one guy is piss angry and rants about when he was a kid. "I had a father like you and he knocked me around and shit and you know what? You know what?"

Harry says nothing.

The man steps toward him, points and says, "I got bigger. Your boy, he's gonna get bigger."

"He ain't my boy," Harry barks.

But the man doesn't care about that information. He turns and stomps toward me. He says, "You're gonna get bigger."

I don't know what to say to him because he's so strong and gruff and I'm afraid but I know he's on my side and I know he is good.

I nod. "Okay."

"No, not okay. You need to keep this in your brain every time that asshole comes at you: You're gonna get bigger. Remember that. This won't be forever because you're gonna get bigger!"

Number Seven.

The two men and woman wait with me until my mom and Lisa show up. Harry stands off to the side smoking. The woman tells my mom the story and my mom finally gets angry. She yells at Harry and he promises it won't happen again. My mom keeps on him, telling him off, that he needs to stop being such an ass, and Harry nods and agrees and apologizes to her. He repeats over and over that it won't happen again. Eventually, my mom accepts this and the men and the woman reluctantly walk away.

The drive home is quiet. My mom falls asleep in the front seat and Lisa conks out in the back. I want to tell Lisa about Number Seven, had wanted to do it when we were walking away from Rolling Thunder, but didn't get the chance. Still, the revelation is perfect without anyone knowing yet: I'm gonna get bigger. The whole time Harry's been around, I never thought of it.

Now I'm not afraid. I scowl in the back of the car, shooting death thoughts at Harry, hoping they get delivered. *I'm gonna get bigger. That's right, asshole, I'm gonna get bigger.*

I rest my chin on the open window and let the wind blow into my face.

END

Harry avoids me. I'm sure this won't last for long but I know he won't be in my life forever, just like the guy at Great Adventure said. And to my surprise, my mother postpones the wedding! "I think the spring might be a better time to get married," she says to me and Lisa, but my sister reminds me that anything can change. "Don't start taking those stupid pills again, Danny. Don't get your hopes up." Still, I start high school with a new mind-set: I'm going to be good. I even see Mr. Cage on the second day and say hello to him.

He stops me and asks how my lawn business is going.

"I owed my mom some money and I had to pay her back so I didn't save much." I did pay her back for the couch, but I deducted fifty dollars because I know patching up the wall didn't cost that much.

Richard Plimpton strolls by holding Erin's hand. I guess they're in love. "Hey Danny," Erin says but Richard just waves. His head is up now. She's given him confidence.

I continue speaking to Mr. Cage. "Fall is coming and I plan to rake leaves and charge more. Then I'm going to do snow shoveling." I thought about this the other night, after I paid my mom back. I may be able to get some guys to help out, like

Bobby and maybe even Gordon. I bet Gordon, being as big as he is, can really shovel some serious snow. I'd pay them well. I tell Mr. Cage this.

"Interesting."

We're standing in the hallway and kids are whisking by us. I even see Janine and she waves. "Hi, Danny."

I haven't decided whether I'm going to continue having a thing for her. I might look elsewhere.

Still I wave back. "Hey Janine."

Mr. Cage smooths his handlebar mustache with his hand. "So you're a regular businessman with a business plan? Impressive."

"Yes."

For the first time, Mr. Cage smiles. Really smiles. So wide, I see his teeth and notice he's missing one on the far left side. His teeth are crooked, too, like mine.

Jimmy Horak passes us too but I pretend I don't notice him.

"I also plan to behave better this year," I say. "I don't want to fight anymore."

Mr. Cage nods, his smile completely gone. It was like his smile was a rare sighting, a shooting star in the night. "I think that's a good plan, Mr. Zelko."

He walks away but quickly turns back and points at me. "By the way, looks like you got a little taller."

"Really?" I say.

"Yeah. Not much, but some."

On Saturday, after I finish mowing two lawns, I ride over to Tyrell's house and attempt to convince him to go to Baskro with me. I really want to be friends again. He's hesitant but he comes outside and we sit on his front porch. I tell him the story of Great Adventure he loves it. He even makes me repeat the part about the man saying, "You're gonna get bigger."

"That's so cool," Tyrell cheers. "It's like Superman swooped in and saved you."

I laugh because it's so stupid.

Or maybe not.

"Two Supermen," I correct him. "And a Wonder Woman."

"Ha ha!"

I also tell him how I saw Iris Cruz at Great Adventure with her family.

"Damn," Tyrell says, *cursing!* "I wish I was there."

"Next time."

"No way. I'm not going anywhere near your mom's boyfriend. He's psychotic."

I chuckle. "Thanks, dude. Makes me feel better that I live with a psycho."

"He moved in?"

"No, but he will."

"That's bad." Tyrell fixes the collar on his polo and thinks for a long moment. "Well, if it gets too much, come stay with me."

Huh? I'm not sure what to say here.

So I say nothing.

I stretch my legs out in front of me. Two younger boys stroll by the house, bouncing a basketball. I want to say something to Tyrell, something that's been in my brain but I don't know how to get the words out without sounding like a jerk. I want to say that I know it's easier being friends with people who are from the same neighborhood and it's harder to be friends with people from a different neighborhood. That I'm sorry Harry is in my life but I can't kill the guy, no matter how much I want to. That my mom might never get rid of him. That Harry will probably be a dickweed again. That he may even say another terrible remark like the "spook" neighborhood thing but, me, I don't think and talk that way. That I'm not him. But I'm glad you're offering to let me stay at your house when things get bad because I know I'm gonna need somewhere to go. And when I turn eighteen, I'm going to get my own apartment and you can finally hang out at my place because I know you won't ever come to my house again. And that I understand.

It's as if Tyrell reads my mind: "I'll say this—life's been dull without you around, Danny. A guy can only read so much before he gets bored."

Tyrell puts his dad's aviator glasses on and we hop on our bikes and ride out to Baskro where the girls are, their boom box blasting some song I don't know. Dawn, Janelle, and Beverly are doing their dance in the late afternoon sun with a nice breeze blowing off the lake. Even Iris gets up and joins them and Tyrell in his aviator glasses and me with my hand shielding my eyes watch as they twirl around, their hands in the air, then on their hips, doing their routine. Our high school has a talent show every year and the girls plan on winning.

"We're gonna be fantastic," Beverly chimes. "Because I'm fantastic."

"I don't know about that," I say, grinning.

"Be quiet, Rocky," Beverly snaps.

I want to tell her that I'm not going to fight anymore. I've got control over myself. I have a plan. A future. Hope.

I lie back on my towel and close my eyes.

In the evening, as I ride through my neighborhood streets, I see Janine Finn walking alone along the road toward me. I cruise by her and she calls out, "Did you get rid of Harry?"

"Not yet," I answer.

"I might have some ideas," she calls back and I circle around and stop, watching as she keeps walking away from me, her long black hair flowing behind her.

Who cares if she kissed a lot of guys? I can still have a thing for her.

In late September, the air has turned chilly and I need to switch my shorts for jeans. I haven't worn them since May and when I pull them on, I notice the bottoms are just above my ankles. Mr. Cage was right.

I pretend talk to my dad, who is wearing his old greaser jacket and his jeans, leaning against the wall.

"They're too short," I say.

He grins. "You got bigger, son."

ACKNOWLEDGMENTS

This book never would've happened if it weren't for writer Thomas Pluck. A few years ago, he invited me to write a story for his anthology, *Protectors*, and when I sent him my story, he turned it down because it was too dark. He said he had a lot of dark stories and he was looking for something a tad bit lighter. So I went back to the computer and wrote a short story called, "Seven Ways to Get Rid of Harry." This novel and that short story have the same basic plotline, although the short story was for adults and it took place in one day. Later on, after that story was published, I decided I could expand it into a book. When I told Thomas Pluck that I had turned the story into a novel, he was very supportive and excited and has been one of the biggest champions of this book.

I'd also like to thank my fiancé, Jay, for giving me so many ideas for Danny. The cigarette in the eye, the bike on the basketball rim, and also the sadness of losing his own father at ten years old came from his own experiences. I'd also like to thank him for being patient and kind and always ready to listen to me while I bang out a story line or chapter. Much love to you.

To Eric Campbell and Lance Wright of Down & Out Books—thank you for taking this on and giving the book a home. I will be forever grateful. I'd like to also thank my editor, Chris Rhatigan. He did a bang-up job, sharpening up my writing and catching my mistakes. Thank you, again.

To the writers of the crime fiction community. Your fabulous support and faith in my writing has been a godsend. I wouldn't be anywhere without your friendship and professionalism. I'm a lucky writer to have met you all.

I'd also like to thank my family. My son, Jack, for always being patient and asking, "Whadda you writing? Read me some of it." To my dad, who gave me the writing bug with your unending love of movies and good books, and my sister and her clan for cheering me on.

And lastly, to my mom, who always loved a good story. Wish you were here. Still.

JEN CONLEY has published many short stories in various crime fiction anthologies, magazines and ezines. Her short story collection, *Cannibals: Stories from the Edge of the Pine Barrens*, was nominated for an Anthony Award in 2017. She lives in Brick, NJ.

jenconley.net

BOOKS

On the following pages are a few
more great titles from the
Down & Out Books publishing family.

For a complete list of books and to
sign up for our newsletter,
go to DownAndOutBooks.com.

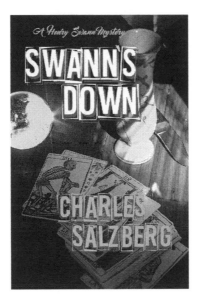

Swann's Down
A Henry Swann Mystery
Charles Salzberg

Down & Out Books
May 2019
978-1-64396-011-1

At skip-tracer Henry Swann's weekly business meeting with Goldblatt at a local diner, his inscrutable partner drops a bomb. He wants to hire Swann to help out his ex-wife, Rachael, who's been swindled out of a small fortune by a mysterious fortune-teller, who has convinced the gullible young woman that she's made contact with her recently deceased boyfriend.

At the same time, Swann receives a call from an old friend and occasional employer, lawyer Paul Rudder, who has taken on a particularly sticky case...

Walkin' After Midnight
Joe Ricker

Down & Out Books
May 2019
978-1-948235-83-9

This collection of stories is set in the darkest corners of New England, where the damaged American underbelly emerges.

The characters in these stories will challenge every notion you have of right and wrong, and you'll quickly realize that you've probably passed some of the characters in these stories on the streets.

Be glad you kept walking.

The Hurt Business
Stories by Mike Miner

All Due Respect, an imprint of
Down & Out Books
March 2019
978-1-948235-75-4

"We are such fragile creatures."

The men, women and children in these stories will all be pushed to the breaking point, some beyond. Heroes, villains and victims. The lives Miner examines are haunted by pain and violence. They are all trying to find redemption. A few will succeed, but at a terrible price. All of them will face the consequences of their bad decisions as pipers are paid and chickens come home to roost. The lessons in these pages are learned the very hard way. Throughout, Miner captures the savage beauty of these dark tales with spare poetic prose.

The Furious Way
Aaron Philip Clark

Shotgun Honey, an imprint of
Down & Out Books
May 2019
978-1-64396-003-6

Lucy Ramos is out for blood—she needs to kill a man, but she has no clue how. Lucy calls on the help of aged hit-man, Tito Garza, now in his golden years, living a mundane life in San Pedro.

With a backpack full of cash, Lucy persuades Garza to help her murder her mother's killer, ADA Victor Soto. Together, the forgotten hit-man hungry for a comeback and the girl whose life was shattered as a child, set out to kill the man responsible. But killing Victor Soto may prove to be an impossible task...

47153452R00137

JUL - - 2019

Made in the USA
Middletown, DE
06 June 2019